Orange as Marmalade

Orange as Marmalade

Fran Stewart

Orange as Marmalade

1st edition: © 2003 Fran Stewart
2nd edition: © 2004 Fran Stewart

Map Design: Penpoint Newsletters, Jasper, Georgia

ISBN: 978-0-9749876-1-3

This is a work of fiction. Any resemblance to any person living or dead is purely coincidental.

Information from *The Nature of Animal Healing* © 1999 by Martin Goldstein, D.V.M., published by Ballantine Publishing Group, reprinted with the permission of the author.

The name *Wayside Gardens* used by permission. (www.waysidegardens.com).

This book was printed in the United States of America

To order additional copies of this book, contact:

Doggie in the Window Publishing
PO Box 1565
Duluth GA 30096
www.DoggieintheWindow.biz

First edition and autographed books are available through this website.

To Harriette Austin,
who lit the fire

Acknowledgments

To say that writing this book was a labor of love is like saying that the *Mona Lisa* is a picture. I am deeply indebted to the following dear souls who helped make the process considerably smoother than it would have been without them.

Theresa Sherburne Rice was always ready to read, to comment, and to suggest. She's responsible for all the menus (except the sandwiches), and she cooked the soups for me so I could taste what I had written. Her piquant questions helped to shape what was a somewhat fuzzy first draft, and her laughter helped bolster my spirit when it flagged.

Darlene Carter, my Monday morning MasterMind partner, held the vision of completion for me throughout the process.

My sister, Diana Alishouse, and my niece, Erica Jensen, read the early drafts and peppered them with notes such as: *Why is it veggie soup at the top of this page and chicken noodle soup at the bottom?*

Millie Woollen. Good editor, who first was my good friend. Good friend, who first was my good breath coach. *Good* is an understatement.

Saskia Benjamin at the High Museum of Art in Atlanta, located the date of *Ansel Adams – the Early Years* and sent me to the right person in Boston for more information.

The curator of The Lane Collection at the Museum of Fine Arts, Boston, who asked to remain anonymous, confirmed my memory of *Wind*, the earliest known photograph by Ansel Adams, circa 1919. I had seen it at the High Museum's Folk Art and Photography Gallery in Atlanta at an exhibition in February 1994.

Eveleen Cecchini, founder and Director of Outreach for Earth Stewardship (www.ofes.org) checked the details about birding and kept me from calling it *bird-watching*.

Kathi and Terry Moon are the creators of *The Personal Boundaries Training*™ www.ThePersonalBoundariesTraining.com. I borrowed some of their concepts to raise the personal power level of the main women in this book.

Dr. Marty Goldstein, author of *The Nature of Animal Healing,* gave me permission to use his name and quote from his book. I borrowed the information about Edward Bach from Marty. Please note: I know that my story is set several years earlier than when his book was published in 1999. This is, however, a work of fiction.

Rev. Andrea Kay Smith, the Global Coordinator for the Planetary Consortium, gave me permission to use her name and information about internship in the Inner City Gardens Project. (www.PartnershipsInPeace.org)

Nancy Welshimer gave much-needed advice about light; Jonathan Oertle suggested a Nikon F-1; and the folks at my local Wolf Camera showed me just what size an F-1 is.

Judy Huebner, of my favorite bank, Fidelity National in Lawrenceville, Georgia, gave me some of the details about safety deposit boxes.

The whole wonderful staff of Loving Touch Animal Center in Stone Mountain, Georgia, took me seriously when I asked them how many mice a cat can eat per day, and how to treat a certain injury.

Peggy Strong at Pets, Etc. in Duluth, Georgia, answered my questions about parakeets.

Chris Luke told me about wine.

Diana and Cassandra, two women who sat beside me at the Atlanta Airport several months ago, helped me choose the model of Glaze's Honda as I sat there revising the sixth or seventh draft.

Juan, a young Army man who sat beside me on a flight out of Atlanta, asked that I not use his last name. He set me straight about which basic training camp to use, and where to send Harlan and Buddy.

Any factual errors are my responsibility alone.

And my special gratitude for the cats who have adopted me, and who help me with my manuscripts by:

a) making me laugh a lot and

b) typing for me"]]]]]]" " whenever I" 0S0o0m0e" turn" " ';;';''''';;" aside to p;;pp;[[[llollolololo" " " answer a phone call.

This *is* a work of fiction, so the usual disclaimer about resemblance to persons living or dead certainly applies. I feel compelled to mention, though, that I borrowed lavishly from friends, relatives, neighbors, folks at Unity, and people in the Atlanta breathwork community.

I proclaim loudly, however, that no one person is shown whole and complete. If I borrowed your nose or your hair, I put it on a totally different character. If I borrowed a story from your past, I changed it around and then gave it to someone who doesn't look or sound like you. If I borrowed your name, at least I gave your first name to one person and your last name to another. The exceptions to this rule are Dr. Marty Goldstein and Rev. Andrea Kay Smith, both of whom are real people.

My son, Eli Reiman, shows up in various ways in two or three characters, including the description of the young man who ends up being the dead body. I've already apologized to him and to anyone else who needs an apology, but I'll do it again in print: "Forgive me, y'all. It was done in love."

One final thank-you is due to Nanette Littlestone, who edited this second edition, and who liked it a great deal. Thank you for your encouragement, Nanette. And for your patience.

I have already completed the second book in the series, *Yellow as Legal Pads,* and have started the third one, *Green as a Garden Hose*, as well as the book that will eventually be the ninth or tenth Biscuit McKee mystery, *White as Ice.* That's the one that will finally solve the mystery of how and why Martinsville was founded. I invite you to come along on this journey with me.

Fran Stewart
At my new house on the side of
Hog Mountain, Georgia
July 2004

List of Plant Names

Acer palmatum dissectum	Japanese Laceleaf Maple
Caulophyllum thalictroides	Blue Cohosh
Cimicifuga racemosa	Black Cohosh / Bugbane
Cortaderia selloana	Pampas grass
Daphne odora	Winter Daphne
Hemerocallis	Daylilies
Herbs	Parsley, fennel, dill, oatstraw, chamomile
Ligustrum lucidum	Glossy Privet Bush
Osmanthus fragrans	Sweet Olive
Passiflora incarnata	Maypop / Wild Passionflower
Petunias	Rebecca Jo, Esther, and Sadie
Pieris floribunda	Fetterbush / Mountain Pieris
Pieris japonica	Japanese Pieris
Stachys byzantina	Lamb's Ears
Toxicodendron radicans	Poison Ivy
Viburnum carlesii	Korean Spicebush
Vinca Minor	Periwinkle

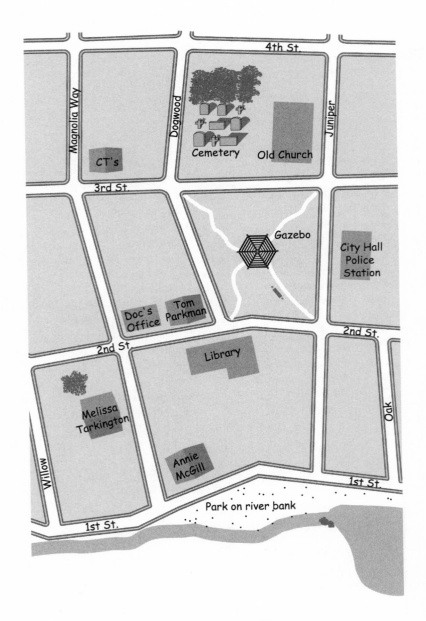

Martinsville

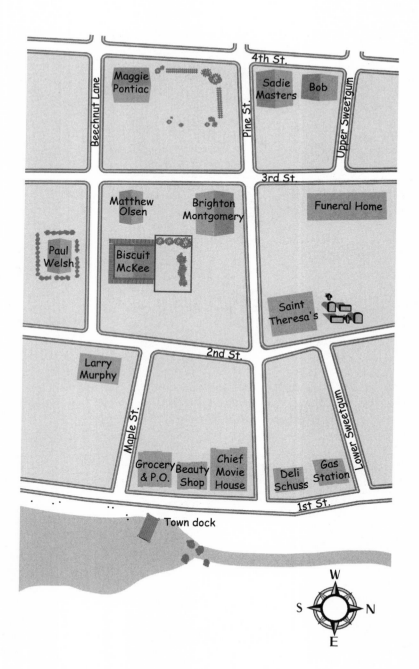

Chapter 1

There had definitely not been a body on the second floor landing when I had run upstairs to the attic earlier in the evening. But there definitely was a body, and a rather messy one at that, as I sauntered downstairs after a leisurely snack. I have never been very squeamish, but I do admit to pausing a moment before I stepped gingerly over the leg that jutted out on the hardwood floor where the stairway turned down to the left.

The blood was just beginning to congeal. Now, did that mean he had been dead only a moment or two? An hour, maybe? How long had I been upstairs? Most of my experience with blood involved rather fresh stuff, and I had always cleaned it up right away. I am meticulous about such things.

You may not think of blondes as being able to deal with blood, but actually I am not really a blonde. I tend more toward the brassy tones. And I do admit to having patches of white here and there. While we are on the subject I might as well tell you, I am on the tall side. My hair is short. My nails are long. My voice is perfectly silky. I love my job. And my name suits me well.

Where was I? Oh yes, the body. Youngish adult. Male. Human. Sandy blond hair, parted on the left. He looked like a man who over-exercised a lot. You know the type. Proud of his biceps. Flexes them every time he sees himself in a mirror. Yecch! Already I did not like him. But, since he was dead, it hardly mattered what I thought.

I have a keen sense of smell. Usually that is a good thing, but in this case, I did not want to stick around smelling the faintest whiff of motor oil that I picked up. Most people would not have smelled it at all. Of course, most people are not like me. I took one more sniff as I walked over him, though, and noticed a woodsy earthy foresty smell. How did that go with motor oil? Ahhh, the oil was in the background, but this man had been in the woods recently. I am not opposed to changing my mind about someone. I was liking him more. Too bad he was very, very dead.

Good clothes. Probably did all his shopping in the city. Deer-skin vest, but this man was not a hunter. He had an interesting medi-cine pouch around his neck. I could tell it held a little piece of antler that he must have found in the woods. I told you I have a very keen sense of smell. Well, his luck had certainly run out. There was a big knife handle sticking out of his middle.

I could not figure out how he had gotten inside. He could not have been in the building when the doors were locked, because I had made my usual rounds right after closing. Did I tell you I am the night watcher here? Very important position because of the dam-age that could be done by intruders. I have been on the job for a year now, and we have not lost a single asset in the last ten months. It took me a while to get rid of all the bad ones right at first. I have probably killed two hundred of them all told, most of them in the first month or two. I did not eat all of them, of course. Only thirty-seven of them.

But, a year ago, at the time of that dead body I had been there a month and a half. I was just getting used to the new staff person. Not that I didn't like her from the start. No, we have been good friends all along. But she did not have my – well – routines down. Some-times she used to check the same places I had already looked, in case there were lost kids. Or sleepers. Or hiders.

At that time there were still a lot of the intruders that I had to take care of. I started bringing them to her as I killed them and leaving them beside her desk. But this one was just too big a body for me to handle, so I left it lying there. Anyway, I had not killed this one. I never take credit for work I have not done myself. It is a matter of pride.

Saturday, April 20, 1996 - Martinsville, Georgia

There had definitely not been a body on the second floor land-ing when I'd closed up the library that Friday night. It was last year. April 28, 1995, to be exact. I always locked the doors and then took a final look around the rooms so I wouldn't miss a kid who was hiding out or someone who'd fallen asleep in the comfy old armchairs.

Being librarian in a small town was never my major goal in life. I have to admit, though, that I love the job, although finding that body last year wasn't fun at all.

Actually, I suppose Marmalade found it. Nowadays I leave the final check-up to her because she's so good at it. She found the little Armitage girl once when the child hid under a desk in the research area. Led her down to my desk as if to say, "Look what we have here, and what are you going to do about it?"

Marmalade is the rather tubby library cat.

Tubby??? You think I am tubby???

She's something of a legend around here. When Miss Millicent died in late 1994 and left all her books and her old Victorian mansion, with its crannies and gingerbread and turrets and gables, to the town council with the stipulation that it be used as a *fine town library*, they took her at her word. They sold most of the excess furniture at an estate auction, and tried to set up the library themselves. But they had no clue how to do it, so they hired me in April of 1995 to repair their mistakes. I wasn't even really a librarian then, although I'd taken a few courses, but I was the only applicant.

The house, one of the oldest in Martinsville, Georgia, had been overrun with mice for a long time, and the little critters had chewed up a number of fine old volumes. Maybe they liked the bookbinding glue. . . .

Yes, and they use the paper to line their nests.

. . . Come to think of it, maybe they tore the paper up for their nests. Anyway, one day about three weeks before I was hired, Marmalade came strolling in off the street through the open front door and started killing mice as if she'd been hired to do it. The town council decided they'd just saved the price of an exterminator. Poor Marmalade had to catch her own dinners.

Mice all taste alike. It gets boring after a while.

The first day I walked into the place, a year ago this month, I saw her at work. I'd hate to be one of those mice. After a day or two, she started bringing dead mice almost like offerings of peace and leaving them in little piles beside my desk. What a sweetheart. She's a gorgeous yellow-orange, with white tummy and feet and chin. She's always been perfectly polite to me, never showing her claws, but I know they're very long and very sharp.

Now, dead mice are not my favorite presents. I much prefer for-sythia, daffodils and a branch of wild cherry blossoms in the spring. Goldenrod in the fall, mixed with some sweet autumn clematis. In the summer, bring me zinnias and marigolds, pungent and prickly-looking. Winter is the time for a bouquet of dried grasses, with a little frost still on them. My husband Sol used to bring me the love-liest little bouquets, just gatherings of roadside flowers, really, but he seemed to have put his heart into the gathering of them.

He sounds nice. Did he like cats?

Sorry, I just got sidetracked. We were talking about that body. Well, this little town was in a buzz, believe me. They don't even have parking meters – and here was a murder. It was the first dead body I'd ever seen, except for funerals. The very first dead person I ever saw was Miss Harkness, who died when I was ten and Grandma Martelson dragged me to the funeral home where she kissed the body of that woman she hadn't even liked in real life, which made the undertaker lady cringe. Even I could tell Grandma was messing up all the work it had taken to make that shriveled-up cranky woman look pudgy and peaceable.

This body, however, which looked quite surprised, didn't seem like it would cause any trouble for the undertaker. I remember it clearly. He was good-looking, even dead. He had a rather Roman nose. Actually, I thought he looked a bit like a handsome camel, with his prominent nose and longish face. But he was untidy-look-ing as a body. His left arm was pointing off toward Biographies, while his head was hanging sideways over the edge of the staircase and his right foot sprawled in the general direction of Histories. There was an amulet bag around his neck that must have gotten twisted around in back of him as he fell. I could see the edge of it poking out from under his very well-developed shoulder. The bag was a light grayish leather . . .

Mouse-skin, obviously.

. . . with some beadwork on it. The beads were as orange as . . . as Marmalade here. We found out later it held some small stones and the tip of an antler.

I knew that.

The knife was easy to spot. The handle looked like a big hunt-ing knife, and it was sticking up at an angle through a leather vest that probably cost an arm and a leg. I have a problem with deerskin

vests. When *Bambi* first came out, I was very young and very im-
pressionable. Then, when my son wanted to learn to hunt when he
was still pretty young, I rented the video to show him what happens
when you kill a mommy deer. Of course, I know full well that the
whole movie was wildly imaginative; papa stag and young son would
have fought it out instead of that Hollywood-ish magnificent abdica-
tion at the end. But I felt better not having a son running around the
woods with a gun. We started him on rock-climbing lessons instead,
and he practiced on the big cliffs near here.

I have to admit I felt a little funny about having a body in my
library. Actually, I suppose I'm sounding too calm about it. Keep in
mind though, that it's been a full year since the murder. Everybody
in Keagan County was talking about it, and some people even started
locking their doors at night. We discussed everything we knew and
quite a bit that people made up or guessed at. Of course, since I was
new to the town, some folks thought I might have done it, although
Bob never thought so. The detectives who were called in questioned
me (and everybody else) thoroughly. One of them sat asking questions, and the other one took notes. Even though I was innocent, I
remember feeling like a deer caught in the headlights.

Or a mouse in my sights.

You see, I'm a reasonably flexible person, but murder wasn't a
part of my usual vocabulary at that time. I've led almost fifty years
of a fairly quiet life, after all. My long ash-brown hair is liberally
sprinkled with gray. I have a slightly rounded tummy, and a bustline
that used to be a lot higher. I was widowed five years ago, after
almost twenty years of reasonably happy marriage. Three kids, but
they're all grown up now. All of my kids were born in February,
three years in a row. Karla Michaels, my best friend from grade
school, who ended up living next door to Sol and me (until she got a
divorce and moved to Phoenix), made a number of not-so-oblique
references to "what went on around the Brandy house every May." I
figured it was just the result of all those springtime scents in the air.
That and simply loving the man I'd married. And now I have two
grandkids and one on the way. I don't believe in hanging onto kids
as they grow. Let them blossom their own way. Raise 'em right as
you can, feed them enough, give them room, and see what they turn
into. Like gardening, you can get a wonderful harvest that way.

Speaking of gardening, I'm in pretty good shape because I do
heavy gardening. I'm talking wheelbarrows and shredder and weeding by hand.

Built my own three-bin compost pile. It's not fancy woodworking, but I can sure wield a hammer. Anyway, when I took this job I had no real strings attached to me except the yard I loved at the old house in Braetonburg. My daughter's taking good care of it though.

Sol's financial sense had left me with a modest income for life, and the Braetonburg Women's Investment Club I helped start twenty-one years ago has really paid off. So my finances are secure, but I wanted more than just staying at home, more than just volunteering on various committees. The library job had sounded ideal. Why, you might ask, didn't I just drive down the valley the five miles from home each day? Good question. I wanted a change. You see, the old house I had shared with Sol still felt lonely to me. I wanted new horizons.

Working here in the Martinsville Library sure kept me busy at first. It took a lot of effort those first few months to set it up, but now it's just Monday, Wednesday, Friday on the job, plus Saturday from ten till two. Tiny salary, but a new town to get to know. Stretch my wings. Wonderful.

Running up and down those stairs in the library helps keep me active, too. Three floors and an attic, but only the bottom two floors are used for the public. Library records and office stuff take up part of the third floor. The rest is pretty much unused. The town council wanted to lock all the upper doors, but I reminded them that Marmalade needed to have access to the entire place to keep down the rodent population, so they just put up some "KEEP OUT — STAFF ONLY" signs at the bottom of the stairs to the third floor. Effective enough for a small town where nothing ever happened.

I'd like to turn the place into a haunted house for Halloween some year, but the trustees who hired me aren't ready for that yet. They're a stodgy lot. Can you believe, they almost didn't hire me because of my name? Too unusual, they said. Didn't sound like a librarian. I was just a woman from the next town with too much time on my hands. Could I help it if my mother was a potter and named me Bisque after the unglazed ceramic ware that she loved?

Of course, once I was in grade school I became Biscuit, and that's what I've been called ever since, Biscuit McKee. My first husband's last name was Brandy, and long before the wedding I told him I absolutely refused to change to Biscuit Brandy. It sounded like a snack and a shot, so I kept McKee at a time when women didn't routinely do that. At least not women from around here. But Sol never minded, and it was just our business after all. The kids decided not to bother with hyphens and such, so they all three grew up as Brandies.

Next week, I'll still be Biscuit McKee, even though I'll be marrying for the second time. Bob said he thought my name fitted me. Nice guy.

Yes, he is.

Marmalade seems to like him a lot, too. Anyway . . . I say 'anyway' a lot, don't I? It's a good word, though. As I was saying, the knife was obvious, but there was a lot less blood than I would have expected. Oh, there was blood all right, a few splashes and a small puddle on the hardwood floor. But most of it seemed to be confined to the front of his all cotton shirt. That Banana store, maybe? She, Marmalade that is, had met me at the front door that morning and marched me right up the stairs. There was no misunderstanding her instructions. She seemed to expect me to know what to do. After one quick look I hurried downstairs to my desk and dialed the number for the police station. I didn't want to alert the volunteer fire fighters, so I didn't call 911.

Funny that a little town like Martinsville, Georgia, has access to that nine-one-one number for emergencies. It was only a couple of decades ago that all the towns along the Metoochie River, which is not much more than a large creek, were upgraded to individual phone lines. Before that, everyone was on party lines. Now, if you've never experienced a party line, you just haven't lived. At home in Braetonburg when I was growing up, our phone line was shared by four other families whose rings we heard, and five families whose rings we *didn't* hear. How did we know who the phone was ringing for? Simple. It was sort of like a Morse code, or like audible Braille. When the call was for us, we heard one long ring followed by two short rings. Karla, my best friend, had one long, one short. The grocery store was three short. Mr. Johnson was one long. Auntie Blue's ring was two short. If you wanted to make a phone call, you had to listen first to see if anybody else was talking. Of course, some people just listened all the time regardless. It's very hard to have a secret in a small town.

From the Statement of Bisque McKee
to the Georgia Bureau of Investigation
Saturday, April 29, 1995

Yes, I found the body when I came in to work
this morning. . . . About 8:30. . . . No, I
didn't. I could tell he was dead. . . .Because
he looked dead. . . . No, I did not. I went
only about half-way up there, then I called
the police station. . . .Last night? I went to
bed about 10:00. . . .I wear size 8½ medium.
Why? . . . No, I'd never seen him before. . . .
No, I don't know why he was here in the library.

Chapter 2

Saturday, April 1, 1995

Harlan paused a moment, then gently pressed the button on his Nikon F-1. The anole lizard didn't even blink as the camera gave out a barely discernible click. Perfect. He eased back from where he had been leaning over the edge of a stone outcropping and ran his hand through his sandy blond hair – at which movement the six-inch lizard turned a questioning glance in his direction. "Sorry, little friend," Harlan whispered, and the breeze carried his words to a female goldfinch perched on the newly leafing-out tulip poplar tree that grew at the base of the small hill. The bird fluffed up her feathers, suddenly looking twice her diminutive size and launched herself into the morning light.

Harlan had a head full of medium-length dark blond hair. His long jaws were clean-shaven, but even now, soon after dawn, a wide shadow under his high cheekbones showed that his beard would come in darker than his hair. He wore khaki hiking shorts that exposed his muscled legs. Those legs, stretched out now before him in the early morning sunlight that was fitfully shining between hazy clouds, sported a light feathering of curly hair. His sturdy gray boots, laced up above the ankle, were of good quality and were obviously well-used.

A dozen pockets covered the khaki vest the man wore over a plain beige short-sleeved cotton shirt. Harlan shifted carefully into a more comfortable position, turning to lean back against an already sun-warmed rock.

Weather is funny, he thought. Three years ago about this time there was an ice storm raging through Georgia. He balanced his well-loved Nikon next to his left side, not expecting another shot to present itself. He'd had a chance to buy a used Nikon F-5, which was the absolute top of the line for the nature photography he did. But he'd chosen to stay with his tried and true F-1. He still got great pictures from it, and he didn't need all the fancy gewgaws. Just a couple of lenses, and he was happy.

Just over a year ago he'd driven to the High Museum in Atlanta for an exhibition of the early work of Ansel Adams. The first photo that pioneer of nature photography had ever taken, with a little box camera, was of a windswept landscape. One tree on a hill with a mountain range in the background. That simple image, called *Wind*, sepia-toned with old age, had shown clearly the incredible eye for composition that the young Adams already possessed. Harlan had studied every book he could find about Adams' photos, determined to show the soul of nature through his lens.

He loved this area. It was isolated, and he hoped it stayed that way. He'd seen too many communities succumb to the sprawl that had enveloped Atlanta and Athens, and was threatening Asheville and the western Carolinas. Luckily, his hometown of Garner Creek, even though it was the Keagan County seat, with a little courthouse on a tree-lined square, was nestled far enough into the valley not to be too noticeable to folks who were looking for a suitable vacation spot or a site for 'development.' Harlan had often thought that *change* was not necessarily synonymous with *progress*.

He was getting ready to reach into one of his myriad pockets for the flask of water he always carried, when off to his right, three deer stepped quietly from a small copse of white-trunked river birch. They paused on the edge of the small meadow that stretched from the knoll where Harlan sat, to the pine woods fifty yards northwest of him. The late spring grasses of the meadow waved gently toward Harlan. Good, he thought. I'm downwind from them.

It was sheer luck that he had been using his 70-210 lens to get macro shots of the lizard. Now, even at this distance, he'd be able to capture the translucent ears of the first doe, if he could just have a little bit more light.

Slowly and without discernible movement, he reached for his Nikon, all the time watching the two females with the gangly-legged fawn. As he raised the camera ever so slowly into position, a second fawn poked her dainty head from behind the farther doe. 'Move a tiny fraction forward, little one,' he urged her mentally. 'And, please, I need a sunbeam.'

Harlan Schneider had been photographing animals for fourteen years. He'd always been a big boy, tall and strong for his age, with shoulders that broadened early. Some of his friends had started hunting early, with guns their dads had given them. But Harlan hadn't been interested. Instead, he had spent hours practicing with the bow that had once belonged to his great-grandfather. His grandmother had given it to him on his tenth birthday, when he was almost strong enough to bend it and string it.

By the time he turned thirteen, he could place his arrows in the bull's-eye of the target seven out of every eight shots. His father had finally insisted that he put his skill to "real use," which meant killing something. That first kill had been his last. As he lifted the lolling head of the six-point buck, he noticed the play of light and shadow across its lower jawline. His own face was already lengthening into its adult shape that would remind many people of an Arabian stallion because of the prominent, aquiline nose he had inherited from his father's Austrian ancestors. His well defined cheekbones came from his Indian grandmother. They held the same kind of shadows as the small buck, but his were the shadows of life rather than of death. Harlan knew the size of the deer herd had to be controlled, but he did not want to be the one to do it.

His mother, who was half Cherokee, and his grandmother had tanned the deerskin for him and had made him a vest that embarrassed him at first because it was too big for him. "I'm making it for the man you will become," his grandmother had told him, and now he appreciated her far-seeing plans. His father mounted the six-point rack and hung it in the living room proudly. One night about a month later, Harlan snuck downstairs, took the rack from the wall, and carried it out into the forest, snapped it off its backing, and left it to be consumed by the tiny forest animals, mice and shrews and such. But first, he broke off a two-inch tip from the longest prong, and put it in the medicine pouch he always wore around his sturdy neck.

It was still there, on this early April morning, the pouch holding the bit of antler as well as some stones he had gathered to remind him of special events in his life. As he breathed quietly, he could feel the weight of the pouch against his chest. His grandmother had decorated the little gray pouch, which she had made from the skins of four large mice, with beads made of the red Georgia clay.

They had lightened when she fired them in the kiln in her backyard, so now they were more orange than red. Mice stood for scrutiny in the animal totem, an ability to pay close attention to detail. His grandmother had seen that ability in Harlan even when he was a baby, lifting his head to peer at the ribbon in her braided hair.

The day after he shot the deer, Harlan walked down to the Garner Creek General Store, a wonderful conglomeration of groceries, hardware, knick-knacks, gifts, clothing, postcards, hunting apparatus, and – what Harlan wanted – cameras. He bought himself a basic Kodak 35mm, paying for it with money he had earned working in the small auto-repair shop that his father and his uncle ran next to his uncle's house.

After a day of cleaning carburetors and gapping spark plugs, changing oil and rotating tires, the young Harlan would escape to the wooded hills behind his family's house, and spend the rest of the daylight hours teaching himself about light and shadow, always hoping to capture on film the grace, the agony, the grandeur that he had first seen in that stag's final breath.

He spent entire weekends camping out in the woods, leaving his family's good-natured bickering behind. He photographed ants and squirrels on tree bark, feral cats in sunlit tall grass and house cats balancing on fences, frogs in misty early morning marshes and snakes on sun-dappled fallen leaves, dragonflies on bright swamp lilies and finches perched in fluttering disarray on tree branches at dawn.

He learned through trial and error. He studied old copies of National Geographic. He spent most of his wages on buying film and having it developed. He named every photo he took, having found a photography book once at the school library in which almost every photo was called *Untitled*. He thought that showed very little imagination on the part of the photographers.

The year he got his first camera, he started saving to buy his own darkroom equipment. In the meantime, the county high school had a photography class, and he managed, while he was still in eighth grade, to weasel his way into the Photo Club so he could use the high school's darkroom after school. He was still proud of that accomplishment. The first picture he created start to finish was of an anole lizard squatting on a rotting log, arching its neck as it investigated a nest of mealy bugs. Somehow or other, Harlan, at age fourteen, had shown the lizard's dignity. That photo was his monumental apology to the stag he had killed before its time.

After almost a decade and a half, Harlan was still fascinated with the process of taking a moment in the life of an animal, and turning it into a statement of truth. He always had been able to wait patiently for the exact detail, for the precise moment. This April morning he was waiting again. Then a cloud shifted just as the second fawn took a delicate step toward her playmate, who was looking back over his shoulder as if to call her to romp a bit in the long grass. The asked-for sunbeam illuminated the first fawn, but left the little female in a shadow of indecision. Click. Perfect. Harlan's mind was already deciding ways he could take that negative and turn it into a story in and of itself. He would probably call it *Invitation to Play* - no. *Friends* - no again. *Invitation* period. Perfect.

> From the Statement of Emily Snow Schneider
> (Mrs. Paul Schneider, mother of the deceased)
> to the Georgia Bureau of Investigation
> Saturday, April 29, 1995
>
> No statement is available. Mrs. Schneider just sat and looked at the floor in her house. When we finally gave up on asking her things, she stood, turned, walked out the door into her back yard, and sat down under a tree next to her mother, Snowfeather Freeman (Mrs. Ian Freeman). She never said even one word.

Wednesday, April 17, 1996

Now that the murder was about a year old, I found myself thinking back as I waited for my sister to arrive, remembering the details of those days. Even now, as I knelt next to the mounds of zucchini vines in my sun-drenched garden, with Marmalade sniffing the ground beside me, my mind wandered back twelve months, and I clearly recalled the first words I ever heard from Bob.

"Martinsville Police Station. Bob Sheffield. May I help you?"

I remember thinking, 'What a soft-spoken man.' His voice reminded me of the *Stachys byzantina* I'd grown in the border near the front porch, so the kids could play with the woolly leaves. *Stachys* was my son Scott's first real word. He had crawled over to me one day, pulled on my pants leg and said "Say kiss." So I'd bent down to kiss him, praising him for speaking not just a word, but a sentence. He'd squirmed away from me, and it took his older sister's interpretation for me to understand. "Mommy, he wants to touch the lamb's ears." I taught all three of my kids the botanical names of plants right from the start. There's something so sweet about a three-year-old saying *"Cortaderia selloana"* when she wants to wave a Pampas Grass plume as she marches around the yard.

"May I help you?"

"Oh, I'm sorry. I found a body here in the library, and I don't know what to do with it."

"A body? Who am I speaking with?"

"I'm Biscuit McKee, the new librarian, and I found a dead man with a knife sticking out of his chest on the stairs when I got here a few minutes ago."

"Leave the library right now. Walk out the front door and wait by the street. I'll be there in about two minutes."

I took an extra moment to scoop up Marmalade, but then, as it occurred to me that whoever had killed that man might still be in the library, I rushed outside. Once there I stopped to catch my breath, and hadn't waited more than half a minute when the dark blue Martinsville police car drove up. Out stepped my lamb's ear voice. How could I have lived here three weeks, in a little town like this, and not met him yet? Of course, I'd spent most of those three weeks inside the library. He stood there, with his hand still on the car door, just looking at me. He was probably wondering if I was the murderer.

He was taller than I was by half a head. Black hair, liberally sprinkled with silvery gray. A nose that must have been broken once or twice, since it had a crook in the middle of it. His ears stuck out a bit, and his mouth had laugh lines around it. Gray-blue eyes behind no-nonsense glasses. He kept watching me as he closed the car door.

Bob Sheffield was the town's only police officer. He walked forward, introduced himself, and asked me to stay outside while he looked around the library. As we shook hands, I saw that he had clean fingernails. By this time I was sure that if anyone had still been inside the library, Marmalade would have known it. So I followed Bob up the walk telling him that theory. Surprisingly, he seemed to accept it, and we walked in together.

I set Marmalade down and led Bob toward the stairs, answering his simple questions as I went. What time had I arrived, did I see anyone near the library, did anything seem out of place, and so on.

The man must have been somewhere in the library before it closed. Or else he had broken in after closing. I hadn't even thought to throw a towel or anything over his face, and there he sprawled, his half-open eyes looking up at the ceiling. When Bob first saw the body, he bounded up the twelve stairs, crying out as he went, "No! Not Harlan!" I was so startled by his outburst, I stopped at the bottom and simply watched as he bent down and lightly touched the young man's shoulder. It hadn't occurred to me that he might know the person, but he obviously did.

I could see the moment when Bob suddenly remembered my presence. Or maybe he was just remembering that he was a cop, as well as a friend. He straightened up, shifted from his left foot to his right, pushed his glasses up higher onto the bridge of his bent nose, turned to look down the stairway at me, and said, "Thanks for not covering this up. You might have disturbed some evidence. How close did you get to the body?"

"Just to there," I said, indicating the third or fourth step down from the landing. "I didn't want to get any closer." I'm not particularly squeamish, but I hadn't liked smelling the blood that had made trails down his clothing and dripped onto the floor. We didn't have any air conditioning in the library at that time, and you know what late April weather can be like around here. Also, my stomach was objecting.

I didn't want to hang around close to the body, but I didn't want to get too far away from Bob either. At that moment I really didn't care how the guy had gotten into my library. I just wanted him out of it.

Bob must have realized that I was beginning to feel unnerved, so he suggested that we go downstairs while he called the doctor. Of course, a little town like Martinsville didn't have an official medical examiner, but Bob explained that Dr. Nathan could make out a death certificate. On the way down, Bob asked me if I'd ever considered that in movies people were always killing a person here and dumping the body there, carting it around as if it didn't have urine running all over everything. It was an unusual topic for a first conversation.

When we joined Marmalade, she was pawing at the papers on my desk. I moved her aside and pushed the phone over toward Bob. Not knowing what to do, I simply leaned against the edge of the old rolltop desk. The pigeonholes were still stuffed with papers that had been left behind by the Millicents. Someday I'd get around to sorting through them.

"The people who go to those movies . . ." Bob was rambling. Why would a cop be nervous? ". . . want to see blood and guts, and they think what they're seeing is exactly like the real thing. Even though I've been the town cop for twenty years, and I've seen lots of dead bodies, they've mostly been car accidents or people who died after long illnesses. This is the first time I've seen a newly murdered body." Maybe he was simply trying to keep me calm. It was working. I found myself watching the play of sunlight that came in from the east window in the Children's Books section, and spilled across the slightly raised blue veins on the back of his left hand.

"I took over this job when my dad died of a heart attack. He was writing a speeding ticket at the time. I was thirty-four years old, working with my brother part time, so I just moved in and ran the station until they could find someone to replace him. That was twenty years ago, and mostly what I've done is write a few tickets and figure out who painted Mrs. Hoskin's mailbox purple. It's usually Tom Parkman's nephew, Roger, or some of his friends. I know all the kids in town, and they know I care about them. They also know I'm watching. Of course, I know all the parents, too, and all the stories. But this is the first murder here in modern times."

"Who is this guy, anyway? I don't think I've seen him in town."

Bob took a deep breath, almost as if he didn't want to put the thought into words. "His name is Harlan Schneider. He was here only for a couple of days. He lives and works . . ." Another deep breath. ". . . lived and worked in Hastings as an auto mechanic, but he was house-sitting for Matthew Olsen, next door to Mrs. Hoskins and her mailbox."

I knew Matthew Olsen. He came to the library once a week, and we usually chatted for a while. He told me all about his pet parakeet, Mr. Fogarty. And Buddy, his son. Each week Mr. Olsen checked out a biography. Margaret Mead. Jonas Salk. I love biographies, too. The week before he left on his trip, he checked out *Truman*. Good reading. It won the Pulitzer prize a couple of years ago. But LONG! It'll keep him busy for a while. I looked up into Officer Sheffield's eyes and almost lost my train of thought. Again.

"Why would Mr. Olsen get a mechanic to house sit?"

"His son Buddy was baby-sitting the parakeet . . ." He paused when Marmalade jumped from my end of the desk and landed right in front of him, meowing loudly.

You have to baby-sit a parakeet?

He idly scratched the back of her head and went on with his sentence. ". . . while Matthew drove to Ohio for a couple of weeks to visit his daughter."

"Why do you have to baby-sit a parakeet?"

"Because pet parakeets are supposed to be handled every day. And Mr. Fogarty seems to like the attention."

Thoughts of the dead body up the stairs kept me determined to keep talking. That way I wouldn't have to think about the blood that I didn't know how I was going to clean up. "You mentioned Ohio. Is the family really spread out?"

"For a while." Bob glanced out the window, obviously looking for the doctor. "Buddy's sister married a local boy who joined the Air Force. He was transferred to Wright Patterson Air Base in Ohio last year. No telling where they'll go next."

"What does this have to do with Harlan?" My mind wandered back to that dead face. It looked like alabaster. Surprised alabaster.

"Buddy met Harlan when they were in boot camp almost ten years ago, right out of high school. In fact, that's when Matthew bought the parakeet – to keep him company while Buddy was gone. Buddy and Harlan became good friends. When Buddy was called out of town on business yesterday, he asked Harlan to come over and stay with the parakeet. It was just going to be a day or two, since Matthew was due to come home yesterday or today."

"How would you know all that?"

"Buddy called me to let me know Harlan would be there. People in town usually check in with me when they're going to be gone for awhile."

"What a horrible homecoming, to find that your son's friend has been murdered."

"It's worse than that. Matthew often said that Harlan was like a second son to him. I'll hate to be the one to tell him. Harlan had everything going for him. He was a great mechanic and a gifted photographer. He was well liked. He told me once that he had a girlfriend, but she had to get a little older before they could date. He was willing to wait, apparently."

"Who was she?"

"No idea. He never said."

Bob withdrew into himself for a moment. I could sense the wheels turning. When he spoke, it was almost as if he'd forgotten I was there. "I don't know why he was killed. I don't know who in this town would do such a rotten thing. And," he added under his breath, "I don't know how to find out."

"You might consider just asking everybody questions. Isn't someone liable to know something?" Was that strident voice coming from me? "What do the police manuals say to do?"

"Ms. McKee, the police manuals weren't written with small towns like this in mind. Sure I know how to gather evidence, but I live here with these folks. I'll be calling in the GBI to handle the investigation."

Officer Sheffield was being patently patient with me, but I couldn't keep my mouth shut. I'd like to think it was just nerves that made me blurt out, "Can't you do your own murder investigation?"

We heard a car pull up outside, and as the young doctor walked up to the front door, Marmalade was purring like an old steam train. If I didn't know better, I would have thought she was saying "Watch your mouth, girl."

That's right.

Chapter 3

Monday, October 3, 1994
Garner Creek, Georgia

"We need just one more signature here, if you please," Ben Alexander said, indicating the line below the husband's name.

The woman took the proffered pen, bent her head, and wrote her name painstakingly on the line. It was so close to the line above it, and her large rounded script looked cramped and confined as she wrote.

"How many keys will we get?" Sid asked as Sarah pushed the form back across the desk toward the gray-suited bank manager, who reached out and added it to the pile of papers in front of him.

"Two, of course, since there are two signatories. I'll bring them to you in just a moment." Ben gave both new customers a friendly smile as he gathered up the stack of papers and tucked them into a manila folder. As he left the room, he turned back once again to glance at the petite auburn-haired woman who had been watching his receding back.

Once the door closed behind the banker, Sid held out his hand and said, "Hand it over to me. We're going to put your mother's ring in the box, and I don't want you arguing about it anymore."

"I like having it where I can see it," his wife objected, "even if it doesn't fit me very well."

"You wouldn't want to lose it. Believe me," he said, "it'll be safer in here." After a moment, Sarah slipped the ring from her fore-finger and placed it reluctantly on her husband's palm.

The banker bustled back into the room, with the folder held firmly under one arm. He sat down at his desk and withdrew two long keys from a small orange envelope that had been tucked into a slot in the folder. He smoothly double-checked to make sure the two keys looked identical, then withdrew a second orange envelope from the top drawer of his desk. As he inserted one of the keys in the second envelope, he smiled again at the young woman. When he started to hand one of the enve-lopes to her, he was surprised that the husband reached out and took it from him. The woman held her breath for a few moments, let it out in a barely audible sigh, then bent her head to look at her hands, as if they held the answer to a question she hadn't quite formulated yet.

Without missing a beat, the banker said, "Yes, well, here's the other key, Mrs. Borden. Now you'll each have one," and held the second envelope out toward Sarah.

Again her husband took the key before his wife even lifted her head. "I'll keep one on my key ring and we'll put the other one in a safe place." Turning to face the bank manager directly, he said, "My wife has an unfortunate tendency to lose things." The banker thought he saw a movement, almost as if the woman had started to shake her head, but when he glanced over at her, the fringe of auburn hair hung still, shielding her eyes from view.

After a moment, during which no one breathed, Ben suggested that they move into the vault to locate the box and to be sure both keys worked. Number 146 was one of the medium-sized boxes, about four feet off the floor, halfway down the left wall of the small vault. The bank manager inserted a key from a large ring and turned it counterclockwise, then spoke to the husband.

"Now, Mr. Borden, would you put one of your keys in this slot on the right and turn it all the way to the left?" As the husband removed the key from one of the envelopes and stepped forward to slide it in the lock, Ben noticed that the fluorescent lighting in the vault made the man's sallow skin look greenish. 'He looks like a loser,' thought the banker, 'and he's a lot older than his wife.' Aloud he suggested, "Try turning it around. The flat side of your key goes toward the hinge side of the box."

Sid didn't seem to appreciate the help, but he turned the key over and twisted it in the lock. "Now," Ben said, moving to take hold of the little handle, "we'll slide the box out. As you can see, it's completely empty. We'll take it out here," he said, leading them to a small cubicle and motioning them inside it. "You can take as much time as you need to arrange your special items in your box. When you're through, just open the door." Ben backed away from the little room, closing the sliding door as he did so. He walked back to his desk, shaking his head slightly. 'Such a quiet little woman,' he thought.

Inside the small chamber, Sid took three or four white envelopes out of his inside jacket pocket and placed them in the box. Reaching into the left pocket of his jacket, he extracted the little ring. There was one small but exquisite diamond, surrounded by a circlet of tiny diamond chips. They caught even the fluorescent lighting and magnified it. The woman looked once at the twinkling light of the ring, then turned her head away. Sid placed the ring under the top envelope, the one marked H.M.

Without looking back, she slid open the door and stepped into the lobby to wait while her husband, accompanied by the bank manager, returned the box to its slot. This time, he used the second key, saw that the box was locked, worked that key onto his key ring, patted his jacket pocket, shook hands with the banker, and left the vault.

As he walked past the cloth-covered table with cups and a coffee maker on it, Sid tossed the empty orange envelope into the trash can. Sarah glanced up once to meet the banker's eyes before she turned to follow her husband out the front door of the First Community Bank of Keagan County.

Saturday, April 20, 1996
Martinsville, Georgia

"So, why couldn't he do his own murder investigation?" my sister asked me.

"Because, along with everybody else in town, he was a possible suspect. But he was cleared right away."

"That's good. It would have put a damper on your wedding."

"Anyway," I said, ignoring the sarcasm and pausing for a moment to take a deep breath and a sip of tea, "that's how we first met, over a dead body. It's hard to believe I never told you the story before."

"It's not as if I ever bothered to keep in touch, other than birthday cards." Glaze, my sister, also has a pottery name. She's five years my junior, but a universe away from me in experiences. Twenty-some-odd years ago, when Sol and I were married, she was in the hospital trying to recover from another suicide attempt. We didn't even think of postponing the ceremony because she had been so far from us for so many years.

Even since her recovery, she and I hadn't spent any real time together. Just brief phone calls and periodic letters. Then she called me last month, in late March, asking if she could come early for my second wedding, assuring me that she would be a model guest. As we talked, she finally told me something of her return to full health after having been diagnosed at age thirty-six with bipolar disorder. Manic depression was what I'd known it as, but I simply never realized she had it. I agreed to the visit, quietly breathing a heart-felt "thank you" because this was my answer – I'd been wondering how I was going to get the curtains up before the wedding. Not that it was necessary. I just wanted the house to look its best, and my sister could sew. But that was another story. . . .

It was a long phone call. She was enthusiastic when I asked for her help and told her about all my plans – café curtains in the kitchen and office, some long, sweepy curtains in the living room, some lacy ones at the front door. I know, it sounds like I'm stuck several decades ago, but I happen to like lace at the front door. I'm not alone. Here, in northeastern Georgia, you can still see a lot of lace when you walk along the lanes in the evening, looking into the lighted front rooms. I'd already measured all the windows and bought all the material, including some extra just in case, but hadn't found the time yet to do the cutting and sewing.

She was two days late getting here, though. She called on Wednesday to say that her car was dead, don't worry, she'd get here in a day or two. Apparently she got a good deal on a used Honda, and had driven it down yesterday. Now her green Civic was parked at the front curb, and she was parked at my kitchen table, one week exactly before my wedding day. My *second* wedding day.

We spent a few moments just looking at each other. When she looked at me, I know she saw a middle-of-the-road, middle-aged, ordinary-looking woman. My long hair has lots of gray in it, but from a distance, you'd say 'there's a lady with brown hair' because the gray is all blended in. I'm five foot seven, only an inch or so taller than Glaze, and I think I'm a little stockier than she is. She holds her weight well. Maybe it's her clothes. I wonder how she does it? Sally, my younger daughter, thinks I have the fashion sense of an aardvark. I suppose she's right. My idea of high fashion is when my socks match my turtleneck in winter, and when my dress is long enough to hide my legs in the summer.

I have *vitiligo*, a condition that means I have no melanin, no pigment in my skin, so the sun burns me rather than tans me. It took me a long time to come to peace with that. When I was young I used to be a sun worshipper, always with a gorgeous tan from May till October, but when I was pregnant with Sandra, my first child, a little patch of non-tanning area appeared on my forehead. I covered it with my hair swept down low and toward the right. But then it migrated to around my mouth, down my neck, here and there on my arms. I spent a lot of years looking like a map of the Alaskan Archipelago, but gradually I lost so much pigment I began to look like one of those English ladies, as if I always wore a hat in the sun. It doesn't bother me any more, but I had to grow into the peace of accepting myself the way I am. All except for my dead white legs. I haven't gotten peaceful about them yet.

Glaze was still gorgeous, in a quiet sort of way; not spectacular, knock-your-socks-off gorgeous. Just the most incredible bone structure, with a nose the Venus de Milo would envy, and those deep-set eyes that looked striking even without makeup. Her short wavy hair had been styled simply to frame her face. It wasn't salt and pepper like mine. No. She got her silver hair straight from Grandma McKee, our dad's mother, who'd had white hair at twenty-eight. Glaze was wearing a brilliant yellow crew-necked shirt that fit the energy of her happy smile. My sister's eyebrows were pretty much perfect. Her ears were small and hugged her head. She had a light quality to her voice. It was pitched fairly low, but had such a nice clarity that she never sounded like one of those over-trained TV voices.

"Are you through looking yet?" she laughed at me.

"No, I feel like I need to make up for lost time. I'm so sorry we were so far apart for . . ."

She stopped me with a wave of her graceful hand with its tapered fingernails. "Let's make a deal right now. The past is the past. What happened, happened. Let's just move forward." She stretched her hand out toward me, obviously requesting a handshake. "I agree to forgive you for being a typical big sister, if you'll forgive me for being a typical little sister. Is it a deal?"

"Done deal," I breathed gratefully. I hadn't wanted to dredge up my lack of care for her in the past. When I entered my teens, she was only eight, so I'd pretty much ignored her, other than to be amazed at her astonishing capacity for guzzling milkshakes. Come to think of it, we had enjoyed occasional games of Scrabble played at a kitchen table much like this one.

We never saw it when her quiet withdrawing ways switched into depression. Mom despaired at her hopelessness, and Dad just kept on believing that his little jewel would "see the light someday." Hardly a prescription for getting the needed help. There weren't any counselors in our small town, and all the doctors were sorely undereducated about depression in those years. We just thought she was a very difficult person to live with; and since she stopped coming home for visits after she was about nineteen, it was easier to build our lives without her. She and I had spent more than twenty years estranged.

When I married Solomon Brandy in 1971, Glenda Harvey was my Matron of Honor, not Glaze, who had spent that April day crouched in a corner at Mainwaring Regional Hospital on the fifth floor, where they put the suicidal people under lock and key.

Now here she sat, this Saturday morning, across the kitchen table from me, still marveling in a life that didn't hurt her all the time. Her depression had been controlled for years with medication and counseling, and she seemed so much calmer than I ever recalled. She was interested in everything. It wasn't so much that I didn't recognize her. It was more that I didn't recognize the new kinship I felt for her. I'd never had a sister before. Not really. Now I had one. It felt good.

Yesterday we hadn't known exactly when she'd be arriving, but Marmalade had scratched at the front door about half past four, warning us that we had company, so I straightened myself up and ran out to meet Glaze before she was even halfway up the walk. As we hugged, I inhaled the most delicious scent. "How can you possibly smell this good after a long car trip? I'm so glad you're here! Whatever happened to your hand?"

She chuckled. "You're going to find out my secrets. I keep a bottle of vanilla extract in the glove compartment so I can dab some on whenever I want to. That way I always smell like a cookie! It wasn't that long a trip today, and I'll tell you about my finger when I'm sitting down."

"Well, no matter what you smell like, you're welcome here. I'm just glad you finally got here."

"Me, too."

"Luckily you made it just ahead of the rain." There had been scattered clouds all day and even some lightning, threatening more showers. One thing about spring in Georgia – when it decides to rain, it generally keeps working on it until everything is soggy. We'd been having a five-year drought so far. Heavy rain just runs off extra-dry soil, so I was voting for slow, gentle rain that would soak in.

Bob, who had stopped by about 4:00 to bring me a lovely bouquet of daisies, walked calmly down the front steps, took the small flowered valise out of Glaze's left hand, gave her a brief hug and a big smile, inspired no doubt by the cookie smell. As we walked up toward the house, I turned to take a good look at my sister, and was surprised to realize that we were both about the same size. "My gosh, you've changed. Whatever happened to my *little* sister?"

"Oh come on, you've seen me since I grew as tall as you."

"I'm not talking about height. You just always seemed so fragile before. Sort of like a waif." I groped for words to explain how strong she looked, even with her bandaged finger. "Now, though, you seem more real, if that makes any sense at all."

"That's because I feel more real, more like the person I'm supposed to be."

"Well, we don't need to stand on the front walk all afternoon. Come on in. Bob's going to put your case upstairs. Did you pack light, or are there six more suitcases in the trunk?"

"I'm here only for a week. Why would I need more than this? I do have my Maid of Honor dress hanging in the back seat and a suitcase in the trunk, but we can get those out later."

As we stepped up onto the deep front porch, Glaze turned back, taking a deep breath. If it had been late winter instead of mid-spring, she would have gotten a whiff of the *Daphne odora*, but April meant she smelled mostly the *Viburnum carlesii*, better known as the

Korean Spice Bush. She breathed out a contented sigh. "It's so quiet here. I'm glad I came." There was a huge clap of thunder. "Well, maybe it's not so quiet," Glaze said as the rain started in torrents. "Whew! Thank goodness for this porch!"

"If you're going to stay here, you'll have to call it a verandah."

"You must be kidding."

"Not at all. Mrs. Hoskins, the woman who's selling me the place, told me that calling it a verandah makes it feel bigger."

"Well then, verandah it is." She shivered a bit in the cool wind that had sprung up when the rain started.

"I'll give you a quick tour of the house and then feed you some hot soup if you're hungry from the trip."

"Do you still think soup is the only food worth cooking? If I remember, you ate more soup than anyone I ever met."

"There's nothing wrong with soup twice a day."

As I stepped back to let her precede me, I could see Glaze's eyes crinkle up as she laughed in response. "There's nothing wrong with milkshakes *three* times a day, either. Now point me toward a bathroom before I bust, and then you can feed me soup to your heart's content."

We walked inside, and I pointed out the doorway to the right that led to the kitchen, then steered her to the left into the living room. "The powder room's over here, tucked near the stairs. A big bath with tub and shower is upstairs, but this'll do for the essentials." Marmalade had been shadowing us the entire time, so I took a moment to introduce them properly. "Marmy, this is Glaze. Glaze, this is Marmalade."

"How do you do, you elegant wonder?"

You smell very sweet, and I like your voice. You are very welcome here.

"Come on into the kitchen when you're through. We'll do the tour after we eat. I made some vegetable barley soup. I hope you like homemade pumpernickel bread."

"Yummy!"

"No milkshakes today, but we'll find one tomorrow, I promise. Give me your car key and I'll ask Bob to bring your other stuff inside once the rain lets up a little."

She fumbled in her purse, and handed me a ring of keys. I turned to go, but not before I heard her exclamation of delight as she walked into the little blue and white nook that was my pride and joy.

I've been in this house only about a month. When Bob and I decided to get married, we knew my year at Melissa's bed and breakfast would be ready to expire, so we found this house - it's a long story - and I moved in with my shredder and reel-type lawn mower and some of the furniture from Braetonburg. My daughters and their spouses came over to help, thank goodness. Bob and I signed a rental agreement with option to buy, but Bob didn't move in with me. Maybe I'm old-fashioned, but I wanted a wedding ring first. Anyway, it's a small town.

Of course, as soon as I moved in, I wanted to tackle everything at once, but knew that I needed to take it one step at a time. In years past my decorating sense had taken a back seat to raising the three kids, and Sol hadn't cared much about fancy wall finishes and such.

The first faux finish painting I did was four years ago, when I helped Sandra, my oldest, fix up the nursery before Verity was born. Verity is my oldest grandchild. Sandra and I painted the room a gentle light green, then mixed green with some faux glaze and a little bit of white paint. We read in the folder from the paint store that we could use a crumpled up plastic bag to dab a texture into the glaze coat as we rolled it on over the solid green. It ended up with the feel almost of leather, and gave a soft mottled look to the nursery walls.

Then Sally, my second daughter, who lived in Hastings, wanted help painting her living room. We used a sponge instead of a plastic bag, to get a heavier, blotchier look to the top coat. Orange, she'd wanted. My gosh, who'd want an orange living room? It did turn out well, though. Probably because it ended up looking more like a soft salmon color.

By the time I got around to doing the little powder room that Glaze was admiring so much, I was willing to try a fake marble finish. It was really just a matter of choosing the paint colors carefully, and then putting them on with a roller in patches over the base coat. I'd chosen a light, light blue as the first coat, then layered on swipes of white and four shades of gray. I finished it with fine silver and gold lines painted with a teeny brush that had only about five bristles.

Feeling a warm sense of accomplishment, I joined Bob in the kitchen, gave him a big hug, and took the jar of vegetable soup out of the fridge. As I did so, the light bulb went *pzzzt*. Of course, when I opened the junk drawer that I've always managed to have in any kitchen I've ever cooked in, there was no extra bulb. I shrugged and dumped the soup into the big pot that Grandma Martelson gave me when I married Sol. I added four or five large spoonfuls of cooked barley, then turned to the cutting board. As I was slicing off some of my special pumpernickel, Glaze walked in, took a sniff, and said, "Wow! That smells divine. I didn't think I was very hungry yet, but now I'm not so sure."

We all three settled around the big table, Bob with his enormous blue coffee cup. I had my big red mug, with the hearts on it, full of raspberry tea. I'd given Glaze the mug mom made six years ago, the one with the green leaf pattern. Bob asked her, "Did you have any trouble finding the place?"

"No, you gave really great directions." She paused as if considering whether or not to continue her train of thought. Apparently the answer was yes, because she said, "I suppose you ought to know . . . I didn't want to worry you on Wednesday, so I didn't tell you the real reason I didn't get here. A really nice woman named Sarah ran a red light in Garner Creek and plowed her little light blue Escort into the passenger side of my car."

"Were you hurt?" I asked as I stood up to ladle the soup into big bowls.

"Sort of. She totaled my car and put both of us in the hospital."

"Hospital?" Bob queried, but I interrupted him.

"Glaze! Why didn't you tell us? You were so close. We could have driven up to get you."

"Well, I knew you had enough on your plate with the wedding plans. Anyway, all I had was this broken finger and a bunch of scratches and dents from the airbag. Luckily, all my bruises are in discreet places. Sarah was hurt worse than I was. Her left knee was banged up pretty badly."

"How can you feel sorry for her if she totaled your car?"

"You sound like a mama bear protecting a cub, Biscuit. I'm okay, and I heal fast. Sarah and I got along just fine once she realized I wasn't going to sue her pants off. She seemed really frightened at first, but then we just seemed to hit it off. She's a really good listener." Glaze paused to lift another spoon loaded with vegetables to her mouth. "Yummy. You *do* know how to cook!"

"Thank you."

"We both like to read a lot," Glaze continued after she swallowed that mouthful, "so we talked about our favorite authors. When her husband got there after he got off work, she was afraid he'd be mad at her for wrecking the car. I could tell he was upset, but that makes sense. It was only a Ford Escort, but that's still money. He turned out to be a used car salesman, so I bought my green Honda from him after I got out of the hospital."

"Garner Creek doesn't have a hospital," I ventured.

"It wasn't really a hospital, I suppose, more like a little clinic, but they had about six beds, three of which were empty."

"You must mean the Montrose Clinic," Bob interjected. "Good little outfit."

"When did you get out?" I asked her.

"Yesterday afternoon. Then I went car-looking and dealt with insurance stuff, and I found a little bed and breakfast place to stay in. Early this afternoon I retrieved my dress from my old car and picked up my new car. Luckily it wasn't damaged, the dress I mean, but I'll need to do some touch-up ironing."

"I'll do the ironing. Your hand looks uncomfortable."

"It doesn't feel too bad, but if it'll get me out of ironing . . ."

"How," I asked her, "did you manage to get admitted to the clinic if you weren't hurt that badly?"

"I guess that's the advantage of a small-town hospital. They wanted their doctor to check me, but she was out of town for a day. They figured it was easier just to admit me so I'd be there at six-thirty in the morning when she came on duty. If they'd been full up, they probably would have released me right away, but I was hurting a lot right at first. I don't know if my insurance will cover it, but it was worth it even if I have to shell out some money."

"Did you have any trouble driving here?" Bob asked. "I noticed it was a stick shift."

"No, it's a breeze to drive, even with my right hand banged up. The gears are as smooth as . . ."

They talked comparative car models for a while, but I tuned out on that. Since they stopped making '57 Chevy BelAires, I firmly believe the automotive industry has gone totally downhill. That was the best car ever made. We got one when I was ten years old. It was black and white. They called them 'skunk cars' that year. I loved those fins. Mom and Dad babied that car, and I learned to drive on it six years later.

Bless my dad. One day when I was seventeen, I was running some errands over in Hastings for Mom, and I got all discombobulated trying to get out of a parallel parking space. There was a pickup truck parked in front of me, and the edge of the road was kind of slanted down toward the curb. I must have connected with the tailpipe. I ended up putting a long scratch in the passenger side door.

I thought I could relate to how Sarah must have felt in the hospital, because I was so scared of telling my dad what I'd done. Dad just took a very long breath, and said, "Well, Bisque honey, I'm glad you weren't hurt." The Chevy still had that scratch when I went to college the next year. I think Dad left it there as a lesson. Or maybe he just didn't think it was all that important.

When we finished eating, I rinsed all the dishes and showed Glaze through the house. The rain had slowed to a minor drizzle, so Bob retrieved her bag and dress. It's really nice to have a man who likes to do such things. That is not, however, the only reason I love him. He returned her keys, then left after the tour. Glaze and I took two spoons and a pint of vanilla ice cream out onto the front porch, curled up and sat foot to foot on the swing, with Marmalade between us, listening to the slow rain and talking till bedtime.

Gratitude List – Friday Night

Five things for which I am grateful:
1. Having a sister
2. This gentle rain
3. Ice Cream!
4. Marmy
5. And of course! Bob

My Gratitude List:
my two humans
this new one
the bird feeder
rain
the swing

Chapter 4

June 1985

Harlan worked for his father and uncle all the way through high school, but left three weeks after graduation for army boot camp. He was very bright, but he was not interested in college. He loved to work with his hands. He could listen to an engine and sense where the balance was off, just as he could look at a forest glade and gravitate toward the ideal vantage point, the best hiding place for getting the perfect camera angle. College was books, mostly. Not for him.

The army hadn't been his cup of tea, either. For one thing, they taught him how to shoot people. Luckily he hadn't been called upon to perform that service in any sort of combat situation. He'd made a few friends, including Buddy Olsen who had come from Martinsville, the little town fifteen miles down the valley from Garner Creek, on the other side of Hastings, where Harlan's mother's cousin owned a car dealership. The two had known each other by sight at Keagan High, but hadn't become friends until they'd been stuck in the same platoon, sleeping across the aisle from each other in the spartan dormitory at Fort Jackson in the center of South Carolina.

They had both been assigned to the same post out of basic training, and had left on a bus for Fort Knox, near Louisville, Kentucky, with the high spirits of the young off on an adventure. Buddy, who had almost flunked the typing class that was a requirement at Keagan County High School, became a clerk assigned to the Paymaster's office. "Heaven help the army," he had joked to Harlan when the assignments were posted. Harlan ended up working in the motor pool. "Maybe there's hope for this outfit yet," Buddy quipped.

Harlan soon found the base newspaper and volunteered to be the photographer, to fill in for a young sargeant who had just been transferred. The editor of the Post News was delighted, especially once he saw that Harlan knew his way around the darkroom. So, for the next couple of years, Harlan's life ran in the same predictable pattern. After a day of motor oil and engine noise, he took up the Nikon F-1 that his parents had bought him as a graduation present, and headed out to photograph parades and tanks, flags and softball teams, lines in the mess hall, cooks at work, pilots lounging in the hangars, infantry drilling in full battle gear, and MPs directing traffic on and off base.

He usually got together with Buddy for dinner at the mess hall, and there was a group of "regulars" that gravitated around them. Harlan dated some of the WAC's, but never got really serious about any of them. He felt shy around women. Buddy, on the other hand, dated most of them and wasn't shy at all.

Buddy Olsen, Private First Class, had red hair, a gift from his Irish mother who had died when Buddy was fifteen. He was as full of blarney as anyone Harlan had ever met. The two balanced each other. Buddy provided the lift and Harlan the stability. Buddy the corny goofing around, and Harlan the thoughtful assessments. Buddy knew all the tunes, and Harlan knew all the words. Buddy was curly haired and cute, while Harlan had the aristocratic bearing of his mother's Indian heritage and the blond good looks of his Austrian great-grandfather.

Harlan loved to photograph people listening to Buddy. They were usually laughing or singing along boisterously, but occasionally Buddy would bend over his guitar and launch into an Irish fisherman's lament that would bring tears, quickly brushed away, to the eyes of the young servicemen and women in the lounge at Fort Knox.

From the Statement of Bartholomew "Buddy" Olsen
to the Georgia Bureau of Investigation
Saturday, April 29, 1995

He was my best friend. . . . I can't believe this happened. . . . It's my fault. . . . Why? Because if I hadn't asked him to feed Mr. Fogarty, he wouldn't be dead now. . . . My dad's parakeet. That's his name. . . . Yes, sir, we've been friends for something like ten years now, ever since we got to know each other in boot camp. . . . Library? No, I don't know why he was in the library.

Saturday, April 20, 1996
Martinsville

"Were there other people working in the library when he was killed?" Glaze asked me.

I was startled out of my reverie by my sister's question. The Saturday morning sun was shining in the east windows of the kitchen, and I had to shift mental gears before answering her.

"No. The volunteers weren't there that day."

"Volunteers?"

"Yes, bless their hearts. The first week I was here I was the only staff, and it was overwhelming, but then three women came to me one day and said that they were charter members of the Martinsville Ladies Book Reading Society. They stood there in their flowered housedresses looking like a collection of petunias, and when they offered to help me sort and label all the library books, 'free of charge, my dear, because we just love literary things,' I agreed immediately.

"One of them, Rebecca Jo Sheffield, the one I thought of as the Head Petunia, turned out to be Bob's mother. That day she was wearing a white dress with lavender flowers and green leaves all over it. At the beginning she was there all the time, but now she's pared down to just Fridays and Saturdays."

"Who were the other two?"

"The second Petunia was Esther Anderson. She helped the most with the cataloging. I shouldn't use past tense. She still volunteers two days a week, Wednesdays and Saturdays. The woman's a walking memory vault. Thank goodness she was there almost from the beginning."

"What color was she wearing that day?"

"Sort of a bilious orange background with marigolds and sunflower designs all over."

"Amazing," Glaze said to her teacup. "They didn't get arrested?"

"For the murder? Of course not."

"No, I meant for the clothing."

"It wasn't that bad. Sounds worse than it looked. They were kind of cute standing in a row. I truly couldn't have gotten all that work done without them."

"My sister, Miss Patience . . ." Glaze started, then switched to a question. "Who was the third Petunia?" That finger must have been hurting her. She kept rubbing the splint and massaging up and down her arm.

"Sadie Masters was the third one. Don't worry. You'll meet her. She is simply a card. First of all, she wears yellow all the time. Doesn't own a single piece of clothing that isn't yellow. Even her car is yellow."

"Sort of like that guy in the water skiing show at Cypress Gardens?"

"Who?"

"Some guy who wears yellow all the time. He started trick skiing in the water show when he was fifty years old. Last I heard he was still doing it, and that's been almost thirty years. The guy must be pushing eighty."

Doesn't it amaze you to learn what tidbits of information some people hold in their heads? "Glaze, how on earth do you know that?"

"I heard it on public radio once. They interviewed the guy. Really interesting. Anyway, tell me more about Sadie."

"Thanks for keeping me on track," I commented dryly. Taking a moment to collect my thoughts, I conjured up a picture of Sadie in my mind as I poured yet another cup of tea from the blue-ringed white teapot my mother – our mother – had made as a gift for me when Scott, her first grandson, was born.

"Well, Sadie rattles on to herself in an undertone all day long. Works at the library every Wednesday and Friday, and we can hear her muttering happily away as she trundles around with her shoelaces invariably untied." I nodded at Glaze's unspoken question as she raised her eyebrows. "Yes, her shoes and shoelaces are yellow, too. She can't drive worth a tom turkey, but she refuses to walk anywhere. Once she had to go to Brighton Montgomery's house . . ."

"Brighton Montgomery? That sounds like an English butler. 'Brighton, serve the scones in the parlor.'"

I would rather have fish.

I reached out to stroke Marmalade, who had just jumped up on my lap. "Wouldn't it be 'Montgomery, serve the scones in the parlor'? I thought they called them by their last names."

"Brighton sounds better. Who is he, anyway?"

He is the one with the black tomcat.

"He sells insurance. Sadie had a payment due that day. He lives two houses down from her, and I'll be darned if she didn't get in her Chevy and drive there, pay her bill, and then drove back home. Bob saw her do it, since he was parked across from Brighton's house at the time. She almost clipped his fender on her way back up the street. It's a miracle she's never killed anybody."

"At least if she's all yellow, she'll be easy to spot."

"Yes," I agreed readily, "we all tend to pull aside when Sadie drives by."

As often happens in relaxed conversations, we roamed off to a discussion of the weather patterns for awhile, then returned to the topic of the new library.

"Mrs. Sheffield was a great help. She filled me in on a lot of the history of the house. Miss Millicent had been an avid reader, just like her parents. They'd all lived together in that house 'Simply forever, my dear, there were always Millicents here.' That family must have saved every book they ever bought. The house was absolutely stuffed with books."

And mice.

"Sort of like my bedroom when I was a kid?" Glaze asked innocently, as she reached for a croissant.

Did you have mice in your bedroom?

"No. Nothing could be as stuffed as your room. Where on earth did you collect all that junk?" I asked as Marmalade licked a flake of croissant off the front of my purple polo shirt.

"It wasn't junk. Well, not exactly junk. I liked it at the time, but now I live in a Danish Modern sort of townhouse, with a roommate who likes the Japanese style. You know, one small table, a few cushions, and a perfect vase with three stalks of bamboo in it."

Any windowsills?

"Sounds lovely."

"Well, Yuko did shame me into throwing out a big bunch of clutter."

"Yuko? Is she Japanese?"

"Third generation. Yuko Tanaka." Glaze shifted in her chair, stood up to take a quick stretch, resettled herself, and said, "Tell me more about your Petunias."

Two of them make a lot of sense, and the other one forgets to tie her shoes.

"They helped me go through the house, room by room, usually with Marmalade here leading the way." I stroked the soft fur bundle that was purring loudly in my lap. Patting a cat reduces blood pressure, I've heard. "It didn't take us long to figure out the reading patterns of each of the Millicents. Old Mr. Millicent had filled his office and his den with histories and mysteries, while old Mrs. M leaned toward the sciences and biographies – and more genteel mysteries, with fewer bodies and much less blood than the mister's."

But they did not have a cat.

"Old Mrs. M was still reading avidly well into her nineties. At her 86th birthday someone in the book club gave her a lurid romance novel as a joke. Turned out she loved it. The next week, she got a friend of hers to drive her to the bookstore in Hastings, where she bought about fifty more of the things. 'The steamier they are, the better I like them,' she'd told Mrs. Sheffield. 'They keep me warm on winter evenings.' I think we both would have loved her, Glaze. From everything I've heard about her, I guess she was a real hoot."

But she did not have a cat.

"Too bad she didn't have a cat," I commented. "That would have cut down on the mouse population."

You've got it.

"Even without a cat, she sounds like a great role model," Glaze suggested. "I love hearing about older women . . ." she paused with a rueful grin on her face. "That means older than I am."

"That includes me, then."

"Older women who stay active and alert as they age. That's the way I want to be." She twisted a strand of her silver hair around her left index finger. "I consider my gray hair a mark of wisdom, not of age."

"Well, between the two of us, we must be pretty wise. I've got a fair amount of gray too."

I stick to orange and white myself.

"Did you know I'm the only woman in my office who's never colored her hair?"

I thought back to my stint in corporate life in Boston. "I guess I was the only one in my office, too. Most of them were blondes, although the last two months I was there, the redheads seemed to be gaining favor."

I know what you mean. We have two Irish Setters in town now. Talk about red . . .

"So tell me about the old lady's daughter," Glaze asked as she got up to refill her teacup. "Was she as much a reader as her parents?"

"Yes, but she was more the intellectual type. She deplored her mother's plebeian tastes, although she was quite careful about mentioning that. Of course, I heard that once she told the book society women, it was all over town – but discreetly, which simply meant that people talked about it in pairs rather than in groups."

"Typical small town gossip?" asked Glaze.

"We prefer to call it sharing of information." When Glaze snorted that *humph,* she sounded just like our Grandma Martelson.

"The daughter's contribution," I went on, "was mostly in the realm of philosophy and literature, leaning heavily toward essays, plays, and poetry. We still don't have all of it catalogued. It's only been a year. There's a lot of Shakespeare, Milton, the transcendentalists, although she didn't particularly approve of Thoreau, and certainly not of Whitman, whom she once described as far too racy. She did have some books of Persian poets in there, though, which seemed pretty racy to me, although those might have been acquired by the old Mrs. M. What a shame she had to die when she was only 98, the year before her daughter died. About two years before I was hired."

About six months before I was born.

"Biscuit, I want to hear the rest of this, but my rear end's going to sleep with all this sitting. Can we walk around the back yard or something?"

Good idea. I will show you the bird feeder.

"Sure. Great idea. I'll show you the garden. Mrs. Hoskins was so glad to have a gardener move into her house. No wonder she gave me such a good deal on it. She and her dog used to spend hours out there every day. Even in the summer, they'd be outside right after dawn to get in a couple of hours of gardening before it got too hot." As I slipped off my sandals and pulled on the tennies that were parked beside the back door, I said, "I'll show you the compost bin I built. First, let me put on some more water to boil so we can have fresh tea when we get back inside." *I think I drink way too much tea. . . .*

Try drinking just water. It is good.

. . . Maybe I should drink more water.

"Garden, yes," Glaze proclaimed, "but I may want to pass on the compost pile."

"Ouch, you hurt my gardening heart. Don't you know a compost bin is the central pillar of a garden?"

Actually, it is the bird feeder.

"Lead me to the pillar, then," said my sister, the city dweller, slipping on a pair of loafers as I refilled the tea kettle.

Once outside, we passed the bird feeder that sat a few feet from the back steps. Marmalade paused there while Glaze and I gravitated toward the vegetable garden that I had inherited from Mrs. Hoskins, bless her heart. "While we're here, we might as well do some weeding," Glaze volunteered. Would I ever say no to an offer like that? Even from a city-girl? Luckily the spaces between the rows are well mulched, so it never gets muddy. So here we were, two young-hearted women, squatting amongst the rows of pepper plants, pulling up odd weeds, and running our hands over the nearby tomato vines. After Marmalade checked out the bird feeder, she joined us in the garden.

I held my fingers up to my nose, inhaling the summery smell of tomato leaves. "Is there anything more wonderful than this?"

Yes. Fish.

"Too bad the tomatoes aren't grown yet. It would be great to have some for . . ."

"Are you already thinking about eating? We haven't digested breakfast yet!"

"Guilty as charged. Come on. Let's pick some of the snow peas, a few cucumbers, and a bunch of lettuce. Maybe we could have a pizza and a big salad tonight."

"I give up," Glaze said. "Can we have a milkshake to go with it?"

We left the veggies there in a pile beside the garden to gather up on our way back into the house. I love this time of year when the dogwoods, azaleas, and Yoshino cherries are in full bloom along the edge of what I call my forest at the back of the yard. This lot is huge. The fenced-in back yard takes up almost the whole center of the block. Of course, a lot of it is a woodsy area at the back, but I like trees. Maybe someday I'll clear a little trail to wind through there.

"Anyway," I said, as we started to wander along the line of tall Leyland Cypress that separates this back yard from Mr. Olsen's to the west, "to get back to the library . . . we didn't have many books for children, and we were sadly lacking in mathematics, physics, and such. The Petunia Brigade put fliers in all the businesses in town, and in the church bulletins, asking for donations of 'gently used' books. I don't know whether it was generosity, or whether a lot of folks just wanted to clean out their bookshelves, but we were inundated. After that the Petunias and I had several busy months of trying to get everything catalogued. What we didn't get to is still piled up in the third floor office."

Thank goodness I had gotten rid of most of the intruders by then. Otherwise you would have a real mess on your hands.

"The body showed up about a week after the Petunias started helping me out, so of course they had to be questioned, which thrilled them no end and caused quite a flurry in the ladies' book club. . . ."

Would you believe they asked Looselaces, but they did not ask me?

". . . Eventually everyone in town was questioned one way or another, but, as I said, nothing much came of it."

"Were you scared?"

"Scared?"

"Well, you had a murderer running around town. And it sounds like you still do."

Her comment made me pause in my tracks. I hadn't really thought about it. "Maybe I'm just naïve, Glaze, but I don't think I was ever afraid after I met Bob." Glaze is really very good at rolling her eyes.

"I have to ask this, Biscuit. Why does a little town like this have a cop? We didn't have one in Braetonburg."

"Good question. Watch out for that little clump of poison ivy," I interrupted myself, pointing to the bright green leaves poking up through the grass.

"What? No Latin name?"

"If you must know, it's *Toxicodendron radicans*, but if I'd taken the time to say that, you would have stepped in it already." There was a long pause.

"What were we just talking about?"

I'm glad I'm not the only one who forgets a conversation within three seconds if something else comes up. But this one I did remember. "You asked me why we have a town cop. Well, the answer lies in the town history. The families that built this town wrote it into the charter that the town has to maintain *an officer of the peace*."

"Why?"

"Nobody knows. They must have thought it was important. They also stipulated a town jail, so we have one cell in the little house on Juniper that's been called 'city hall' as long as anyone can remember."

"If you don't mind my asking, how can the town afford their own cop?"

"They can't. The salary's diddly-squat. But Bob's grandparents were really well-off, and they left modest trust funds for their one child – Bob's father – and all of the grandchildren. Bob has done some pretty successful real estate developing down in the Atlanta area. It's a fast-growing area, and he's making sure that the land he buys is treated respectfully. He won't allow the contractors he hires to clear-cut the land. So his houses end up selling for scads more money because of the beautiful old trees and the fact that each house is unique and suited to its site."

"How can he build houses in Atlanta if he lives way up here?"

"He travels there periodically. And his brother lives there and oversees the operations. They're partners."

"You said 'all of the grandchildren.' Who else is there?"

"He has a sister, too. You'll meet both of them at the wedding."

We had just about circled the fence line, and we paused for a moment behind the shed. In our purple and yellow shirts, we probably looked like a big johnny-jump-up to any birds passing overhead. I smiled at my compost bin.

A three-section compost bin is a gardening work of art. All the kitchen peelings and trimmings go into it, along with any grass raked up out of the yard. Never add meat scraps or dairy stuff to a compost bin. That might attract rats and neighborhood dogs. Bob and I usually leave the grass trimmings on the lawn to work their way down between the living grass blades to form mulch. He's a dear about helping me with the mowing, but once in a while a lawn needs a good combing, too, and all that dead grass will go into the right hand side of the bin.

I sprinkle in some dirt, add any veggie peels on hand, toss in some shredded leaves from the pile in back of the tool shed, and maybe water it lightly if we haven't had much rain. After a couple of weeks of "cooking," the pile's ready to be turned over into the middle bin. I use a pitchfork, which helps to aerate the pile. Of course, the sides of the bin are heavy chicken wire, to let air in so it won't just rot.

Actually, if you have enough dead leaves to counteract all the nitrogen in the green grass clippings, it shouldn't get slimy and smelly. It just begins to cure into wonderful dirt. I start adding all the new stuff to the first bin, on the right hand side. When it's time once again to turn that first bin, I pitchfork the middle bin into the left side, turn the right bin into the middle one, and start all over again. Does this make sense? *This* bin, of course, is just getting started, since I built it only a month ago when I moved in. Hopefully, it will be ready for its first turning by the time Bob and I get back from our honeymoon in Savannah.

Ideally, with enough sun, a little bit of rain, and good earthworms working their way up into the pile from the soil below, the third bin becomes usable compost that I add to the topsoil around plants or mix into the planting hole for shrubs or veggies.

"Biscuit, your compost pile is beautiful, I admit it. Now stop staring at it. Don't we need to get the peas and lettuce inside and washed off before they start drying out too much in the sun?"

"Oh my gosh, I forgot the veggies!"

As we gathered up the garden pickings, Glaze returned to our earlier conversation. "Whatever happened to the dead man? Who killed him?"

The guy who sneaked out the back door.

"Don't we all wish we knew . . . nobody ever confessed. Nobody ever got caught. It certainly wasn't the perfect crime, there were clues, but they just didn't seem to point to anyone in particular. Bob called in the Georgia Bureau of Investigation, too. They sent someone up even before the body was taken out of the library. There was a detective who thought that Margot Schuss did it, but she had a cast-iron alibi."

"Nothing came of it?"

"No, but I think it was someone in this town."

"Why a local person?"

"Only someone who'd lived around here for a while would have known that there was a back entrance that didn't look like a door. Even I didn't know about it, and I'd worked there for three weeks."

That is because you did not look carefully.

Glaze perked up her ears at that. "What do you mean – didn't look like a door?" she asked as she stepped around Marmalade, who had started up the stairs before us, but then turned around to look at us rather pointedly. I wondered what that was about. In the kitchen we dumped the peas in the sink. I'd forgotten about the boiling water, which was filling the room with steam – not what I needed on a warm April morning. Glaze turned off the burner as I carefully laid the lettuce on the counter beside the sink.

Then, before answering her question, I stepped through the office into the powder room to grab a big hair clip from under the sink so I could wind my hair up into a loose twist on top of my head. Much cooler. Even in April, sometimes we get 80-degree weather. I hope it'll be cooler for the wedding next week.

By the time I got back into the kitchen, Glaze was already rinsing off the cucumbers in the sink, using her left hand to keep the bandage dry. I never use pesticides, so we didn't have to worry about heavy poison removal. Just rinsed off the dirt and the worm poop. She handed the rinsed ones to me so I could lay them out to dry off on an old tea towel.

"You were getting ready to tell me about the door that didn't look like a door," she prompted, as she looked out the side window at the swing on the porch. Verandah.

"Oh, there was some sort of old conservatory room out back that we'd turned into a reading area. It had some trompe l'oeil wallpaper, and it turned out that the door that looked like it was just part of the wallpaper actually opened into a little space behind a big *Ligustrum lucidum*."

"Biscuit, would you please speak English?"

I decided to tend to the tea making rather than retort to such a sophomoric complaint. I agree with the British, who contend that drinking hot tea in the summer opens the pores and actually cools one off. I think it has something to do with sweating, but I've never been afraid of a little perspiration. Actually, sweat doesn't smell too much if there's no fear involved, since the apocrine glands under the armpit are responsible for removal of fear toxins. Interesting, isn't it? On the other hand, there's not a lot of evaporation when the relative humidity is 97%.

"It's a big Glossy Privet bush," I explained as I rinsed the teapot to warm it, added some oat straw and chamomile, and poured in the boiling water. "All anybody had to do was duck behind the bush, open the door and walk in. They checked there for fingerprints, but there were only smudges. The ground didn't show any footprints, but that didn't mean anything, since the *Vinca minor* was fairly thick and springy, unusual for that shady an area. It generally needs more light."

"My sister, the botanical encyclopedia," Glaze moaned, crossing her eyes.

Chapter 5

June 1986

On Friday evenings, right after work, the two friends would grab their tents, leave Fort Knox in Buddy's pickup truck, and head out to the little state parks that were dotted all around northern Kentucky and southern Ohio. Harlan would spend his time taking pictures, and Buddy would sleep late and then schmooze with folks in the campgrounds and play his guitar around the campfires that always seemed to spring up at night. They could usually depend on some sturdy mama-type to ply them with marshmallows and chocolate – "do you two know how to make s'mores, or do I need to show you?" – and sometimes to follow that up with an invitation to breakfast the next day. The two young men always said yes to that.

One Friday evening they'd been sitting at a campfire, toasting marshmallows of course, when the middle-aged man across from them asked if they'd ever been on a birders' hike. No, they hadn't, they admitted. "There's one tomorrow morning, and you're welcome to come along. I even have an extra pair of binoculars you can share." He added a few more details, then ended with, "Well, I'm turning in. If you want to join us, we're meeting right here at four o'clock."

"Four in the morning?" Buddy croaked in disbelief.

"That's right. Don't worry, we'll have some coffee brewed, and we leave at 4:30 sharp."

Buddy wanted to skip it, but Harlan persuaded him that it would be a new experience that he couldn't pass up. "Anyway," Harlan said as the clincher, "I'm used to looking at birds, so I'll let you have the binoculars all to yourself."

"Whoopee, whoopee," grinned Buddy as he danced around in an imitation of delirious excitement. "I can't wait."

"Right. We'll see if you still feel the same way at oh-three-fifty."

At four o'clock precisely, both newcomers to the event of the birdwatch stepped out of their pup-tents to join the small ring of hushed but expectant men and women, all of whom sported layers of warm clothing, cameras, binoculars, and assorted field guides. The leader of the hike, who was a middle-aged ornithologist of some renown from the nearby college in Yellow Springs, gave a few concise instructions, including "call me Connie," before she turned to head up a well-worn trail into the surrounding woods.

By the time a hint of light was just beginning to touch the eastern sky, the group was well up into the woods, on the edge of a meadow. For the next hour, the birders commented in undertones about the various birds they heard or saw. "Did anyone catch the eye color on that Vireo?" Connie would ask in a whisper. Harlan heard Buddy mumbling to himself quietly. He figured it was something about what the heck difference does it make what color eyes he has. A few moments later Connie remarked about the low-pitched call coming from the middle of the meadow.

Harlan pointed out a Brown Thrasher, the state bird of Georgia, that no one else had noticed sitting on the lower branches of a sumac. Connie glanced at him and gave an appreciative nod. Buddy leaned over and whispered, "Two points for you."

Once, when they spotted a medium-sized gray bird with a striking white breast, black wings and tail, and a big band of black running from the beak to behind the ears – "Where are a bird's ears, anyway?" Buddy had muttered to Harlan – Connie informed the group of mostly puzzled birders that this was a Loggerhead Shrike. There were quick notations in life-list notebooks, while Connie continued quietly to explain that the shrike was carnivorous, eating mice, grasshoppers, or even small birds. "Often," she declared brightly, "the shrike will hang its prey on thorns or on barbed wire fences." At that Harlan lowered his Nikon, and Buddy grumbled that he wished he'd stayed in the tent.

The usually effervescent Buddy had been pretty subdued ever since dawn. At the beginning of the walk he had listened avidly, even if a little sleepily, to the chirps and tootles and tweets, trying to find even one he could identify. Poor Buddy was new to the art of the outdoors. He had never been one to range the forests around Martinsville and had seldom paid any attention to anything feathered, unless it was, minus its feathers, being served for dinner. About thirty-five minutes into the walk, there had been a moment of almost total silence, as the first hint of light pierced through the forest leaves. Off in the distance a drawn-out call sounded its clarion notes. Buddy brightened visibly, and spoke out, too loudly, "I know what bird *that* is!" Fifteen sets of eyes had swiveled around at him. Fifteen heads had wagged in disbelief and pity. Everyone there had heard the call, but no one had whipped out a life list notebook. Harlan really felt sorry for Buddy, who had for a moment been so happy to identify the *cock-a-doodle-doo*.

From the Statement of Matthew Olsen
to the Georgia Bureau of Investigation
Saturday, April 29, 1995

I don't know what to say. He was like a second son to me. I loved that boy. . . . Yes, he had his own room here. He was such a good influence on Buddy, too. It's my fault he's dead. . . . Why? Because if I hadn't wanted to go to Ohio to see my daughter, Harlan would be alive today. . . . He didn't leave when I got home because he said he wanted to stay an extra day to take some pictures of Mr. Fogarty. . . . My parakeet. . . . When I got here he was out taking pictures somewhere. . . . Yes, we did talk last night. He came in when it started getting dark. That's when he told me he'd stay till tomorrow. Today, that is. . . . No, I don't know why he went out later. I was already asleep. . . . No, his bed hasn't been slept in. . . . Library? No, I don't know why he was in the library.

Saturday, April 20, 1996
Martinsville

"*Vinca minor* is Periwinkle to non-Latin-speakers," I explained
to Glaze. Actually, some of the botanical names are of Greek origin,
but I figured that was not information that Glaze wanted to hear. My
idea of fun is to read my *Wayside Gardens* catalog from cover to
cover. I have big plans for the grounds of the library, but I'm having
to start small so I don't offend the trustees, whose idea of landscap-
ing is a ring of petunias around the bottom of every tree. I started by
placing some small-leafed hostas in amongst the petunias and edged
the walkways with zinnias. This year I planted some dahlias in the
front corner–not the kind that are so over bred the bees can't get
through all the frills to the nectar, but some of the sweet older spe-
cies, which have much more sensible flowers.

I'm tucking an herb garden in the sunny area in back, with lots
of room for parsley and fennel and dill to serve as host plants for the
butterfly caterpillars. Last month I put in an *Osmanthus fragrans*
where it will soften the northeast corner as it grows. Ahhh, the leaves
of the Sweet Olive may be a bit prickly, but the smell in a couple of
years will be divine. If I set a few benches here and there, we can
make little outdoor reading nooks. I wonder if I could get away with
letting the *Passiflora incarnata* grow along the picket fence in front,
so the Gulf Fritillary butterflies could lay their eggs on it? Maypop.
What a silly name for a vine that has such an exotic looking blossom.

I came back to present time with a start, and looked fondly around
my kitchen. Other than needing to make curtains for the four windows, and someday replacing the solid back door with one that has
windows in it instead of a tiny peephole, I like this room just the
way it is. It's large but cozy at the same time. Glaze and I had ignored the big table in the center and gravitated to the little nook at
the north end that holds a miniscule round table, just big enough for
breakfast for two, if you serve the food from the stove. It's perfect
for sisterly chats, as the two of us were discovering.

It has great windowsills, too.

The bay window that forms the nook looks out over the big fronds
of the *Cimicifuga racemosa*. The plant is tall, but the top of it is
open enough to let us see through to the great view of the garden,

which is far enough out into the yard not to be shadowed by the
house. Blessings on Mrs. Hoskins for all her hard work that I was
getting the benefit of. There's another, taller window, almost floor
to ceiling. It's on the east wall, back in the corner of the kitchen, to
the left of the sink. The cross ventilation is wonderful when I open it
to the back of the shaded verandah. A Lady Banks climbing rose
shields that corner and softens the early morning sunlight that peeks
through the window. That rose is the home of a nest of little purple
finches. Even as Glaze and I talked, I could hear the baby birds
cheeping like crazy. Yesterday they were trying to flutter their wings.
That means they'll be gone today or tomorrow. I'm so glad my yard
is bird-friendly. Except for having a cat, although I've never seen
her chase a bird. . . .

*I do not like to eat birds. They are too feathery. Did you ever
have feathers stuck to the roof of your mouth?*

. . . That corner window has a wide sill that's low enough for
Marmalade to sit on, grabbing a few rays of sunlight before the wide
overhang of the porch eaves cuts off the sun.

I love that porch. Yes, it does darken the rooms a bit, but it cuts
out so much glare and so much of the summer heat that it's well
worth the loss of bright light. Glaze must have caught my mood.
"This is a wonderful room," she said. "What's that tall, wavy-look-
ing plant outside the bay window?"

*It is the home of the garter snake that ate a baby toad yester-
day.*

I started to say that it was *Cimicifuga*, but decided to forestall
her predictable comment on the Latin. "It's Black Cohosh. The roots
can be made into a tea that is great for relieving hot flashes."

"I thought it was for inducing labor and helping to tighten the
uterus after birth," Glaze commented, running her left hand through
her hair. As far as I could see, the mussing up hardly made a difference. She still looked great.

"How did you know anything about that?"

"Yuko, my roommate, is an apprentice midwife, and I quiz her
on her lessons."

"Well, you're right about cohosh, but there's a big difference
between black cohosh, which is growing out there," I said as I nodded toward the back yard, "and blue cohosh, which is what your
roommate will use for women in childbirth." I couldn't resist the
opportunity to get in a plug for botanical names. "Even though they're

both called cohosh, the black is *Cimicifuga racemosa* and the blue is *Caulophyllum thalictroides*. They both taste terrible, but they're effective. I used the blue cohosh when Scott was born at home, so I know from experience." I paused to try to pick up the original thread of our conversation. "But we were talking about the disguised doorway."

I dispensed the tea through the bamboo strainer to catch all the stray oat straw bits, returned the teapot to the counter, put a couple more of the croissants on a blue-ringed plate in the middle of the table, and sat back down. "Bob's the one who showed me that back door. Even Marmalade seemed surprised when he opened it after the ambulance had taken away the body. She darted through it, in and out a couple of times, purring like a generator."

I was not surprised. I was trying to tell you that two people had left by that door. Don't you ever listen to me? I saw the one who came in later and cried over the body.

"She sounds like a generator now. You said there were lots of clues. Like what, for instance?"

"The knife belonged to Mrs. Hoskins, who lived here. She's the one whose wooden mailbox kept getting painted strange colors. We'll walk out front later so you can see it. No telling what color it'll be today. Bob usually can figure out who did it, and he gets them to go back and paint over it so it'll be black again, the way Mrs. Hoskins liked it. That old mailbox has so many coats of paint on it, it probably weighs fifteen pounds. If I remember correctly it was spray-painted with neon orange just before the murder. Her knife had been missing for a day or two. She thought that maybe she'd just mislaid it when she was separating her *Hemerocallis*. I always use a sharp shovel for that job, but she liked to use her husband's heavy old hunting knife. They're out near her mailbox – the daylilies, I mean – so anyone could have picked it up if she left it there."

"Any fingerprints?"

"Only one partial. It was on the blade, just underneath the hilt. The murderer had wiped the handle, but missed that one print. The only problem was that it didn't match any prints on record."

"I'd hardly call that a clue, then," Glaze commented as she munched another croissant. "These are yummy; are they from that little deli place I passed coming into town? It had a strange name."

"Yes, they make them fresh each day. It's called the DeliSchuss."

"Delicious?"

I spelled it for her. "It's pronounced sort of like *delicious*, but put a little bit of accent on the first syllable, so it means the deli owned by Mr. and Mrs. Schuss."

"Is she the one you said had the alibi?"

"Yes. She and her husband are a Norwegian couple who used to live in New York and then gave up the big city to move to our little Martinsville. They stay busy all the time. They had a dinner party for her brother from out of town the night of the murder. That reminds me of another clue. There was a deli napkin in the dead man's pocket. He had written the deli phone number on it, and the number 2330. The napkin wasn't all wrinkled up, so it didn't look like it had been in his pocket for very long, but he hadn't been in the deli that day. *DeliSchuss is Delicious* is their slogan. It's printed right on the napkin, which is why we knew it was from there."

"Oh come now, Biscuit. Surely the guy could have walked in to get a cup of coffee, picked up a napkin, and nobody had to notice him."

"Glaze, you don't realize how the town rumor mill works. I started telling people two weeks ago who you were and when you were coming to visit, so they wouldn't invent a jillion scenarios to explain you as you drove into town yesterday . . ."

They did it anyway. You should hear some of the things they're saying.

". . . I should have just let it go to see what they came up with. No, people knew the dead man because he was Buddy Olsen's best friend, but he didn't live here, so he would have been noticed. He had *not* been in the deli that day, but he had their unwrinkled napkin in his shirt pocket."

"How do you know he's the one who wrote on it?"

"He had fairly distinctive handwriting, and his grandmother had saved all the letters he wrote her when he was in the army. She wouldn't give them up, but she did let Bob and someone from the GBI look at them."

"GBI?"

"Georgia Bureau of Investigation."

"Okay, so you have a knife with an unidentifiable print and a napkin with the victim's handwriting. Big-time clues. What was the dead guy's name?"

"Harlan Schneider. He used to live just up the river. He came from Garner Creek originally before he landed a job as a mechanic at a car sales place in Hastings. He was identified by Mr. Olsen, who lives next door here. Harlan was a good friend of Mr. Olsen's son Buddy. They'd been in the Army together and had kept in touch. Harlan was a hiker and an amateur photographer. He was pretty good at it. He even had his own darkroom." I remembered all the details easily because Bob and I had been so involved in the drama of the murder for months after it happened. It was daily discussion for the whole town, in fact, from April through the end of last summer at least.

"Mr. Olsen," I continued, "was visiting his daughter in Ohio, and Buddy was house-sitting for him. But then Buddy was called out of town on business, and he asked Harlan to come over and fill in for him for two or three days. Harlan ate at Mr. Olsen's house and spent the early evening hiking around in the woods with his camera."

"Did they have to call Mr. Olsen in Ohio to come home to identify the dead guy?" Glaze asked, obviously fascinated by this year-old saga.

"No. He returned unexpectedly the evening of the murder, and Harlan decided to leave the next morning, but he went and got killed instead."

"What was on the film?"

"What film?"

"You just told me he had a camera."

I'd forgotten that part of the puzzle. "They never found his camera. They even searched the woods around here, but it hasn't shown up."

"Think the murderer took it?"

"Probably."

"Then maybe Harlan had taken a picture the murderer didn't want him to have," Glaze speculated into her teacup. "Was he maybe a closet bad guy? A quietly unsavory character?"

Just the motor oil smell.

"No. Everybody thought he was a really nice guy . . ."

Everybody except the one who killed him.

". . . He was Buddy's best friend, but there must have been something going on for him to sneak into the library and get himself killed like that."

Glaze took a moment to lick some crumbs off her thumb. "So maybe someone here in Martinsville had hired Harlan to photograph somebody. Harlan tried to blackmail the man who hired him, and . . ." Her voice faded away from her improbable story as I peered at her over the rim of my mug.

"When you're done inventing, would you like to hear the other big clue?"

"No, I like my story better – and your so-called clues didn't get you anywhere if you don't even know who did it."

"Okay, I won't tell you that there was a footprint in the blood of a size five woman's shoe."

"Oh come on," Glaze whined. "You can't tell from a footprint whether or not it's a woman's shoe."

"Well, then, this mysterious other guy was wearing high heels."

"Oh." But Glaze wasn't defeated yet. "You're trying to tell me that a woman with teeny feet plunged a great big hunting knife up to the hilt into the front of a guy who had to have been a lot bigger than she was?"

No, she did not kill him.

"No, I'm trying to tell you that a woman with teeny feet was with the guy who killed Harlan."

No, she came in later.

"Or she was with Harlan when he got killed."

Why do I keep trying, when you do not listen to me?

"Or she came in afterwards and found the body."

Yes.

"That's what Bob thought," I continued, "but there was no way to prove it."

You could have asked me.

"What's up, Marmalade? What are you yowling about?"

"Great, so now we have three people in on this murder."

"Only two people, Glaze – the killer and the woman."

"I'm including Harlan. It seems a shame to exclude him from the formula, since he had such a major role, being the body and such."

"Glaze, you are strange."

"I'm not the one who likes getting dead mice as presents from a fat cat."

I leaned my head closer to the orange head in my lap. "You're not fat, are you Marmy?"

From a Journal Entry Dated Thursday, May 11, 1995

I finally told Mama what I did. She didn't like it,
and she's grounded me FOREVER, but she's not going to tell Papa or anybody. Luckily she said she
would help me get rid of the shoes. So I'm safe, but I
don't feel like smiling ever again.

June 1988

When Harlan, resisting the incentives thrown at him by the overly
enthusiastic re-enlistment officer, left the Army after the requisite
three-year tour of duty, he had considered roaming around the country for a few years. He and Buddy even discussed heading up into
Minnesota, until Buddy heard about winters that sometimes reached
thirty below zero. He decided that Georgia was on his mind after all.

Harlan, too, found himself wanting to return to his home state,
wanting to look around for someone to date. He had tried joining a
gym near Fort Knox, thinking he would meet women who were
healthy and active. He found, though, that he wasn't interested in
the young females who had practically thrown themselves at his long-
faced good looks. Instead, he wanted someone with some *life* to her
rather than just a lot of adrenaline. Hefting car parts around, hoist-
ing tires and climbing under car hoods was workout enough, so he
quit the gym. Hiking for miles at a time kept him in better shape
than many young men his age. No, Harlan didn't want to date casually. He was willing to wait to find a kindred spirit.

He returned to Georgia in June of 1988 and got himself a job ten
miles away from home in the little riverside town of Hastings. He
lived in a compact apartment over the bakery, which was where he
ate most of his breakfasts.

Buddy ended up back in Martinsville, living in the big old house
that his dad had floated around in ever since his wife's death, and
especially now since Buddy's sister Millie had recently married and
moved to Wright-Patterson Air Base with her Air Force husband.
Buddy got a job in a small catalog sales company in Russell Gap, up
the road a ways. He commuted the twenty-five miles, glad that he

didn't have to buck heavy traffic to do it. He was so personable, he soon became their top sales person. Occasionally he had to run special weekend training classes for new personnel, since the company grew so fast it expanded into other types of merchandise. Buddy became the company's liaison with the various suppliers.

The two friends still got together frequently to go to movies in Garner Creek or at the Big Chief Theater in Martinsville. Or they'd camp for a weekend in the hills above either of their hometowns. Sometimes they'd hang out at the deli in Martinsville. Miranda, the quiet black-haired girl who worked there made great sandwiches, and when she had time, she'd stop to talk with them. She was still pretty young when they first met in 1990, but Harlan wondered if maybe, someday when she was older . . . He was patient, though.

Every few months Buddy's dad would drive over to Hastings with Buddy and take the two of them to dinner at Buster's Barbeque, up in Garner Creek. He liked Harlan, and was glad that his son had a friend who was so dependable. Sometimes Mr. Olsen thought that Buddy was a little bit too happy for his own good.

Chapter 6

Saturday, April 20, 1996

*Y*ou *are right, Widelap. I am* not *fat. My tummy is a little rounder than it's been in the past. Even running up and down those library stairs could not counteract the effect of all those mouse dinners, and you have been feeding me very well since I moved in with you. I have to admit I like living here, knowing that I do not have to catch my own dinner, and having your soft, roomy lap to jump onto whenever I need it.*

The purr stopped for a moment, then continued.

I hate to admit it, but I am as stumped as my humans are. I must have been in the attic stalking that really sneaky mouse with the white whiskers when the murder happened. I probably should have heard something. Ordinarily I would have, but I was so intent on my hunting, I suppose I might have missed a quiet *murder. Maybe I was finishing off the mouse while Antlerbagman was getting killed. What* I *did was not a murder; it was an execution. A fine point, perhaps, but I am meticulous about such things.*

I remember stopping at my litter box on the third floor right after I left the attic. Then I strolled halfway down the stairs before I smelled the blood–and the car oil.

It was then, I think, that I heard the sound of that unfamiliar door opening and closing. Later, when I met Softfoot and led him to the funny door, I ran in and out to show him how the Sneakman and the other one had left that way. I am happy to say he seemed to understand because he carefully checked the ground where their smells were.

I looked down again at the silky bundle purring in my lap. About a month after the murder, when I hadn't seen a mouse, dead or alive, for a week or so, Marmalade followed me out the library door late one afternoon. Always before she had walked me to the door, purred a good-bye, and stayed inside to hunt as I left for home. But that day she must have known the rodent problem was under control . . .

Of course I knew it. Once I caught whitewhiskers, it was just a short clean-up campaign.

. . . and she wouldn't be needed on the night patrol anymore. She strolled out onto the porch with me, sat down as if to wait for me to lock the door, and then followed me down the block to Azalea House, where I was staying with Melissa Tarkington.

Melissa ran the closest thing to a bed-and-breakfast that Martinsville has ever known. She didn't rent to just anyone. No, she had a few regular customers who came the same time every year. She used to joke that it was almost like one of those time-share condos in the junk mail ads.

When I was hired last year, Melissa was without her regular March/April/May clients, who had left on a year-long jaunt around the world. That meant they wouldn't be there for their usual three months in 1996 either, but they wanted to reserve their space, so they asked Melissa if they could pay half their usual rent for 1996. Melissa agreed, with the understanding that she could rent the rooms to someone else for that time period. She'd heard that the library trustees were looking for a cheap place to rent for the new librarian. They figured the salary was so small, they had to sweeten the pot a bit. Melissa told them she'd rent them the rooms for half the usual monthly amount. Nobody ever stayed there through the summer anyway, so Melissa came out on the sweet end of the deal. Her half-price clients were happy, the town council saved money, Melissa made extra money, and I didn't have to worry about housing for a year. It was a case of win/win/win/win.

The best thing was that Melissa and I gradually became very good friends. I cooked soup for her. She cooked breakfast for me. In the evenings, we spent a lot of time just talking, sharing pots of tea, solving the problems of the world. We laughed together and sometimes cried together. I'd been there only five months when her favorite nephew was killed in a car accident. A drunk driver from Enders, a town down the river from here, rammed the boy's bike off the road and over that steep embankment between here and Braetonburg. The guardrails didn't help Jake at all, but they saved the drunk driver from going over the edge.

Anyway, that first evening that Marmalade followed me home, I asked Melissa if it was okay for me to keep a cat. She knew Marmalade from the library and agreed right away, especially since the regulars had a cat that came with them every year.

Long white hair. Lazy as the dickens. Smells like canned tuna. Likes to sleep on the long bench in the sun.

Later that evening Marmalade and I sat together on a curved garden bench beside the *Acer palmatum dissectum*. The Japanese laceleaf maple tree was surrounded by the banks of flame azaleas that the bed and breakfast was named for. And the late afternoon sun threw the maple-leaf shadows over Marmalade's fur. She watched my face as I talked to her about the way I was feeling about that sweet policeman who was investigating the murder. She acted like she knew what I was talking about, and she purred her encouragement.

You will figure it out some day.

A week or so later I took her up to the vet in Russell Gap to have her spayed.

From the Statement of Melissa Tarkington
to the Georgia Bureau of Investigation
Sunday, April 30, 1995

Of *course* I've talked about it. *Everybody's* talking about it. . . . Yes, she's living at Azalea House, my bed & breakfast. . . . Yes, I do remember. She went up to bed a little after ten o'clock. . . . I think she's a lovely lady, and we're getting to be good friends. . . . Yes, I've started going to the library at least once

a week. . . . No, I don't think I ever saw him there.
. . . I wear a seven, more or less. It depends on the
style. . . . No, I don't know why he was in the library.

Saturday, April 20, 1996

It's hard now to believe how much has happened in just a year .
I had an operation, for one thing.
. . . and, looking back, I realize that Bob didn't really ask me
out or anything, not at first. Yet we ended up spending a lot of time
together. We had several discussions at his office or at the library
and often at the deli. He kept saying that he had to get the full picture for the murder investigation. But we'd find we were talking
about the way we'd grown up in nearby towns without knowing each
other existed. He's only five years older than I. He'd tell me about
wanting to play baseball, but not being able to see the ball. Getting
glasses in seventh grade. Entering the science fair his freshman year
with a project on diabetes, and having his poster board, with its
little packets of sugar, eaten by mice . . .
You just can't trust those critters. They can get into anything.
. . . the night before the judging. He said he really understood
what Marmalade was up against.
I told Bob about my mother the potter, and my dad the music
teacher, both of whom had loved me enough to let me shoulder the
responsibility for my own decisions. "Write your own music, and
then play it with passion," is what my dad had told me on my 14th
birthday. He gave me a packet of composers' paper, with the pre-
printed five-lined staffs. I don't think he meant for me to write music literally, but just that he was trusting me to listen to the music in
my heart. When I told him, close to my 23rd birthday, that I was
going to marry Sol Brandy, his only question was, "Does this guy
make your heart sing?" And I'd said yes.
Marmalade listened to most of those discussions that Bob and I
had. Sometimes I'd be the one with the cat on my lap. Sometimes
Bob would hold her. Sometimes Marmalade would just crouch off to
one side, with her tail curled around her feet. That tail outlined where
the carrots would have been if she'd been a meatloaf.

It took Bob six months to get around to proposing. We got along so well, although he usually drank coffee. I usually drank tea. . . .

I always drink water.

. . . He was a cop. I was a librarian. He knew people. I knew plants and books. He'd been divorced after six years of an early unfortunate marriage. I'd been widowed. He liked Mahler. I preferred Mozart. Neither of us had or wanted a TV set. We both liked to walk. We both treasured silence. He kept a journal that he wrote in each morning, and sometimes at night. I kept a journal that I wrote in each night, and sometimes in the morning.

His first gift to me was a dozen *Allium giganteum* bulbs. He said if I planted those giant onions, they'd grow taller than my granddaughter, and she'd like that. I guess he had me pegged right from the start. Last month I dug up some of the bulbs of the huge onion-like plants, which *had* grown taller than four-year-old Verity, to bring here. They're planted between the front steps . . .

Where the cricket sings all the time.

. . . and the sweet-smelling Winter Daphne bush.

We both wanted a cozy house right from the start. His house on Upper Sweetgum Street was way too small, and my rented rooms at Azalea House had been a temporary landing place from the moment I'd moved to town. I adored the lovely yard with the bench under the Japanese maple. I appreciated its proximity to the library, but it was still only a temporary shelter.

Before we started house hunting, we put together a treasure map. I'd read about that process (self-help section, third shelf in the red room), but Bob said he had done it before. I found out months later that he'd made a treasure map, a dream board, of his ideal life partner several months before I showed up in town. He had wanted a self-sufficient, companionable woman in her mid forties. He wanted someone with gray hair, and what he delicately called "an ample armful, easy to hug and hold." He also wanted someone who would hug back!

I was talking about the house, though. We'd wanted it to be within easy walking distance of the town center, with a generous sized front yard, a big back yard with room for a garden, a deep porch with enough room for a swing and a couple of rocking chairs. One good-sized bedroom, one office-sized room, one sewing/craft room. No guest bedrooms, because we didn't plan on having my kids *ever* come to live with us, but we did want a comfortable sofa that would make out into a bed for temporary guests, so we needed a big enough living room to accommodate it. No formal dining room, but a kitchen large enough for a table. We needed a big laundry area so we could put a litter box in there. All our wants said "big," but we wanted all of it arranged in a smallish-sized house.

Except for the "small" part, we got what we wanted. Mrs. Hoskins, of the multi-colored mailbox, moved to the new retirement center in Hastings, and her house was up for sale. There was, besides the mailbox – green the day we looked at the house - a wide porch, which she insisted on calling the verandah, on three sides, two big bedrooms upstairs, as well as an area for a sewing center, an office downstairs, a big living room, a small and very dark powder room under the stairs, the eat-in kitchen with a nook tucked into a bay window, and a huge attic that holds some old trunks that were left by the previous owners. Mrs. Hoskins didn't want to deal with them, so she just left them. I'll probably get around to tackling them next spring during the cool weather.

The back yard was completely fenced in. Mrs. Hoskins had a much loved dog, named Barley, that had lived with her for years. As a pup he played all over the yard, fetching sticks and balls as long as Mr. or Mrs. Hoskins would toss them. After Mr. Hoskins died suddenly of a ruptured appendix, Barley was a comfort to the widowed wife. He always sat with her while she gardened. As he got older, he began to plod around the perimeter of the yard, marking his realm on all the fence posts every day, maintaining his rights as the ruler of his backyard kingdom. Sometimes he'd snooze under the line of Leyland Cypress trees, shaded from the afternoon sun.

Mrs. Hoskins had wanted to move to Hastings for years, but the retirement center wouldn't accept dogs. So she stayed here until Barley took his last walk around the fenceline, came back to where she was sitting on the porch steps, and died quietly in her arms. He's buried under the dogwood tree in the back yard. The next week, Mrs. Hoskins asked Paul Welsh, who lives directly across the street behind that huge hedge of *Ligustrum lucidum*, to replace a couple of broken fence posts so she could put the house on the market.

Marmalade liked her laundry-room, and she's liked the rest of the house, too. So have I. The one-year lease was up at the bed & breakfast last month, so I went ahead and moved in here. I'm renting it, and we'll close on it after the wedding.

When I moved to Martinsville, I kept the old house in Braetonburg. My Sally and her Paul were tired of renting, so they moved in to house-sit until I decided what I wanted to do. Now it looks like I'll be selling them the house. A good deal for them, and I'll enjoy having them there. Of course, Sally will probably paint a couple of rooms orange. She wants to change some of the 'mama decorating' to make the place more her own. I understand. As long as she doesn't sell the big bed. It has too many good memories, but it belongs in that house, not in this one.

Speaking of which, Bob comes to visit a lot, but he doesn't spend the night here. I'm old-fashioned, as I've said before, and so is he. Also, I'm the librarian and he's the town cop. We have a lot of eyes on us.

After our wedding next week, Bob has promised to build a whole series of Bob's Original Cat Trees and Scratching Posts to grace some of the corners. Meanwhile, Marmalade's pretty good at levitating to the top of six-foot bookcases, so she has her own baskets up there. Last week one of the baskets crashed onto the office desk. Luckily Marmy bailed out on the way down, but Bob came over that evening and anchored them with ingenious little dowel and wing-nut devices of his own invention.

To continue with the house tour, I love this "vestibule" as Mrs. Hoskins calls it. Inside the front door is an ample greeting area, as wide as it is deep. There's room for the elegant old oak drop-leaf table that Mother Brandy gave me as a wedding present when I married her son. She had received it on her wedding day from her mother-in-law. A good tradition. I'll pass it on to Scott's wife, if he ever gets married. . . .

Why don't you just keep it? I like the legs. They have those bumpy edges. Great for rubbing my sides on.

. . . Right now he's having so much fun living in Alaska, climbing glaciers and working at the University there, I wonder if I'll ever see him again. For now, there's room on the table for a huge vase of forsythia or dahlias, or whatever is blooming. I'm going to keep flowers there all the time, like the daisies Bob brought me yesterday.

Good idea.

Above the table, which Marmalade loves to rub against, by the way, is the staircase. It rises from the left to the right. We have to walk over to the left, toward the living room, to get to the bottom of the stairs. If we walk to the right instead, we enter the kitchen, which stretches along the east side of the house.

The stairway heads up to a landing, then turns and parallels itself to the second floor, where the bedroom will take up the whole north side of the house, when we knock out a wall or two. Mrs. Hoskins told us to be sure to investigate the attic, although I haven't gotten around to that yet. There'll be plenty of time for all of that, once the house is really ours.

> From the Statement of Paul Welsh
> to the Georgia Bureau of Investigation
> Sunday, April 30, 1995
>
> Sure, I knew him pretty well. . . . Yes, that's right.
> I live one house down the street, directly across
> from Elizabeth Hoskins. . . . No, I was out of town.
> I took my son to visit his great-grandmother in
> Americus. . . . She lives in a nursing home there.
> . . . We stayed with my brother. . . . Yes, I picked
> Cory up after school on Friday and we drove
> straight there. . . . Today. We pulled in about two
> hours ago. . . . Of course he wasn't in any trouble!
> He was a great guy, and I liked him a lot. . . .
> Library? No, I don't know why he was in the li-
> brary.

June, 1988

Hastings was a small community, but it had many businesses, such as the retirement home, that served the entire county. Cherokee Motors, the car dealership owned by Tony Cecchini, who was the cousin of Harlan's mother, needed a good mechanic. Of course, Harlan stepped into the job as if it had just been waiting for him to leave the army. He felt like he'd been training for it all his life. He was well-liked right from the start by the other mechanics at the dealership. The women in the front office liked him too. Both of them wanted to marry him off to their daughters, but he quietly re-fused their frequent invitations to meals.

Tony Cecchini, whose Cherokee mother had married an Italian guy from Long Island, was a big, brash, loud-spoken man with a heavy head of straight black hair that he pulled back into a pony tail, thereby going against the grain of this conservative community. Not only that, he offended almost everyone in sight with his taste-less television ads. When he first came up with the idea, in the fall of 1988, he tried to talk his cousin's son into playing the lead role in the ads, but Harlan had taken one look at the script and declined. Respectfully, but definitely. Every six months or so, Tony wrote a slightly different version of the ad, each one worse than the one before. By 1995, Tony was striding onto the screen each night, barechested and carrying a huge hatchet, right before the 6:00 news. Harlan cringed every time he saw it.

"This is Tomahawk Tony, down at Cherokee Motors in Hastings. We're slashing prices right and left to give you the best deal ever." Tony waved the hatchet and let out an ersatz war whoop. "Remember, we're the ones who kept *our* word, white man. You can count on us at Cherokee Motors for the best deals in the county. New or Used, you can trust a car from a Cherokee."

It was horrible. It was worse than horrible. It was disgusting. Apparently, though, it was just zany enough to capture the notice of the masses, who flocked to Hastings to buy their vehicles from that weird guy on TV. Each buyer received a card, suitable for framing and personally signed by Tomahawk Tony, that said:

"You did us wrong, but we do you right."

From the Statement of Anthony "Tony" Cecchini
to the Georgia Bureau of Investigation
Monday, May 1, 1995

What else can I tell you? Yes, he worked for me, but he was *family*. . . . He was the son of my cousin, my mother's sister's grandson. We were close. Our whole family is close. . . . I don't know, but when I find out who done it, you may have another murder on your hands. . . . Library? What do I know about a library?

Chapter 7

Saturday, April 20, 1996

"She's not a fat cat," I said again to Glaze as I stroked Marmy's soft ears. "She's just comfortably padded. Anyway, I'm going to be a lot more comfortably padded than she is if we don't get off our duffs and take a walk. I'm going to show you downtown Martinsville. Put on your walking shoes, and let's get going."

I took just a moment to wash up the cups and plates, and put them on the drainboard. Drying dishes is the only job I know of that, if you don't bother to do it, it does itself.

"We'll just stroll around town a little bit. It'll raise our spirits and get us breathing. Maybe we'll go through the beauty shop and then walk up to the deli for some lunch."

"Beauty shop?"

I turned to Glaze to explain. "Sharon Armitage owns the gift shop between the grocery store and the movie theater. Everybody in town calls it the beauty shop because Sharon put a beauty parlor in the side room. The gift baskets always smell a bit like hair coloring, but it's a fun little store to visit just because Sharon is such a friendly soul. Also, you'll get to meet every woman in town if you drop in there often enough."

"I imagine one drop-in will be enough for me. I might want her to do a wash and blow-dry for me before the wedding, though, as long as she doesn't turn everybody's hair into a blue helmet."

"Don't worry about an old-lady hairdo. Sharon was another refugee from the cities. She worked with some of the best hairdressers in New Jersey and New York, until she and her husband Carl moved here ten years ago to get their little girl out of the suburbs. Ended up having three more kids once they got here – must be something in the air. Carl owns the gas station on the north end of town, and runs the movie theater three nights a week." As I spoke I was filling Marmalade's food dish.

Feeding a cat dry food is the best thing in the world from a convenience standpoint.

I like chicken better.

. . . Cats won't overeat unless they have a dietary imbalance of some sort – I read that in that great book by Martin Goldstein. As much as I talk about her being tubby, she's not really. Oh, she was when she first adopted me, but now she's sleek and slim and just right. Her thick hair is what makes her look full all the time.

Glaze and I waltzed down the front steps in high spirits a little before ten o'clock, and we turned right when we got to Second Street. We crossed Oak and Juniper, then paused at the corner entrance to the town park, admiring the daylilies by the benches and along the sidewalks. What's with the weather this year? Daylilies never bloom this early, yet there we stood looking at bright orange blossoms and a few deep red ones. Of course, I had to tell her the whole story. There have been daylilies in Martinsville for at least two hundred years. One of the oldest books in the library, a real treasure that turned up in response to my Petunia Brigade's call for used books, was a set of diaries that were started in 1797 by Ida Peterson's great-great-great-great-grandmother's younger sister, who was born here in Martinsville in 1787, the year before Georgia became the first southern state to ratify the constitution.

According to the diary, Faith and her sister, who were twelve and fourteen years old, talked their father into ordering some daylily bulbs from Savannah. They were delivered by cart in 1799 to the general store, which was run by the girls' father. That October the two sisters planted twenty-four daylilies here and there around town, and they bloomed the following summer, the first summer of the new century. "Every five years after that," I told Glaze, "as long as they lived, the sisters divided the plants and replanted the flourishing roots. You'll have to come back in the summer to see this place when all of them are blooming. It's a riot of colors."

Glaze and I stood looking at a lush stand of vibrant orange day-lilies, wondering for a moment if any of these had roots that came from the original two dozen. "That diary must have been pretty interesting," Glaze commented. "Were there lots of good stories?"

"Yes, quite a few. The one that touched my heart the most started on the day before the fire that burned down the church in 1814. Faith, the diary writer, wrote that her fourth baby was starting to come. She was twenty-seven years old at the time and already had three sons. The next entry, written by Chastity, the older sister, said that the church had burned down but that she and Faith had missed it because Faith had been trying to get her baby birthed for twenty-four hours. After the church was gone, she finally delivered a baby girl. The last sentence for that day read, 'Faith held her child, kissed her forehead, named her Hope, and went home to the angels.' They buried Faith beside the burned-out building, and then they rebuilt the church."

"What happened to the baby?"

"Chastity raised little Hope and her three older brothers with her own four children."

"It's a shame the diary had to end on such a sad note."

"It didn't. Chastity continued to write in her sister's diary every evening until she ran out of pages. Then she started her own diaries. We have the whole set. They cover a total of seventy-six years, until Chastity died in 1873. She was eighty-eight."

"My sister, the historian," Glaze said, but without the usual teasing lilt.

I turned to look at her. She had bent down to brush her hand across a daylily blossom. "They're all buried at the cemetery on Third Street," I told her. "Maybe we'll walk up there tomorrow so you can see the headstones."

In a much more somber mood we passed by the library. I pointed across the street to the house where Bob's best friend Tom lived. Just beyond that was the little clinic that we were so fortunate to have in town. When we reached Magnolia Way, I couldn't help smiling. Despite the sad story of Faith and little Hope, I was simply enjoying being outside. We detoured across the street to Azalea House, Melissa's bed-and-breakfast where I lived my first year in Martinsville, but there was nobody home. "We'll stop by again some time while you're in town. I want you to meet Melissa. She's a dear friend, almost a second sister."

"Then, shouldn't *she* be your bridesmaid, instead of me?"

"Heck, no, baby sister! You're my first choice." I couldn't resist leaning sideways to give her a quick hug. I didn't have the heart to tell her that Melissa had resigned the job when she found out that Glaze was coming. Now, though, I was glad we'd made the change. I was enjoying this sister of mine.

"Tell me a happy story," Glaze demanded as we turned and walked past the lovely old Japanese maple; so I took the time to tell her as much as I knew about *Heal Thyself*, the health store we were headed toward. It sat on the corner of Magnolia Way and First Street, overlooking the bend in the river.

"Annie McGill was a local girl who read about cruelty to animals in the slaughterhouses when she was in fifth grade, and decided right then that she was going to make a difference in the world. Her mother had been appalled when ten-year-old Annie declared that she was a 'vegetable-arian.' Nothing Mrs. McGill said could change Annie's mind. Annie never went off the deep end with protests and all that. She just quietly started learning how to run a business – I think Margot and Hans Schuss are the ones who helped her formulate her business plan while she was working for them one year."

"Are they the deli people?"

"Yes. When Annie was ready, she went to the First Community Bank in Garner Creek and got herself a business loan to buy the old Simpson house after Mr. Simpson died. She lives upstairs and runs the greatest little herb and vitamin store downstairs. Because she hadn't wanted to stock fresh veggies and stuff that had a limited shelf life, she convinced Ida and Ralph Peterson, the ones who own the grocery store, to start carrying organic meats and veggies, and stuff like goat's milk and cage-free eggs that they buy from Mrs. Pontiac, who lives just a block up from me."

"I never knew a town this size with so many food-related places!"

"You're right. We have a health store, a restaurant, a deli, a grocery store. Everybody in town does eat out a lot," I admitted, remembering all the wonderful dinners Bob and I had eaten at CT's, the restaurant up on the corner of Magnolia and Third. "The deli's open six days a week from nine a.m. to five p.m. The restaurant's open Tuesday through Saturday, evenings only. So, if people don't remember to buy some take-out, they have to cook for themselves on Sundays and Mondays. I really like the way the businesses around here are supportive of each other."

"So the grocery store doesn't carry vitamins?"

"Nope. That's Annie's territory. They're only three blocks apart, so it's not a disaster if you have to go both places to shop."

"Sounds rather British to me. Now all you need is a pub. I forgot to pack my vitamins, so I'll pick some up if Annie has the kind I like."

"Remind me to get some more licorice root tea. It's great for cooling down hot flashes."

"I'm having those, too. Pain in the tutu, isn't it?"

My little sister, having hot flashes? I took a good look at her. We'd both taken after Dad's side of the family, with bodies that were more pear shaped the older we got. But Glaze had mom's neck, long and slender, so her weight didn't look as obvious on her as my weight did on me.

"Did you know you have Auntie Blue's eyes, Glaze?"

"Really? I've never seen her that much. They moved to Colorado when I was in seventh grade."

"You do remember Uncle Mark, though, don't you?" Glaze furrowed her forehead for a moment until she realized what I was talking about. Then we both burst into peals of laughter, startling the sparrows that had congregated in the leftover puddles along the roadside.

Uncle Mark was married to Auntie Blue, who was my mom's older sister. Her name was really Beulah, but who on earth would saddle a girl with a name like that and expect it to stick? Mom couldn't say Beulah when she was a little girl, so she called her Blue, and the name seemed to fit.

One day, while Uncle Mark and Auntie Blue were over at our house, I'd come home in a tizzy because my eighth-grade art teacher told me I didn't have any talent. Mom said not to worry about his opinions because he still had to put his pants on one leg at a time.

Well, Uncle Mark heard that and decided he'd be the first man in history who could put his pants on BOTH legs at a time. So he took an old pair of gardening pants that were kind of baggy, and tried to jump into them, both feet at once.

Later, when we visited him in the hospital, he looked up at the traction pulley and admitted that maybe he wasn't as flexible as he used to be. Mom told him he was just plain pig-headed. Auntie Blue said that the next time he was going to try anything that foolish, please let her know in advance, so she could warm up the camera.

Thursday, July 21, 1994
Garner Creek

Harlan didn't work weekends, except an occasional Saturday till two o'clock. He walked to work, usually ate lunch at the diner down the street, saved part of his money for film, and the rest to invest in a house someday. One of the good things about his apartment over the bakery was the big interior bathroom that he had been able, with the owner's permission, to transform into his own darkroom. He'd had to squeeze things in a bit, but had managed the trays and the special lights and the developer. It had been easy to seal the door completely to prevent incoming stray bits of light.

One Thursday, just as he was leaving for lunch, one of the salesmen from the used car section approached him. Harlan knew him by sight, as he did all the people who worked there. Sid Borden was a sallow-faced, lanky fellow, who reminded Harlan of one of the blue-tailed skinks he had photographed, only not as dignified. He usually stuck to himself, so Harlan was surprised when Sid walked up beside him and said, "I have something I'd like to ask you about. Mind if I buy you some lunch so we can talk?"

"Sure," Harlan shrugged. They walked down two blocks to the little café on the corner and asked for coffee, black for Harlan, light and sweet for Sid. "What's this all about?" Harlan asked after their coffee was set down and they'd ordered a club sandwich for Sid and a cheeseburger with the works for his guest.

Sid smiled as he stirred his coffee, then placed the damp spoon carefully on the little paper napkin. He pulled another napkin out of the holder by the wall and set it beside the one that now had a small coffee stain on it. "I've wanted to talk with you for several weeks. I hear that you're quite the photographer." Sid had a salesman's voice. It was good when the customers didn't realize they were being sold anything. Somehow his customers always believed the purchase had been their own idea.

"Yeah, I guess," Harlan agreed.

"You have your own darkroom, right?"

"Right."

"Would you be interested in making a little extra money and helping out the cause of justice at the same time?"

"What do you mean?"

"You're not aware of this, I know," said Sid, as he glanced around to be sure that nobody could overhear their quiet conversation. "I do some work on the side as a private eye." He figured that Harlan might ask to see his PI license card. That place a block off Peachtree Street in Atlanta where he'd bought the card did good work, but Sid wasn't sure it would stand up to too much scrutiny, so he flipped the card into view from his wallet and then quickly tucked it away.

"I've been tailing a couple of people, two separate jobs, but they both might recognize me, since I've been involved in several high level cases." He might as well make this sound good while he was at it. "What I need is for you to take a few good-quality photos of these people in a couple of compromising places. You know, eating in dark restaurants, and going into motel rooms. These may be evidence in court cases, but you'll need to be very confidential about doing this. Nobody can know where the pictures are coming from." He wondered if he'd gone too far, since there was no overt response from his lunch partner. He bit into his club sandwich, waiting for a response. His sales training told him to present his case and shut his mouth. The first person to talk – and that first person was never Sid — would end up buying the car.

Harlan, however, was thinking of f-stops for the poor lighting in dark restaurants, responding to the challenge of the photography rather than being concerned about the details Sid had so carefully laid out. It simply didn't occur to him to question Sid. He had glanced at the private investigator's license, with Sid's photo laminated on the left side. Tony had hired the guy, so it must be all right. Of course, Tony had written that awful commercial, too. Harlan did wonder for a moment if Tony even knew about Sid's second job as a P.I.

He took a big bite of his cheeseburger, thought for a moment, swallowed, and said, "Sure. When do I start?"

"You can do the first job during your lunch breaks and maybe a little evening work," Sid explained, giving Harlan specific places where the couple had been seen, and showing him a Polaroid of the man. He'd taken it himself at a political rally, so Harlan would be able to recognize the man. This was an up and coming politician named Hubbard Martin. A married man with some little piece of tail on the side, and Sid figured they'd return to the same restaurant, the same motel once or twice more over the next few weeks. He might as well cash in, was the way he reasoned. He handed Harlan an envelope with a small wad of bills in it "to cover any expenses" with the understanding that there would be more when the photos and negatives were turned over.

It took Harlan only two days to get three photos of the two walking into and out of the Russell Gap Hideaway, a motel tucked into the backwater streets of a little town about fifteen miles up the river from Hastings, on the other side of Garner Creek. He'd managed a good shot of the two of them with their heads together over martinis at dinner earlier that same evening. Harlan knew he'd seen the man somewhere, but it took him a few days to realize that he was a politician from Martinsville, running for County Commissioner.

The next weekend, Harlan happened to see the man in Martinsville. Hubbard passed him on the street, and looked closely at him. Harlan couldn't tell if he recognized him, or just was wondering if he could get his vote. Harlan had actually been planning to vote for him, until he'd seen what poor taste the man had in women. 'Come to think of it, I'm not going to vote for anybody who's stupid enough to play around, especially this close to home with an election coming up.'

With the additional money he made, Harlan bought a loupe for his darkroom, so he could see the fine details better. He had been making do without a magnifier, even though he'd wanted one for some time. He tucked the rest of the cash away for his house fund.

From the Statement of Sidney "Sid" Borden
to the Georgia Bureau of Investigation
Monday, May 1, 1995

Yeah, I knew him from work. . . . No, not well. . . Yes, we ate lunch together sometimes down at the corner restaurant. . . . You know how it is, you're headed to the same place. It's crowded, so you sit together. . . . Baseball mostly, or fishing and bowling. You know, guy stuff. . . . The last time I saw him? It must have been Friday. He was in the parking lot when I came out. . . . No, I didn't talk to him. . . . At home with my wife. It was our anniversary. . . . We had dinner out. . . . We were in bed by 9:15. . . . Library? No, I don't know why he was in a library.

Saturday, April 20, 1996
Martinsville

Annie had the vitamins, but Glaze and I took almost an hour just to browse through the cheery little rooms. Annie spent part of the time helping us find the brands we asked about, and the rest of the time sitting in the rocking chair she had tucked into a corner beside the big front window. We chatted with her as we wandered around the little shop.

"Did you make that lovely quilt?" Glaze asked, motioning to the checkerboard fabric that draped across the back of the rocker.

"Yes, as a matter of fact, I did," Annie replied. "I've been interested in quilts ever since I was a little girl. When I was seven I started making one quilt square each month, so this particular quilt is eight years of work–ninety-six squares. At first I had to work at it to turn out one square in four weeks, but later it just became a habit to make a special square each month, no matter what other quilt I was working on. If you look carefully," she said, lifting the quilt from its resting place, "you can see that all the squares are dated. They're in chronological order."

Annie's braid had migrated to the front of her shoulder, and she swung it back out of her way. "My mother insisted that I date each square, and I'm so glad now that she did." Her shy smile couldn't disguise her pride as she pointed out the little embroidered dates. The squares in the upper left corner were obviously the work of a beginner, with simple childish stitches, and large bits of material. As we looked across the rows, rather like reading a book, we could see Annie's sewing ability bloom. There were color phases she'd gone through. "This was the summer I was into purple," Annie said, indicating three squares done in shades of purple and lavender. All of another row was her "green period–that was most of fourth grade." Some of the squares were embroidered with flowers. Some had words like love and peace and friendship sewn in bold colors.

"That's a self-portrait square I did when I was twelve," she said, pointing to a little fabric girl in a gingham dress, with long red pigtails. Annie's hair was still a vibrant copper, although she wore it now in a simple braid that hung down below her waist.

"Where do you do your quilting, Annie?"

"Upstairs. There's a big room right above us that overlooks the river. I have my quilting frame set up there and a big table for cutting and piecing."

I looked up and raised my eyebrows questioningly.

"You're right," Annie laughed. "There's not much room in there to move around, but it suits me just fine."

After we paid for the vitamins and the tea bags, Annie warned us not to drink licorice root tea more than seven days in a row. When Glaze asked why not, she explained, "It can raise your blood pressure. Most people think of herbal remedies as very safe, because they're natural, but herbals can be powerful medicine. They need to be used with care and knowledge. I think people should take responsibility for their own health, and I try to educate my customers whenever I can."

Annie's mouth pursed into a rueful grin. "Sorry if I sound like I'm preaching at you."

"Hush up, Annie. I for one appreciate your expertise and I like getting those reminders."

"Anything I need to know about my vitamins?" Glaze asked as she paused in the doorway.

"Take two each day. One before breakfast and one before bedtime. Also, drink plenty of water between meals, not because it's good *for you*, but because it's *good*."

> From the Statement of Annette "Annie" McGill
> to the Georgia Bureau of Investigation
> Tuesday, May 2, 1995
>
> No, sir. I hardly knew him at all. Of course, I knew
> he was Buddy's friend, but they never came to my
> shop. . . . Size nine, usually. . . . Home, working on
> a quilt. . . . No, sir, I was by myself. . . . Library?
> No, I don't know why he was in the library.

Saturday, April 20, 1996

"Sounds good to me," Glaze remarked as we started along First Street toward Sharon's Beauty Shop. "I always drink plenty of water, although I'd rather drink plenty of milkshakes!"

"Don't worry. We're just a few blocks from the deli."

Every person we passed had a familiar face, and quite a few stopped us to inquire, "Is this the Philadelphia sister we've heard so much about?" If Glaze didn't know that I'd been excited about seeing her again after all those long years of separation, she had no doubt about it by the time we'd walked the three and a half blocks to the gift shop.

In between interruptions and introductions and questions about her bandaged hand, Glaze asked me if it was a unisex beauty parlor. "You know, where men and women both can get haircuts?"

"Not a chance. This is lady's turf exclusively."

"Then where does Bob get his trim jobs?"

"A block up on Maple Street. Larry Murphy is a retired barber who used to have a shop in Hastings, but came here when his father got sick about a dozen years ago. When the father died, Larry, as the oldest of the eight kids . . ."

"Eight?"

". . . yes. Larry inherited the huge old house, so he decided to stay. Retirement wasn't all that much fun anyway, since he didn't like to fish or read. He enclosed the side porch, and turned it into the barber shop. He even painted a red and white barber pole on the door. I'll show it to you when we walk past there on the way home."

"What did all the other kids think about Larry getting the house?"

"Most of them didn't care. They'd all left town as soon as they got old enough. Barry was the second son. He owns a really scrumptious small hotel just upriver from Savannah. That's where Bob and I are going for our honeymoon. I've never stayed there, but it has a great reputation for good food, lovely rooms, and beautiful gardens."

"Big beds?" Glaze asked with a twinkle.

"Hush your mouth, little sister." Was that a blush I felt creeping up my neck? I'm almost fifty years old. I thought blushing had gone out for me a LONG time ago. This was 1996, for heaven's sake. Yet here I was getting all warm and fuzzy-feeling. I *was* looking forward to our honeymoon, though. No, we hadn't 'done it' yet. Not because of any prudishness. Just a deep belief that consecration and vows add depth to...

"Biscuit? Yoo-hoo! Are you with me?"

"To get back to our discussion of the Murphy family . . . "

"And to let the red recede from your face," my sister added gleefully.

"I said there was a whole passle of Murphy kids. Bob's told me about them, but I haven't met any except Larry. Bob said they couldn't wait to get away from town."

"Why?"

"Because nobody ever could think of them as individuals around here. Their parents had named the boys Larry, Barry, Gary, Perry, and Harry."

"That's awful," Glaze groaned. "Surely you jest."

"Girl-scout's honor. Wait, though. It gets worse. The girls were named . . ."

"Let me guess, let me guess," interjected Glaze, tapping my arm. "Umm, there has to be a Mary . . ."

"Right."

"And a Sherry?"

"You got it. And . . ."

"That poor mother must have been pregnant her whole life."

"That poor mother is the one who came up with all these names. She was actually proud of it, or so Bob says."

"So who was the other girl? Nary? Blair-ie? Kwerry? Tipperarey?"

"I think we need to get you out of the sun. No, the last girl was named Derry."

"Ha! I bet she got called dairy-cow in school."

More to change the subject than anything else, I detoured across First Street to show Glaze the Metoochie River. It's really more a creek, especially with the drought we'd been having, but it's been called a river for two centuries. Why change things now? "What does the name mean?" Glaze asked.

"Beats me. I tried to look it up, but the original meaning has been lost. Some people say Metoochie is just a mispronunciation of the real name given the river by the Cherokee. About a hundred and fifty years ago . . ."

"When the church burned down?"

". . . yeah, about that time. Anyway the name got corrupted some-how, and everyone started calling it the Metoochie. That's what it's been ever since."

"Aren't there any old maps that show the real name?"

"Nothing that's readable. I even checked with the state archives. This big river of ours is just a creek to most of the folks in the rest of Georgia. I just haven't been able to find the answer, but I keep hop-ing."

"Nothing in the old diary?"

"No. Both women mention gathering reeds by the river or hauling water from the river, but they never call it by any name."

Maybe I should start being more specific in my journal that I write in each evening. I always write a gratitude list, too - five things for which I'm grateful. I read once that when we focus on what's good in our life, we're more likely to attract more good things. If we focus on the yucky stuff, that's what we get more of. Then, after I write the list, I jot down some musings about what's gone on during the day. If someone reads it a hundred years from now, maybe a great-great-great-granddaughter of mine, will she be able to understand the flavor of my days?

What we focus on . . . Hmmm . . . Even with the rain we'd been having, the water level was still low. A five-year drought, and no end in sight. Maybe I should start carrying an umbrella everywhere.

Ever since a flood washed away five or six buildings about seventy years ago, there's been nothing built on the Metoochie along here, except the town dock, which is really just a medium-sized pier that juts out into the water so the kids have something to jump from. The rest of the waterfront is like a park, with a grassy area that slopes down to the water's edge. People fish, feed the ducks, picnic in the spring and fall, or just walk along and enjoy the sounds of the river. I pointed to the placid pool where the river runs deep, right in front of where we stood. "Bob told me he learned to skip stones right across there before he even started school."

"Is he good at it?"

"Champion quality," I affirmed, having counted sixteen or seventeen skips on a single throw. It's always hard to know exactly how many there are, since the skips get smaller and so much closer together toward the end of the run. There were almost twenty, I knew that for a fact. Upriver and downstream from the pool, the creek is littered with large boulders. No rapids, nothing that dynamic, but rough water nonetheless. Here in front of us, though, some geologic shift had left a deep, broad, quiet pool where people sometimes swam in the early mornings. Of course, during the school vacations, there are always kids in the water. No lifeguards, no real rules. The bigger kids look out for the little ones, and there are always moms patrolling the edge. It works well.

From the Statement of Sharon Armitage
to the Georgia Bureau of Investigation
Tuesday, May 2, 1995

Well, why on earth would you want to know that? .
. . Size nine and a half or so. I'd be six feet tall if I
didn't have so much turned under to walk on! . . .
Yep, I closed up my shop about five and took the
girls home. If my husband Carl's at the station,
which he usually is till six-thirty, they come to the
shop after school and do their homework in the back
room. Some days I let them go swimming after their
homework is done, but not this past Friday. . . .
Yep, once I got home, I stayed there. . . . Library?
No, I don't know why he was in the library.

Wednesday, January 18, 1995
Garner Creek

Here it was Wednesday again, and the waiter knew what she
always ordered. She called that good service.

Sarah looked around the busy little diner. 'Maybe I should eat
here more often,' she thought. 'Not just on Wednesdays.' The first
time she'd stopped in to eat here, almost two months ago, was when
Ben had come in, recognized her as a bank customer, and stopped to
say a friendly hello. She'd been surprised when he'd asked if he
could share her table. Naturally, she'd agreed. The diner had been
crowded that late November day. If there'd been an empty table, he
might not have asked.

He seemed to want to talk to someone, though. He told her how
busy they'd been on Monday and Tuesday. It was because of the
Thanksgiving weekend rush. She understood. She'd been really busy
at Mabel's, which is why she had decided to treat herself to a relax-
ing lunch at the diner.

That first time he sat down, she knew he appreciated her good
conversation. Not like Sid. She knew her husband didn't like her to
talk. Sid didn't talk much himself except to complain. When he did
talk he wanted her to be quiet. So, this was new. This was special.
Of course, Ben usually just talked about his wife. Sarah and Ben had
been having lunch together most Wednesdays, and she'd been happy

to sit and listen, making a little comment now and then. His wife had moved out last August, three months before Sarah and Ben started their weekly lunches. He was still really upset about it. He wanted a family. He loved his wife and didn't know how to get her back.

Saturday, April 20, 1996
Martinsville

As we pushed open the door of the gift shop, the chimes hanging from the handle tinkled happily, and Sharon Armitage trundled out of the beauty parlor, wiping her hands on a towel. "I'm full up, Biscuit. I don't have a bit of time until Monday at 11:30." She extended a damp hand as she echoed the same question everyone had been asking. "Is this the wonderful sister from Philadelphia that we've all been wanting to meet? Well, sweetheart, whatever happened to your hand?"

"Car accident. Not my fault. I don't know about the 'wonderful' part, but I'm Glaze McKee. It's a real pleasure to meet you, Sharon. My sister tells me you're a woman of many talents."

"Havin' four kids was one of my biggest talents," Sharon giggled. "Yep, if I could do that, I figured I could do anything. The gift shop is just because I like dealing with pretty things. Of course, I was trained early on as a hairdresser – knew I wanted to do that from the time I was a little bitty tyke. Yep, I used to comb my mother's hair every evening." She used the back of her hand to brush a stray blond curl away from her face. "Whoops! I've got a perm to check on. Maggie will feed me to her chickens if I overcook her hair. You two just look around, and if you need anything, go ahead and take it and pay me next week. I don't have time to fiddle with the register today."

I laughed at Glaze's startled expression. "That's the way it is around here, Glaze. We live in a time warp, before shoplifting, before bum checks, before credit card abuse. Fun, huh?"

"Too good to be true," she replied with something like awe in her voice.

We spent a couple of minutes wandering around the tiny store, but my tummy was beginning to rumble a bit, and I could tell Glaze wasn't in a gift-basket mood. "Come on, let's head on to the DeliSchuss . . ."

"I still don't believe that name."

". . . to get some of their good soup before it's gone. Maybe the name's corny, but the food's always fresh and wonderful." We walked out the tinkling door into the late morning breeze. "You'll like the staff. Margot and Hans run it during school hours. After school and on Saturdays, the kids do the work."

"Kids?"

"They're always high school kids. Every time one leaves for college, the Schusses just hire a replacement from the sophomore class."

"How can a deli support that many employees?"

"They have only two or three kids at a time, and one of them is their daughter. She's a first-year student at the University of Georgia in Athens. I think I heard she wants to major in biology. She goes to classes during the week and then works at the deli on Saturdays. She lives with Bob's sister in Athens and does chores to earn her room and board."

"What kind of chores?"

"Cooking, laundry, shopping..."

"Lucky of Bob's sister to have a live-in maid."

"It's not quite like that. Miranda's a good worker, and Ilona needs a fair amount of help. She has some medical issues."

"I'm sorry. I didn't mean to sound flippant."

"You didn't know. Anyway, Miranda's a real godsend."

"Will I get to meet her today?"

"Probably, but don't expect a conversation. She hardly says anything – a very quiet girl."

"Who did the Schusses hire to take her place during the week?"

"Ariel Montgomery. She's Brighton and Ellen's daughter, but she never works Saturdays, thank goodness."

"Why? What's wrong with her?"

"Nothing. She just seems to attract hoards of young men. It makes the place pretty crowded during the week right after school."

"So why do the Schusses keep her on?"

"I think they consider it their civic duty to hire local kids. A lot of the businesses around here and in Braetonburg do the same sort of thing. We don't have a single kid in the county high school who doesn't have an after-school job. I know you've heard the old saying that it takes a whole village to raise a child."

"Yeah, but it never seems to happen that way anymore."

"Maybe not in a lot of communities, but around here we take that seriously."

"You mean every kid goes on to college?"

We had paused in front of the Chief Movie House. *Gone with the Wind* was showing. Some things just keep on keeping on. Didn't Tara have a big porch? No, a verandah, with tall columns. "I like my verandah better," I said out loud without thinking.

"I thought we were talking about kids going to college."

"Oh, right. Well, not every kid around here wants to go to college. It's just that we feel they ought to have the skills to live productive lives and to enjoy the work they choose to do. The whole town – well, almost the whole town - seems to have a strong commitment to teaching those skills and responsibility and work ethic to the young folks. Most high school kids help out in their family businesses, but those whose families don't own stores or farms get after-school jobs with other families."

"Sounds too good to be true," she repeated.

"That doesn't mean we don't have some kids that push the boundaries a lot. Remember our fifteen-pound mailbox?"

"Yeah. Most towns have statues that get painted – you have a mailbox. Never mind. Let's go eat. I could use a milkshake."

"Do you still think a milkshake can cure anything?" I asked.

"Of course! I wasn't the milkshake marathoner for nothing." From the time Glaze was about seven until she got out of high school, she drank at least two milkshakes a day. It was the only way mom could get milk into her, and mom believed all the propaganda that said milk built strong bones. She ignored the sugar content and figured the milk was value enough.

We were still chuckling when we walked into the DeliSchuss. The quiet, black-haired young woman making sandwiches behind the counter smiled as we entered. Miranda Schuss was always quiet, but she had a lovely, peaceful smile. Last year she used to come into the library a lot to work on her senior term papers. The first few weeks I was there, I'd see her three or four times a week, but then she stopped coming in. The only time I see her now is in the deli or at Ilona's house when Bob and I visit his sister.

Miranda nodded us toward the only empty booth at the back of the deli. There were a lot of head-turnings as we wove our way through the lunchtime throng. I stopped two or three times to make a quick introduction, but we were both too hungry to dawdle for long over chitchat.

Cory Welsh came over to ask what we wanted to drink. "Hey, Ms. McKee! I bet this is your sister!" A very pleasant young man, although his taste in slacks could have used some improvement. Cory had lost his mom in a car accident when he was only six. Bob told me that Cory's dad was almost always on the road – he sold farm equipment – so Bob's mom (my head Petunia) had pretty much taken over Cory's rearing Mondays through Fridays. She'd done a good job. Cory was what I would simply call a good kid, even if he did look like a cross between a golden retriever and an afghan hound, with his thick blond hair parted straight down the middle. Not by design, I thought. That was just the way it grew naturally. As he went off to fetch a lemonade for me and a vanilla milkshake for Glaze, I turned to the menu. "Some of the open-faced sandwiches are authentically Scandinavian. Some are more German. And some seem to come right out of California. But they're all good. The Schuss family make their own mayonnaise here. The soups are good, too."

Cory quickly sat our drinks in front of us, tossed his head to flip an unruly strand of reddish-blond hair away from his left eye, and snapped open his order pad. Glaze chose an open faced smoked salmon sandwich with avocado, sprouts, and palm hearts. The fresh mayo for her sandwich was blended with capers. I decided on a hearty lentil soup with zucchini bread on the side. There is no such thing as too much soup on any given day. I could guzzle soup the way Glaze could guzzle milkshakes.

The deli gradually emptied until we were pretty much by ourselves. I had quietly told Glaze about Cory's history, and I could tell she was impressed. After we'd eaten our fill, Glaze asked Cory for a doggie bag for the other half of her sandwich. When he brought it back to us, she complimented him on the delicious food and on his efficient service.

"Thanks, ma'am. The Schusses train us really well here, and this is a fun place to work. I like it a lot better than the grocery store. We get to have a lot of responsibility, too. We used to do outside deliveries, well Miranda did them, until last year, but we quit after that guy was murdered . . ."

Beyond Cory's elbow, I could see Miranda look up and frown. Cory was entirely too talkative, but he was fun to listen to. I figured he could stand up to the lecture he was bound to get from Miranda.

". . . because Mrs. Schuss didn't want anybody going out on the streets alone for awhile. Finally they figured it was safe again, but the delivering took too much time anyway, so they decided just not to do that any more."

"You said you used to work at the grocery store?" Glaze asked, obviously intrigued by this garrulous young fellow in baggy black pants that were a contrast to his tidy white shirt. Over the pocket was the deli's logo, a red line-drawing of an open faced sandwich and a cup of coffee, with the slogan in cursive winding above it, as if it were the steam from the cup.

From where I sat, I could still see Miranda eyeing us. I couldn't tell if she needed help, was jealous of her friend's ability to charm the old ladies she undoubtedly thought we were, or just didn't want his talkative nature to bother paying customers.

"My dad travels all the time, and he didn't want me to go into his line of work, so he thought I should try a lot of different things to see what I was suited for. He wanted me to learn how to manage my own business. I like working. That is, when I'm not skateboarding. The first job I ever had was sweeping out the gift shop when I was seven years old. Then I worked in the grocery store as a stock boy. I tried to work in the frame shop for a couple of months, but I just couldn't get the hang of those cutting machines. I think Mr. Snelling was afraid I'd chop my fingers off, so he talked me into leaving before my year was up. This job's the best of all, even though I do have to wear this goofy shirt."

"I admire your professionalism, and I'll bet you're a great skate-boarder," Glaze commented, and Cory beamed. "Do the other young people all work as hard as you do?"

"Ariel's been here weekdays since last summer. She's doing pretty well so far. Miranda is the one who made your sandwich." He indi-cated the girl with the curly black hair who was still behind the counter, this time cleaning up. "She's the owners' daughter. She's been working with her folks since she was a little kid, so she knows everything about the business. She helped train me when I started here." Cory leaned a little closer and lowered his voice. "Ms. McKee, do you remember the time last year when that cat of yours kept fol-lowing Miranda all the way from her house to here?"

"Yes, I certainly do." I turned toward Glaze to explain. "Mar-malade wouldn't leave Miranda alone. For a few weeks she followed her everywhere. I almost thought I was going to lose my cat."

"Miranda was freaked out about it," Cory said, and I could hear the concern in his voice.

"Does she still do it?" Glaze asked me.

"No," I said. "It's like she finally lost interest."

"Stupid cat," Cory blurted out. "How could anybody lose interest in Miranda?"

Hmmm. This seems to be the afternoon for blushing. Glaze was incredibly diplomatic. Quickly, to give Cory a moment to recover his composure, she said, "Miranda must be a good friend of yours."

"Yes ma'am." He wouldn't quite look us in the eyes, but he was getting over the rough spot. "Miranda's nice, but Billy Smith is my best friend. He works for Mr. Parkman over at the restaurant. We're both seniors, and he's great at skateboarding, almost as good as me!"

"Billy's mom," I explained to my sister, "is quite a famous fabric artist. She sells her quilts and stuff in galleries in New York and Chicago."

"Not Judy Smith?" Glaze asked.

"Yes. Have you heard of her?"

"I've seen her work," Glaze exclaimed. "It's fabulous! When I went to New York last year, a friend of mine showed me a gallery where Judy's wall hangings were on display. They were phenomenal."

Cory was beaming at this commendation. "My dad's been dating her, so Billy and I think we might end up being brothers. That would be a lot of fun. I never had a brother before."

"Aren't you about ready to graduate?" Glaze asked him.

"One month, one week, and five days. After that I want to start my own business. Billy's going to be a chef. He doesn't want to leave Holly, his girlfriend, but he's already been accepted at a great chef school in Vermont . . ." Cory's voice faded off as he realized that he might be spending too much time talking to the clientele. Miranda was still staring at him.

Glaze saw that she was about to lose her information source, so she asked him to tell her more about Holly. After all, the deli was practically empty, just two other tables and us.

Cory was easily convinced. "Holly's dad is Reverend Pursey. He's the town minister. Holly's 17, and she's going to Cornell next year. She's going into veterinary medicine, and then she wants to set up a clinic here in town."

"Are there that many cats and dogs in Martinsville?" Glaze asked, unabashedly slurping out the last of her milkshake.

"Oh, no ma'am. She wants to treat cows and horses. You know – farm animals. She'll handle pets, too, if she has to. Maybe you could bring your cat to her, Ms. McKee."

Maybe Holly could hire you to do her promotional work, I thought, as I munched the last crumb of my zucchini bread. Aloud I said, "Of course I will. Do you have any particular plans for this summer?"

"Yeah. Reverend Pursey and Father Ames are getting together a group of kids to go to Atlanta for a week to work as interns in the Inner City Garden Project. The deal is that we help out there, and then when we come back, we're supposed to do a garden project in our own area."

"Do you have a project in mind?"

"Well, some of us thought that we might try to get some trees planted in Enders." He looked over at Glaze. "Since you're from Philadelphia, you wouldn't know, but Enders is the next town five or six miles downriver." Obviously it hadn't occurred to him that since we were sisters, we had both grown up in this valley. I didn't have the heart to set him straight, and apparently, neither did Glaze. Cory went on with his explanation. "You can't get there from here because of the huge bluff just south of Martinsville. You have to drive twenty-five miles back up to Russell Gap, take County Road #4, and then swing south. Enders is in another little dead-end valley, kind of like this one, only it's not nearly as nice. That's why we thought they could use some help." He paused and sent an appraising glance my way. "Say, Ms. McKee, we still need a couple of chaperones to sign up for the trip. How would you like to volunteer?"

Two weeks with a bunch of high-schoolers? Probably not my cup of tea. "I'd have to think about it, Cory."

Cory turned and raised his voice. "Hey, Miranda! Good news! Ms. McKee is thinking about being a chaperone for the trip!"

"Cory, that's not exactly what I said."

"I know, but you'll really enjoy it. We'll have a great time!" He pulled out his order pad, tore off the top slip, and placed it face-down on the table exactly half-way between Glaze and me. "Now I'd better go check the other tables or I'll be in hot water. Here's your check, and I really enjoyed talking with you."

I think I have a problem with setting boundaries. I think I don't know how to say no. I think I'm a sucker. I think I'll probably enjoy Atlanta. I think I see my sister laughing at me. I must be having a hot flash.

As we stood up, Miranda moved unobtrusively over to the cash register, ready to ring up our lunches. Other than briefly asking if we'd enjoyed our lunch, she didn't say anything, just smiled as she handed us our change.

"Hurry back," Cory called out as we left. If I hurry back, I wonder what else I'll get signed up for?

As we turned up Pine Street, a yellow Chevy pulled up beside us. "Let me guess," Glaze said out of the corner of her mouth. "Who could this yellow car possibly belong to?" How can she whisper without moving her lips?

"Biscuit, is this the wonderful sister from Pennsylvania we've been hearing so much about? Well, sweetheart, whatever happened to your hand?" Glaze rolled her eyes before she turned and smiled at Sadie Masters, who was wearing yellow-framed sunglasses.

From the Statement of Judy Smith
to the Georgia Bureau of Investigation
Tuesday, May 2, 1995

Oh, I knew who he was, but I don't think I ever talked with him. . . . Size five or five and a half, but I'm usually barefooted like this when I'm working around here. . . . Only when I attend openings. They're too hard on my ankles. . . . These are some new pieces I'm doing for the Chicago gallery, so I haven't left the house except to go to dinner with Paul once last week. . . . Thank you, I'm glad you like my pieces. . . . Thursday or Friday, I think. We ate at CT's. You'd have to ask Paul. All the days run together when I'm preparing for a show. . . . Yes, Billy was here when I got home. . . . Library? No, I don't know why he was in the library.

Friday January 20, 1995 Garner Creek

Sid paced the showroom, wearing a used-car-salesman-smile on his otherwise murky face. He'd sold only half his quota for the week, and he was angry about that. It was Sarah's fault. How could he sell cars when his wife was cheating on him. He'd called her at work two days ago and was told she was eating out like she did every Wednesday.

That night, as she was making a sandwich for her lunch the next day, he had casually asked her if she had a long enough lunch break to eat her food without having to gulp it down, or did customers interrupt her meal.

"Oh," she said, "sometimes I work through lunch, but usually I just sit in the back room and read a book."

"Do you ever go out for a walk?"

"No, not usually. I'd rather be there in the shop in case they get busy."

Sid decided to talk to Harlan again. This would be easy. 'I'll show him a picture of Sarah, and tell him where she works,' Sid thought. 'He's never met her, so he doesn't have to know she's my wife. He'll think it's just another PI job.'

Just bring him proof, that's all he wanted. Just a few pictures and the negatives. He'd take it from there. He already had a stash to choose from, but this job was more important. He was looking forward to shoving the photos in her face and asking her just what was going on . . .

Chapter 8

Saturday, April 20, 1996
Martinsville

Extricating ourselves from Sadie took a while. We finally just started walking up the hill, and Sadie followed along in her car, carrying on a good-natured monologue until we passed the barber shop and turned left onto Second Street, while Sadie had to continue, as straight as she could manage, up Pine to get to her house.

"Is everyone in town that loquacious?" Glaze wondered.

"Of course not. Remember Miranda, at the cash register? She hardly said a word to us."

"That's because Cory had already talked our ears off. I do have to admit he was interesting. I think he has a lot of promise."

"I hope he and Billy get to be brothers. Judy Smith just wants to be an artist and work out of her house. She hates all the promotional stuff she's had to do. Her work is finally beginning to sell quite well. I think that's the reason she's seeing her way to date Paul Welsh more. They're not officially engaged, but it's pretty obvious to everybody in town that they soon will be."

"I hope Paul knows about it," Glaze commented rather ascerbically.

As we stepped into the vestibule after our walk, the phone rang. It was Bob, inviting us to dinner at Chef Tom's. "Whoopee! What a great idea. On behalf of us both, I say yes. Glaze will love it – and so will I."

"I'll be by to pick you up around 7:30. Does that sound like good timing?"

Perfect.

"Perfect." I reached down to pat Marmy, who had greeted us at the door. "It'll give us time to work off the huge lunch we just had at the deli. See you this evening. And, I love you."

As I hung up the phone I turned to Glaze. Marmalade was winding herself in and out around Glaze's legs. "You're in for a treat, sis. CT's – that's what we all call it around here – is the best restaurant in the county. Bob and I eat there often, but it still feels like a holiday every time. Tom Parkman, the owner, is Bob's buddy. He's an interesting guy. I think you'll enjoy meeting him."

You will love him. He gives me fish.

"I've enjoyed everyone else I've met so far."

"That's because you haven't met Larry Murphy yet."

"Who?"

"You remember. He's the barber – Larry, Barry, Gary, Perry...." Come on in the kitchen so we can put this stuff away," I said, indicating the doggie bag and the tea. Glaze squeezed her bag of vitamins between two of the spindles and left it sitting on the stairs for later, then followed me into the kitchen.

"So, what's wrong with the barber?"

"He comes on with a super-friendly air, says he just loves giving hugs, and then, once he's enveloped you, he'll grope away as long as he can get away with it."

"Which would be about an eighth of a second or less, if he tries it with me!"

"Well, good luck. He's got tentacles like an octopus. I'll warn you if I see him coming. We're safe for this evening, because he never eats at CT's."

"Why not?"

"Tom took Larry aside one evening and told him to keep his hands to himself in the restaurant if he ever expected to be seated there again. Larry left in a huff and hasn't been back since. He tried to badmouth Tom, but nobody would listen to him."

"Is Larry really horrible?"

Yes.

"No, just sort of slimy." By this time I had taken the doggie bag from my sister and walked over to put it in the fridge. Doggone it. I'd forgotten to get a light bulb. "He leaves me feeling contaminated somehow, every time I talk to him. I feel like I have to be protecting myself the whole time."

"I've known men like that. They need a real clear message that such antics aren't acceptable."

How about claw marks on their noses?

"The worst thing is he thinks he's irresistible because he's so cute."

"Do you mean he *is* cute, or he just thinks he is?"

"Well, he's pleasant looking. At least, I used to think he was until I ran into him a couple of times on the street. He even does it at church. He'll never try anything when Bob's around, thank goodness, but I don't want to feel like I need a guard any time I walk through town. I'm thinking of screaming at him from a block away the next time I see him coming."

Launch me at him, Widelap, and see if he ever bothers you again.

"What you need, big sister, is a quick lesson in groper-control. The best defense is to keep him from getting his paws on you to begin with."

With surprisingly little effort, Glaze gave me a lesson in setting firm boundaries. It took me a couple of tries as we did some role-playing. First I pretended to be Larry. As I walked up behind Glaze, she turned, gave me a dazzling smile and fielded my outstretched arms. Then, as she said, "How nice to see you, Larry," she twisted out of range and ended up standing in front of me with her hands very firmly holding my wrist and elbow. If I'd had two extra sets of arms I might have been able to get them around her, but I felt firmly put in my place. She even did it with a broken finger. Amazing.

"Now, I'll play Larry," she said, as she moved away from me. She turned and sidled back, slipping an arm around my waist before I could even think what to do. "No, no, no, Biscuit. You have to anticipate this. Here, you do that to me, and see what happens."

As I walked up on her left side and tried to slide my right arm around her waist, Glaze tucked her right elbow against her waist and then pushed her elbow backwards. At the same time she twisted forward and to her right, reaching out her left hand to grab Larry's (my) arm. Again she was a foot and a half in front of me, holding me away from her. Smooth! She stood there smiling and saying, "It's nice to see you again, Larry." It took me three or four more tries, but eventually I was able to fend for myself. We tried the elbow-tuck defense from both sides until I felt comfortable with it. By the time Glaze finished with me I was almost hoping we'd run into Larry soon. I wondered if there was a boundary technique for avoiding chaperone duties . . .

"What's the dress code at the restaurant?" Glaze asked me, changing the subject. "I didn't bring any fancy clothes, except a couple of nice dresses for the wedding and the rehearsal."

Orange fur is easier. I am always dressed right.

I glanced down at Marmy, who was looking from one of us to the other, almost as if she were following our conversation. "You'll be fine with whatever you want to wear. The dress code is non-existent. Casual, but respectful, as Bob likes to say."

"So, help me look over my extensive suitcase wardrobe, and tell me more about CT's."

You will like it. He serves great fish.

"Tom is Bob's best friend. They go fishing together, and bowling sometimes. When Tom gets a chance he stops in at the station, and Bob drops by the restaurant a couple of times a week."

"That's nice to hear. In the office where I work, there's so much competition going on between the men, it's hard to get a project coordinated."

"I didn't say they don't compete. You should hear the talk about who caught the biggest trout or who ties the best fly."

Like two tomcats on a picket fence.

"Tom is the same age as Bob. They grew up together, were drafted, went to Viet Nam, and then Tom went away to a culinary school in Vermont. Eventually he sold his big New York restaurant for oodles of money . . ."

"Oodles?"

"Yes, oodles, and came home to remodel his parents' big old farmhouse into the restaurant of his dreams. The kitchen is state-of-the-art, all bright lights and stainless steel; but the dining rooms – well, I think you'll like them. They're simple, candle-lit, comfortable, quiet, homey."

"I hope they're not cloying."

"Not at all. They're just – well – nice. Tom doesn't need the money, so he keeps the prices reasonable. Practically everybody in the county eats there."

"Sounds crowded."

"No, it's a huge old house."

Tom was the chef, of course, but he had an able assistant. Several years ago, borrowing an idea from Margot and Hans Schuss, he started conducting a work-study course for some of the local high-school students who might have dropped out otherwise. Two of them, Cory's friend Billy and a young girl whose name I couldn't remember, would be heading to that great New England culinary school in the fall. I filled Glaze in on these details as we puttered around the house, doing some of the little odd chores that precede a wedding. Finally we got spruced up and met Bob at the front door at 7:30. I was wearing my favorite blue silk blouse with my charcoal slacks, and I carried a gray cable-knit cardigan for the cooler evening that was ahead. Glaze had chosen an emerald green polo shirt and her white sweater over silky black slacks. She twisted a green and white silk scarf into a flower shape at her neck, and ended up looking elegant. How does she do it?

The restaurant was just three blocks away, but mostly uphill, so we took our time getting there. As we strolled along Third Street past the church, Bob pointed out the intricate, hand-carved front doors, something of a landmark in town. I mentioned that I'd already told Glaze about the original church building burning down in 1814, so I asked Bob to tell her the whole tale. Bob's a wonderful story-teller, and he loves the town history.

"Two brothers," he started, "became local heroes by wrenching the doors from their hinges in order to save them from being destroyed in the fire. It started when an oil lamp fell over. The story goes that their great-grandfather had been responsible for carving the doors, and their eighty-nine-year-old widowed great-grandmother was calling out, 'Save the doors, won't somebody save Homer's doors!' The boys did manage to save them, but they were both so badly burned in the process that they died within a week of each other and were buried with honors in the little cemetery over here on the south side of the church." We pushed open the small iron gate and detoured into the church yard to look at the monument that stood in the center of the gentle slope.

"The boys are buried here," Bob continued, "next to their great-grandfather, who was the first person buried in this walled-off portion. According to some old accounts, a couple of months after the first families finished building the church the first time, they marked off this plot with this little stone wall." As Bob went on with his story, Glaze and I sat down on the wall, which was just the right height and more than wide enough to form a comfortable seat. "When the boys died, the town voted to bury them here. They added this tall stone column. It's a wonder it's never fallen over in all these years. There's an inscription on the other side." We dutifully stood up to inspect the weathered carving.

Henry & Jason Martin
Heroes in Lyfe, Heroes in Death
The Doors of Heavyn are Open to Them

The dates carved below the epitaph were too worn to read. "They were 17 and 19 years old," Bob said sadly. "They had a younger brother who carried on the family name. One of the town council members, Hubbard Martin, is a direct descendant."

"Hubbard? What kind of name is that?"

"It's a family name of some sort," I broke in to explain before Bob could. "He's the one who didn't want to hire me because of *my* strange name."

"Now, Bisque, be charitable," Bob instructed. "Hubbard's been grumpy ever since he lost the election."

"He was probably born grumpy. He's not a very nice man."

Our conversation was lost on Glaze, who looked up from the inscription. "Martin?" she asked. "As in *Martinsville?* Is that a co-incidence?"

"No, their great-grandparents and five other families founded the town in 1745," Bob explained. "The 'old' Mr. Homer Martin was only twenty-four at the time, but he was the leader of the group, and they named the town in his honor. The church was the first building to be put up, although the doors weren't carved until five years later. The second building in town was a huge barn where the families lived with all their animals for the first year until they could get houses built. It was more important for them to protect their livestock and get the fields planted than it was to have separate houses."

I broke into his story to tell Glaze, "Three babies were born that first year in the barn. One of those babies grew up to be the mother of Chastity and Faith, who planted the daylilies. Their graves are right over here." I turned away from the stone wall and indicated a tidy row of headstones with simple epitaphs, just names and dates. We stood for a moment, then left the orderly little cemetery, closing the gate behind us.

We walked for half a block before we broke the silence. As we crossed Dogwood Street, Glaze asked, "Is the barn still standing?"

"I'm afraid not. The field where it used to be, just beyond Upper Sweetgum on Third Street, holds a funeral home now. Serves the entire county area. There's nothing left of the old barn except the stories."

By this time we were approaching CT's. "The rest of the stories can wait for another time."

We walked in and were greeted by Billy Smith who was, apparently, not on kitchen duty this evening, but was acting as host. He asked us if we wanted our usual spot. Of course we did. So he seated us in the front parlor next to the biggest window, where we had a lovely view of the Metoochie and the forested hills on the other side, bathed in evening light.

We took our time ordering, discussing favorites on the menu, and finally settled on pork chops for Bob, fish for me, and duck for Glaze. Except this is the way it read on the menu:

grilled stuffed double pork chops with apples,
onions, and Calvados
sweet potato souffle with pecans and brown sugar
fried green tomatoes
chilled corn and cumin relish

rainbow trout with baby shrimp in white wine sauce
on a bed of sauteed kale
barley pilaf
sauteed baby courgettes

duck a l'orange with cherry brandy dunk
wild rice with mushrooms and leeks
sauteed baby artichokes with garlic butter

All the meals started with CT's signature bread, which meant exquisite little onion and poppyseed potato rolls, and ended with a big salad. We planned to be there for a long time.

From the Statement of Larry Murphy
to the Georgia Bureau of Investigation
Tuesday, May 2, 1995

No. It's not Lawrence. It's Larry. . . . I worked until
about five-thirty or quarter to six. Then I fixed
myself a sandwich and watched TV till after the
eleven o'clock news. Went to bed after that. . . . I
knew who he was. Everybody around here knows
everybody else. . . . He was okay, I guess. Not anybody I'd go out of my way to talk to. . . . You know,
you guys ought to check out where Tom Parkman
was that night. . . . No, no particular reason. . . .
Library? No, I don't know why he was in the library.

Wednesday, February 1, 1995
Garner Creek

Sarah sat at their usual table at the little diner. At least, she
liked to think of it as 'their' table. She'd arrived a few minutes earlier than usual. Of course, they always had to eat a late lunch because Ben was so busy during the regular lunch hour. So was she,
for that matter. That's why she'd volunteered to work straight through
till 1:30 every day. Myra, who used to have to take the late lunch
period, had been so thankful. Myra was nursing her four-month-old,
and needed to go home at 12:30 to feed him. Sarah thought she
understood. She and Sid hadn't started a family. Sometimes she
wanted a child, but it didn't seem right to bring a child into a family
where there was never any conversation and very little love. Sarah
didn't believe in having babies just to have some company.

Now, however, she had someone to talk to. 'Although,' she
thought as she shrugged her shoulders a little to release some of the
tension, 'he does most of the talking. Maybe I should have been a
counselor.' The thought had occurred to her before, but she had always put it aside because there never seemed to be the time to go
back and finish college. Sid had come along when she was a junior,
and marrying had seemed like the right thing to do at the time. Of
course, he used to talk to her when they were dating. He was ten
years older than she was, and she found herself just going along
with whatever he said. Then one day he'd said, "Let's get married."

Funny how things had worked out. She'd landed the dress shop job so close to this diner. She'd been hired because she had all that experience from working summers during high school. After all this time – six years - she still knew how to work a register faster than anyone else. Mabel's was a popular store. They carried a wide range of sizes, styles, and prices, so women came from all over Keagan County. 'Such a tiny county,' Sarah thought. 'The smallest in the state. All the people here shop in the local stores. We wouldn't even think of going to the city. Maybe that's one reason this is a prosperous county,' she mused as she picked up one packet of sugar. 'We all support each other.'

This time, the waiter brought her the usual decaf with lots of cream. That's what came of eating at the same place once a week for two months.

Some of the other people there were regulars, too. She recognized the blond woman with the little gap between her teeth. She looked like an Organizer. She came once or twice a month and usually met two or three other women. Today it was the short brown-haired woman who always wore tacky polyester scarves. Sarah glanced down at her own simple orange silk scarf. She had tied it in a tasteful off-center bow. 'I bet nobody ever pointed out the difference to her,' she thought. 'I think I'll invite her to stop in at Mabel's for a free scarf-tying lesson.' The lady with the scarf sat down just as a tall gray-haired woman with green eyes joined the group. 'I'll invite all three of them,' Sarah thought, 'so the short woman won't think I'm trying to fix her.'

She took a moment to stir in another little container of cream as her glance continued idly around the diner. There was that real old man with the crooked nose who came in every single Wednesday, just like her. Maybe he came in on other days, too, because he seemed to know the stringy-haired waiter. They were laughing at something. She wished she'd heard the joke so she could laugh, too.

She noticed the man who always wore a black teeshirt, and the young fellow who looked like a powerful race horse. He was one of the new regulars. She'd seen him last week; she remembered his long face and the expensive looking camera that he left sitting on the table beside his sandwich.

As she glanced at her watch, in walked a woman in a blue denim dress. Sarah had already decided weeks ago that the blue denim lady must be taking a class at night school and studying during her lunch hour. Today she was lifting a big notebook and two textbooks out of a totebag that proclaimed, "I'm Proud to be a Grandma!"

Just then, before Sarah could look at her watch again, Ben walked in the double glass door and headed straight to her table. "Sorry I'm late. Got tied up over a loan. Did you order yet?"

"No, I was waiting for you."

They didn't shake hands, didn't touch, hardly even made eye contact. They'd wondered if they should even keep up the Wednesday lunches, but it was so important to both of them. If they never touched and hardly ever looked at each other, surely no one would notice anything, or be suspicious.

"I wanted to ask you something," he said as he sat down opposite her. "It has to do with next week."

The lady with the gap-tooth kept talking to the gray-haired woman, while their friend fumbled with her menu. The man in the black teeshirt took a last bite of his sandwich and left hurriedly. The young man with the big muscles and the camera shifted his seat a little bit to the left, so he could get a clear view of the auburn-haired woman and the man who sat across the table from her, talking earnestly.

Saturday, April 20, 1996
Martinsville

Tom always managed to find the time to saunter around to each table for a word with the patrons, welcoming newcomers and making the old-timers (like Bob and me) feel genuinely appreciated. He would suggest wines to complement the entrée. Bob and I weren't connoisseurs, so we tended to order the wine he told us to, and we always enjoyed it.

Tom wasn't particularly tall, wasn't particularly handsome, wasn't particularly anything, except a nice man. Just light brown hair and dark brown eyes with laugh lines crinkling the corners. A great tan. Wide hands with the kind of surprisingly long fingers that would cause many mothers to look for a good piano teacher.

"Tom, I'd like you to meet my sister Glaze, from Philadelphia. She's visiting for the week."

I could feel an electricity. No sparks, exactly, just an undercurrent that flowed around all of us like that first spring breeze that drifts the aroma of the *Viburnum carlesii* through the kitchen window. Glaze looked friendly and happy and completely oblivious of the impact she was making. Or maybe she's just used to being admired, even if it was very discreetly done.

"Here for the big event?"

"Yes. I came to help out, but I feel like I'm the one being pampered."

"Don't worry, sis," I spoke up. "Tomorrow we start sewing those curtains, and then you might be sorry you came. Thank goodness Tom and his staff are doing all the catering; otherwise you'd be cooking all week, too."

Tom held the handshake longer than I would have expected him to, since he was always so professional in his restaurant. Given my sister's looks, though, I shouldn't have been surprised. Tom gently enclosed her right hand, bandages and all, in both his hands. "What happened to you?" he asked. "Did that orange and white ball of fur chew you up?" He winked at me as he said it. He and Marmalade were great friends, which may have been one of the reasons I liked Tom so much.

Glaze chuckled a bit ruefully, and said, "Car accident. Not my fault."

I knew that Bob would fill him in on the details tomorrow or Monday, so I abruptly changed the subject. "What's the best wine to go with pork chops, fish, and duck?" I asked.

He turned toward me with a pained expression, and slowly let go of Glaze's hand, but not before I distinctly saw him look down at her other hand, searching for a wedding band or an engagement ring.

I gave Bob a do-you-see-what-I-see-happening gaze, and he returned it with his now-Biscuit-don't-start-assuming-things stare.

Tom quickly assured us that we'd all be happy with *Gewürztraminer*, a spicy white wine with a slight grapefruit flavor. Sounded good to me. Tasted delicious. Over two hours later we ended the meal with a baby Bibb lettuce salad with a simple French vinaigrette. At Tom's suggestion, we decided to indulge in a light raspberry and lemon pudding – one dessert with three forks – and coffee. As we left, Tom handed me a little bag. "Give the furball a little treat. It's on the house."

We took our time strolling home – downhill, thank goodness – after that long leisurely dinner filled with conversation that flowed without awkwardness, and silences that settled without embarrassment. After we crossed Juniper, Glaze asked, a little too nonchalantly, "Does Tom's wife do any of the cooking at CT's?"

In spite of her oblivious air at the restaurant, she was at least a little bit interested. I tried hard not to raise my eyebrows too much as I swallowed my triumphal I-told-you-so. Bob turned to look at Glaze, with what I recognized as his I-will-not-laugh-under-any-circumstances expression. "No, Glaze," he said. "Tom's never been married."

There was an awkward silence, the first of the evening, that I rushed to fill by telling Glaze about the first time I'd met Tom. "He asked me if Biscuit was a nickname, and when I admitted that my name was Bisque, his eyes brightened up, and he said, 'as in seafood soup?' I knew then that he was a true chef at heart, and almost hated to set him right about the pottery background." Although I didn't mention it to Glaze, I'd seen his eyes light up almost the same way this evening, and I knew her perfume had been a success.

Marmalade came up sleepily to greet us as we walked in. Glaze walked into the kitchen, so I could have a few minutes with Bob. I loved having her here, but it put something of a crimp on the romance of the wedding couple. Bob enveloped me in one of his wonderful hugs and said, "I'll see you two for dinner tomorrow. You need some time together, so I'm going to spend the day puttering, maybe tie some flies."

"Name one of them for me, dear." As he left, I bent down to pat the warm cat, who had obviously been curled up somewhere napping while we were gone. "Did you miss us, sweetie?"

You have been to see Fishgiver. Did you bring me anything?

"Come on in the kitchen, Marmy. Tom gave me a little treat for you. Wonder what it is? . . . Looks like salmon, you lucky cat."

I knew I could count on him.

"Listen to that purr." As I scooped out a little smidgen of the treat onto a square plate that said 'You Can't Beat the System' – it had a map of the London subway system on it, one of those souvenirs that you bring home and then wonder why - Glaze admired Marmalade from her chair at the kitchen table. "Don't you wish you knew what she was thinking?" I placed the plate on the floor, and Marmalade's dainty little raspy tongue began savoring the offering.

I am thinking I enjoy salmon.

"She's probably just enjoying the fish."

Gratitude List – Saturday Night

1. Walking down to the Metoochie River with my younger sister, Glaze.

'There,' I thought as I wrote. 'That's enough detail to keep my great-great-great-great-granddaughter happy, if she ever reads this journal.' I patted Marmalade's head and finished my list:

2. The right amount of gentle rain
3. Good food and good companionship
4. Flowers that bloom earlier than expected
5. My compost pile

salmon
Widelap
Smellsweet
Softfoot
Fishgiver

From the Statement of Thomas Edison Parkman
to the Georgia Bureau of Investigation
Wednesday, May 3, 1995

Yes, I live across the street from the library. . . . No. I wish I could help you, but I didn't hear a thing.... I closed up the restaurant, walked home, and read for awhile. . . . *Walden Pond*. I'm thinking of a trip to New England in a year or two. . . . It must have been about midnight. . . . Sure, I knew him. . . . He was a really nice kid. Same age as my nephew, Roger, but a lot more responsible. . . .Library? No, I don't know why he was in the library.

Wednesday, February 8, 1995
Garner Creek

Every few months Sid would invite Harlan out to lunch and would turn over more photo jobs to him, always with the admonition that the work be kept strictly confidential. He never reported on the results of the court cases, but Harlan understood that these might not be public knowledge.

One Tuesday in late January, Sid had approached Harlan with a different sort of request. This time it was a woman whose picture he handed over. It wasn't a polaroid. It was the left-hand side of a wedding close-up. The groom had been cut off.

"She works up in Garner Creek at Mabel's Dress Shop. Her lunch hour starts at one-thirty every day. Think you can arrange to take a late lunch so you can follow her to wherever she goes?"

"I can't take that much time off for lunch, if I have to drive there, follow her, get the pictures, and drive back here."

"Okay. See if you can get the day off tomorrow, and I'll pay you extra to cover for that. This is a really important one. We think she may be passing secret information, and she always does it on Wednesdays."

"From a dress shop?"

"That's just her cover."

Harlan didn't have to take the next day off because he managed to trade three Wednesdays for three Saturdays. He didn't have anything planned for those weekends, Tony was okay with it, and Joe, the married mechanic, was delighted to get some Saturdays off for a change. Harlan followed the short auburn-haired woman to the Garner Creek Diner the first Wednesday, and again the following week, getting in a few shots of her meeting with a man in a gray suit. He was only mildly curious, since the two of them looked so ordinary together.

The following week he was a little late getting to Garner Creek, and he was still in his car when he saw the woman on a street corner near the diner. She was just getting into a gray Saab, so of course Harlan followed along and got some good shots of the two of them going into the Hideaway. Dang, that place must do good business, even at lunch time. About half an hour later they came out, got into the car, and drove away, so Harlan drove back to Hastings to develop his prints. The next day he handed them all over to Sid, along with the negatives.

Chapter 9

Sunday, April 21, 1996
Martinsville

Six more days till my wedding. Glaze and I lingered at the little round table in the nook. We had started the day gently and luxuriantly, lounging around in bathrobes and nibbling on the fresh doughnuts that I'd gotten up early to fry, once Maggie Pontiac's rooster up the street woke Marmalade and me. I loaned Glaze my green velour robe, and it matched her eyes. April days can get quite warm around here, but the early mornings are fuzzy bathrobe times. We felt lazy and wonderful.

Marmalade was underfoot a lot, and Glaze laughed that she seemed to be trying to tell us something. Maybe she had a tummy upset of some sort. She'd woken me up once during the night, pawing at the covers, but I'd been too tired to pay much attention. Now, however, I picked her up, plopped her in my lap, and prodded gently at her belly.

Quit poking me and look outside.

It seemed as round and soft as usual, no excess heat, no hard lumps. "I think you're okay, Marmalade." I could have sworn she was disgusted with me as she hopped off my lap and onto the wide sill of the bay window.

I stood up to begin the bread making. I always make three or four loaves from one big batch. I usually braid one with rosemary or scallions in it, put one or two in loaf pans, and I form at least one into a round loaf to bake on a cookie sheet later on in the week. Because I make such a big batch, I end up giving a lot of bread away. Fresh bread is one of the highlights of life. Grandma Martelson's house always used to smell like fresh bread. I remember burying my face into her apron just to inhale the wonderful scent. Grandma had one of those aprons that's all one piece, that kind of wrapped around from her neck almost to her hemline. She would let me try it on when I was little. It reached to her knees, but on me it dragged the floor. And then, one day I tried it on and it almost fit me. I'd grown up without even realizing it. I remember . . .

How about remembering to look out back?

". . . Marmy, stop making that infernal racket. You know I won't let you out there to chase birds."

Then let me out so I can chase that man.

"Marmalade, hush! I can't hear myself think."

I do not believe this. I do not believe that these two humans are unconscious, regardless of evidence to the contrary.

Glaze peered out past Marmalade's pacing form, at the chickadees who were strutting around the sunflower seed tray in the back yard. "Other than dealing with a noisy cat, do you ever get bored living in a small town like this?"

"She's not usually this noisy. She's been acting funny lately." I watched her a moment, then turned back to Glaze. "Do I miss the concerts and the museums and such? Yes. Do I ever feel over-inspected by the town criers who watch what everyone else is doing all the time? Yes. But would I want to live at the faster pace of a city again? I did it once, Glaze, for that year before I married Sol, when I worked in the advertising firm in Boston. Once was enough."

Remembering that I hadn't rinsed the sprouts yet, I stopped measuring the dry ingredients for the bread and pulled the tea towel cover off the jar to check the progress of the radish seeds. They were about ready to eat. Why do the hulls tend to clump together until I'm ready to remove them, and then they spread out and stick to the sides of the jar or to the sprouts themselves?

"I can always visit a city," I continued, "to see the plays and enjoy the museums; but then I can come home here to a place where every face I see is recognizable, even if I don't know all the names. The fancy sights there in the city aren't enough to trade for the quiet evenings here."

I looked down at all the little white radish seedlings clinging to my hands. I'd missed having a garden in the city. Tubs on the apartment balcony just weren't enough.

"It's time to green up these little guys, so we can use them in the salad tomorrow. I hope you like radish sprouts."

"I sure do. They're peppery and wonderful!"

"Think you could do a final rinse with just one hand?" As Glaze moved to my side to take over the de-hulling process, easing the little sprouts into a bowl of water and rinsing them yet again, I noticed that Marmalade was pacing back and forth, faster and faster. She loves watching those birds. "How long has it been since you could see more than twenty or thirty stars at night?"

How long has it been since you have looked for men in your back yard? Look now! He is still behind those big trees! Look NOW!

"In the city? Are you kidding? I never . . .What's wrong with Marmalade?"

"What are you yowling about? Leave those birds alone. They won't bother you."

Glaze picked up the thread of her thought. "I never even look for stars anymore. In the winter I can usually see Orion, and some of Taurus, but that's about it."

I washed out the sprout jar and dried it. Once the hulls were cleaned off and drained, we transferred them back into the jar and put it on the counter nearest the window so they could get indirect sunlight for greening the little leaves. Then I turned back to the bread process, beating an egg to blend into the goat's milk, along with some oil and a little sugar.

"Glaze, I like being able to sit on a park bench day or night without worrying about who might sit down next to me. I could never do that in the city." I measured flour and bran, then warmed the milk mixture before adding the yeast to it, as I continued to recall my feelings when I lived in Boston. "There was a tension that I often wasn't aware of, but it was always there."

I was surprised by the strength of my feelings for this little town, and I knew I was beginning to sound like a real estate broker hot on a sale. I thought I'd already guessed the real reason Glaze was asking all these questions. It wasn't the small town atmosphere. Last night, when Tom had said good night to us, I'd seen her looking at him as if he were pizza after final exams. Her next words surprised me.

"Biscuit, I never had a sister before. I don't want to give away a chance to get to know you better. I don't think I'm ready to move here, and you might not want me this close anyway; but could I come to visit more often?" She paused as if gathering her thoughts. "And, could I stay a few extra days this time around? Maybe I could house-sit while you two are at the beach for your honeymoon."

Not if this guy is still in the back yard.

As I said a heartfelt "Yes," Marmalade abandoned the window to hop up on my sister's empty lap. She placed her paws on Glaze's collar bone, nuzzled her forehead to forehead, seemed to inhale a big breath. My gosh, did the cat love the vanilla, too? Then Marmalade curled up and settled in Glaze's arms, claiming her right to that spot whenever it was in the house. As I turned back to the breadmaking and began to blend the flour and bran into the yeast-laden goat's milk mixture, I couldn't tell whether the contented sigh came from my sister or from the cat.

Both of us.

From the Statement of Margot Schuss
to the Georgia Bureau of Investigation
Wednesday, May 3, 1995

I saw him often in the deli with his friend Buddy. . .
No, I haven't seen him at all this week. . . . Did I like
him? Yes, he was very pleasant. . . . I wear a size five
shoe, but I don't know that it's any business of yours.
. . . Of course he knew my daughter; she works at the
deli. . . . Of course not. She's only in high school and
he must be almost thirty. . . . I was home all evening
and all night. My brother is visiting from out of town.
. . . Miranda? She came home from the deli around
six o'clock and helped me prepare a big dinner. . . .
Of course she was here the whole evening. This was
family time. . . . Library? No, I don't know why he
was in the library.

Wednesday, February 8, 1995
Garner Creek

It was funny, Sarah thought. Last week, about two months after their first lunch, Ben suggested that maybe they should stop meeting in public. He asked her to walk two blocks past the diner, and said he'd pick her up at the street corner. That way, he said, they could have some private time together. He knew a little place where they could go. It turned out to be a motel in Russell Gap, about five miles north of Garner Creek.

She had gone with him, expecting to make love, and then here they were just talking, because having sex didn't feel right for either one of them. He'd pulled out pictures of Sheila, his wife, and he'd asked Sarah's advice.

"Have you told her how much you love her?"

"She ought to know I do. I earn good money. I've always been faithful. I let her work wherever she wants to work. If that's not love, I don't know what is."

"Isn't that funny? My husband could have said the same thing. Sid has been faithful, I'm sure. He brings in good money. He lets me work where I want to work. That's not all there is to love. Most women want to be appreciated for who and what they are. Sometimes love doesn't feel like love if you can't understand how the other person is expressing it. I'm going to give you a list of good books about how men and women communicate differently. And I want you to *read* them."

Sarah stood there in the Hideaway Motel, looking down at the bed she knew they wouldn't be touching. It occurred to her that if she went back to college and finished her degree, maybe she could start getting paid for all this counseling she was doing.

Turning around to face Ben, who was sitting in an armchair on the other side of the room, she told him, "You need to be putting your energy into saving your marriage. Why don't you call up your wife and ask her out to lunch next Wednesday?"

"You mean like a date?"

"Exactly! You love her. It's time to let her know that." Sarah could read Ben's expression. "You're thinking you'll invite her to dinner instead and send her a dozen roses. Don't do that yet. Don't overdo it. Just ask her to lunch and let her see the caring part of you that I see and that I respect."

Just like that, it was over.

Sunday, April 21, 1996
Martinsville

The rest of Sunday morning was a disaster. How any day can disintegrate like that after such a lovely start, I'll never figure out. After the bread was safely rising, I set aside the last three doughnuts and licked my fingers contentedly. We thought about going to church, but then decided we needed a long walk instead. I'd never played hookey with my sister before, and I thought it would be fun. Little did I know.

We scooted upstairs to exchange our fuzzy robes for comfortable pants and polo shirts, blue-gray for me (not my best color) and orange for her (not her best color either) and invited Marmy to join us for a stroll down to the river to walk off the sugar overdose before we started sewing. We never made it out of the front yard.

The mailbox hadn't been painted green this time, or blue or purple or red. It was still black, but it had a crude yet startling skull painted on the side of it. Glaze over-reacted, letting out a banshee wail that curdled my insides and made that third doughnut seem like an even bigger mistake than when I'd eaten it. Even Marmalade, who had followed us out the front door, jumped at the sound.

"My God," she gasped. "He couldn't have known I was here. That crazy, stupid, obnoxious bastard!"

I've raised three kids. I'm usually up to dealing with hysteria in a fairly straightforward manner. This time I blew it. "Glaze, stop that insane babbling right now. What on earth is wrong with you?" Of course, instead of eliciting a reasonable explanation, my question brought Glaze around to stare uncomprehendingly at me for a moment. Then she turned and ran into the house, followed by the cat. So much for our quiet walk.

Before I followed her in, I took a deep breath to steady myself, and bent to look at the source of her anger. At first glance I thought the skull had been painted on the black background, but found that it was a white ink drawing on black paper that had been glued onto the mailbox. Good old rubber cement is easy to apply, which explained how the skull could have gotten there without our being aware of it. Anyone could have walked by last night and casually slapped on some contact cement, then just pressed the paper into place. In the dark, nobody would have noticed anything.

I realized I should have looked around earlier to see if anyone had been watching us as we discovered what they'd done to the mailbox, but of course there was no-one in sight when I turned to survey the street. The skull, when I looked closely at it, was so detailed it even had a wiggly line for the saggital suture along the top. Whoever the weirdo was, he was a pretty good artist. I scurried up the walk, happy to duck into the privacy of the front doorway, stepped over Marmalade, and stopped long enough to call Bob at his house before I went upstairs where I could hear Glaze pounding her fist into a pillow.

"Sis, what's the matter? I'm so sorry I yelled at you. Please forgive me." She raised her head and shook it, not in answer to my request, but rather as if she were trying to clear her mind of garbage. "Can you tell me what's going on so I can help somehow?" Glaze quietly straightened up, then walked into the bathroom to splash water on her face with her left hand. One of the advantages of not wearing much makeup is that one can splash and dry off anytime without doing any damage. One of the advantages of having my sister's bone structure is that she doesn't need makeup to look stunning with or without splashing.

Glaze folded the towel carefully and placed it back on the rack, then leaned her elbows on the counter, buried her face in her hands - although how she managed that with the splint in the way, I couldn't tell - and let out an enormous sigh. I stood, undecided for a moment, then stepped over and gathered her up into a hug, and just held her until she relaxed a bit. Now was not the time for interrogation.

"No more questions, I promise, until you've got a good strong cup of licorice root tea in you. You don't have high blood pressure, do you?"

"My sister, the herbal encyclopedia. No, my blood pressure's fine. At least it was until I saw . . . " Her words trailed off, and I saw her left hand clench.

"Take a deep breath, and then come on down to the kitchen. I'll brew the tea while you make up some highly improbable tale to tell me to explain this. We'll drink the tea, and then you can tell me the truth. By then we'll both be ready to face it. By then Bob will be here and he can hear it, too." I linked my arm through hers as I spoke and maneuvered her down the stairs – bless that ancient builder who believed in wide stairways – through the vestibule, and into the kitchen. As we walked past the front door, Glaze closed it and decidedly turned the lock.

Thank you. It is about time you did that. I have been guarding the door.

I stepped over Marmalade, who was purring mightily, and steered Glaze into one of the comfy chairs at the big table so there would be room for Bob to join us when he came in, locked the back door as unobtrusively as possible, and walked back to the stove to retrieve the tea kettle. As I headed to the sink and turned on the cold water, I reflected on how truly lovely it was to feel safe in my house, in my town. The deep-well water was not only drinkable; it was delicious. The traffic was not only slow; it was downright sedentary. Well, except for Sadie . . .

The animals that meandered across the streets were friendly dogs and cats – each of them known by sight; raccoons might investigate the garbage cans at night, but there hadn't been a case of rabies in the whole county for several generations. I hadn't bothered to make the curtains for the bay window yet, because I'd never felt any threat from the direction of my back yard.

Now, though, I had a sister hunched on the chair with the yellow-flowered seat, looking furious. I'm not, as you well know, particularly squeamish, but this time I had a gnawing ache in my gut that said my safe haven might not be so safe anymore. I decided to add a little lemon balm to the tea. Marmalade was still purring loudly, standing on her hind legs, with her front paws resting on Glaze's knee.

I have been trying to warn you. Maybe now you will listen.

How could anything in Martinsville be a threat to my sister? My sister, who hadn't been here before. My sister who'd left Braetonburg right out of high school and spent the next eighteen years fighting for her life before she was diagnosed as a manic depressive in her mid-thirties. She'd been working in Philadelphia for the past five or six years. Before that she had moved around the country so frequently, I always had to wait for a letter or phone call before I'd know how to contact her. She had often sounded low, but never let her crises carry over into her communication with family. Years ago, Mom and Dad and I had been shocked and panicked when the first call came from an emergency room. We'd flown to her hospital bed three different times in three different states, to bring her home and try to help her, only to have her pack up and leave within weeks. What did we know then?

But now was different. This sister, here in front of me, oblivious even to the cat, wasn't having a bi-polar moment. She was furious,

or afraid, about something that she hadn't seen coming. I hadn't
seen it coming either.

I did.

Martinsville was settled a quarter of a century before the other
little towns in this area of the country. Most of them grew up near a
creek – easy to do, since the run-off from the nearby age-old moun-
tains had crisscrossed the ancient plains with valleys, and had wa-
tered the valleys abundantly. This was a transition area of rolling
hills, but our little valley was deeper and steeper than most. The rest
of Keagan County – the smallest county in the state – was flat enough
for small farming, yet bumpy enough for interest and for keeping
out the developers.

The sister town of Braetonburg, where Glaze and I were raised,
five miles up the river from here, could have been a carbon copy.
One long street hugging the narrow river, five or six parallel streets,
pulled together into a net of cross-hatching by the lanes and byways
that branched up from the river.

Busy highways tend to grow up on the plains and in the bigger
valleys, with longer staightaways and larger towns. Or maybe the
towns grow larger because of the wider, busier roads. But Martinsville
and Braetonburg stayed peaceable and quiet, and gradually became
havens for people who turned their backs on the cities and migrated
to the towns like trout to the deep pools where the currents eddied
around big boulders. People who avoided the interstate highways as
much as possible. People who had the financial resources to live in a
town where the arts flourished, but where the 'natives' needed customers for our businesses. How they find us, I'll never know. We're
in such a narrow valley, there's not a lot of room for new houses, so
we'll probably, hopefully, never have 'suburbs.'

I often have wondered why Homer Martin and the original five
families chose this valley, and how they *found* it in the first place.
Two hundred years ago, it must *really* have been isolated and inaccessible, but they did find the valley and they started the town. Now
people still find us when they need our special brand of peacefulness.

They come from all over, never enough new people to overwhelm
the old-timers, but just enough to flavor the town with a variety of
ethnic backgrounds and arts. Little Martinsville, that nobody outside Keagan County has even heard of, has a Norwegian deli, a prime

quality restaurant, a health store that is chock full of the organic products and herbs and teas I love. We have an old-fashioned home-town grocery store that actually carries cheeses like Ementhaler and aged Gouda year round, and a dance school that every child for miles around attends starting at age three.

We have our own doctor, Nathan Young, the son of one of the town council members, who went away hoping to become a world-famous surgeon, but met a mentor in medical school who believed that doctors should know their patients – the whole patient, the family history, what comforted the person and what hurt – doctors who saw people rather than collections of symptoms, doctors who specialized in caring, and who helped people awaken to their own ability to heal. The office is small, but the care is first class.

We don't have any lawyers. We have one insurance office and one gas station, and two churches. St. Theresa's Catholic Church and our non-denominational Protestant Church. I wish we had a synagogue and a buddhist temple. They would round out the town quite a bit, although their attendance might be a little slim for the first few years. If we want to buy cars, we go to Hastings or Russell Gap. If we want to see a movie, we walk down the street to the Chief Movie House on Thursdays, Fridays, or Saturdays. When I was a kid, some of us used to drive over here to Martinsville on Saturday nights. This is where I first saw *Gone with the Wind*. Grandma hadn't wanted me to see it, since it had a swear word in it. I'd already read the book, though, so I couldn't see that it mattered much.

It was one thing to drive five miles down the valley to see a movie; but it took a major commitment to drive here from any of the big cities in Georgia or the Carolinas, so we never had an influx of fancy summer homes, for the simple reason that getting from point A to point B was too complex for people caught in the fast ruts. When folks moved to our little towns, they tended either to leave very soon, realizing their mistake, or else to stay for long enough to raise kids and grandkids, knowing all the teachers, joining the PTA, telling the old stories. We tend to take long walks in the evening, and we listen to Saturday summer afternoon concerts from the better-than-average town band in the little gazebo on the lawn of the five-sided square. My dad learned to play the trombone for the Braetonburg band when Mr. Johnston had his heart attack, so the Stars and Stripes would sound balanced the coming summer. People said it was community spirit. Dad just thought trombones were fun.

Neither town ever grew across the Metoochie River, for the simple reason that land on the other side is too full of caves and too steep for roads or buildings. Instead, we can look at an old forest of dogwoods and laurels, with some hickory and lots of pine, too inaccessible or undesirable for loggers, but lovely for soothing the eyes on a sunny day.

When I first left Braetonburg to go to the state college, I thought I'd be back. Four years later, though, with a double degree in Marketing and English, it seemed silly to waste all that college-knowledge on a small town, so I'd headed off to an advertising agency in Boston, where life had been giddy and crammed with activity and full of friends and bursting with culture. There, I had longed for the stars at night rather than the city's neon. There, I learned that I wanted the murmuring of the river rather than the whine of traffic. I enjoyed Boston, but soon realized that my heart had a hole that the city couldn't fill.

When I lived there, I couldn't see the Perseides in mid-August, that deluge of meteors that grace the night sky each year. I'd grown up with the Perseides. There were no city lights to get in the way, so on clear August nights, my mom and dad used to bundle us up in the blue and green afghans our grandmother had crocheted. Then they carried us out into the back yard where we'd all four lie huddled together on a blanket and watch the shooting stars whizzing overhead from the north, making brief but startling trails across the night sky. Every time I get a new calendar, I always look ahead to August to see when the full moon will be that month, hoping it's around the first, or not until after the twentieth, so the night sky will be dark enough for me to see the meteor trails.

In the city, though, I somehow forgot to look for the moon, in the sky or on a calendar page. Don't get me wrong. I enjoyed the city for that year, but I wanted a home town to nestle into for the rest of my life. I'd already decided to move back to stay. A week after I came home, I ran into Sol Brandy, who'd been away for four years working in Chicago, with insurance, investments, financial plans and such. He said he had suddenly realized that he missed seeing the meteors in August. We were married the following April. Then we watched the Perseides every year that it wasn't cloudy, until he died.

Braetonburg had been our refuge. When I took the job as librarian and moved here last year, Martinsville also had felt like a refuge a place where I could heal some more after Sol's loss, and learn to laugh again. Even when that murder happened, I still somehow felt a sense of safety, as if it couldn't touch me directly.

But now, I thought as I sat down across from Glaze, Martinsville had at least one person in it that I probably wouldn't want to meet on the street at night. Some one person I wouldn't welcome into my home. Someone who had angered my sister.

Marmalade hopped up into my lap and growled. The sound was so unexpected, I jumped, then realized that she had mirrored my thoughts exactly. Only I didn't know who I ought to growl at.

Try the guy who has been hanging out in the back yard.

Chapter 10

Sunday, April 21, 1996

Glaze hadn't even tried to invent a plausible excuse for her fury. Since sitting down, she hadn't said anything, just patted Marmalade, sipped at her tea, or held it absent-mindedly in her cupped hands. With her bandaged finger sticking out at a funny angle, she gazed across the kitchen to the watercolor on the west wall, my first attempt at "art" which Bob had insisted on framing, since it was bound to be famous someday. I told him the only way it would be famous would be as *Grannie's silly picture*. We both liked the colors, even if the subject matter wasn't easily identifiable. At times it looked like a western sunset, with many clouds. Occasionally we could see in it a pond in a hot summer landscape, or maybe an abandoned sulfur mine? It never resembled the yellow dahlia I'd been looking at last year when I painted it, but it matched the sunny kitchen décor, and provided instant laughter on gray mornings.

Glaze turned her eyes from the picture only when she heard Bob unlock the front door. He walked in unhurriedly, picked a mug off the rack as he went past it, and pulled out the chair at the head of the table. "If you have some more of your rabbit-food tea, Biscuit, I'd like a cup of it." As I rose to fetch the teapot, I could see that Bob was studying Glaze with his you-can-take-all-the-time-you-want-but-I-expect-the-whole-story expression. For a moment she straightened her back as if she would refuse, but then almost instantly slumped back down and let out a heart-rending sigh. Rending *my* heart, at least. Bob just kept looking gently curious.

"His name is Jeff Winslow," she began without preamble. "I started dating him seven or eight years ago. We sort of drifted into a relationship." I saw her clench her jaw for a moment and wondered what the reason was. She took a deep breath and continued. "When I joined a support group for bipolars, I asked him to go with me. He went along to the meetings, but he never seemed to 'get it'. A bunch of us used to go for coffee together after the meetings, and Jeff was the life of the party. He sort of claimed me, I guess, always sitting beside me, always draping an arm around my shoulder. At the time, I didn't mind too much. He was pretty coarse, but he was good at cracking jokes and getting everyone to laugh."

Glaze pushed her mug away. I was going to have to think of something else to serve. Milkshakes, maybe? Lemonade? Gewürztraminer?

"He had this bizarre tattoo of a skull on his right forearm. He drew it himself and took it to a tattoo place to have it duplicated. He was very proud of it. Used to show it off to all the women in the group. It looked just like the one out there," nodding her head in the general direction of the front walk. "As I got to feeling stronger and more sure of myself, I just stopped going out with him, but he kept on asking me. I gave in and went to lunch with him a couple of times. Finally I woke up to the fact that I needed to take care of myself. That did *not* include dating a guy I couldn't respect."

"Why do you say that, sis? What was wrong with him? Other than the strange tattoo, I mean."

"Well, for one thing, he was into drugs . . ."

So he was stupid, huh?

". . . and he was mean about little things. He wouldn't tip the waitresses. He bad-mouthed everyone when they weren't around. He acted like he owned me." She paused, thinking back. "He kicked a dog once . . ."

"Poor dog!" "Oh, no!" *Yuch!*

". . . when we were walking down the street, and this fuzzy little brown and white dog, a pup really, came trotting up to me. I started to bend down to pet it, but Jeff kicked it aside, and then kept on walking."

I stood up and headed over to the fridge for a glass of goat's milk, again having to step over Marmalade, who was standing beside the table with her back arched. If I hadn't known she was just stretching, I'd have thought she looked angry.

I do feel angry.

Glaze continued her litany. "He shoplifted, not because he needed anything, but just to prove he could get away with it." I opened the fridge door. That blinkin' light was still out. Well, the grocery store wasn't open on Sundays, so it would have to wait another day. Glaze grimaced and went on, "He'd step on caterpillars on the sidewalk. I told him I didn't like that, but he just laughed at me."

"The bastard!" "The rat-fink!" *Murderer!* Bob and I both blurted our condemnations out at the same time, and Marmalade yowled again. We must have been scaring her. I bent down to reassure her that we were okay. I'm glad I'm marrying a man who has his priorities right. Anybody who steps on caterpillars is lower than dirt. A poor comparison, though, since I happen to like dirt. Did you know just a smidgen of dirt contains billions of bacteria and may have thousands of yards of fungal mycelia in it? That may not sound very appetizing, but those are very necessary components that help plants survive. So why do we compare bad men to dirt, when dirt is basically good?

"Why do you think he showed up here?" Bob asked her. She turned to him shaking her head.

"I don't know for sure. I think he may have remembered that I have a sister. I know I talked about you in the group," she said looking up at me as I felt about for the goat's-milk carton. "It's a long shot, but maybe he was just traveling around the area and saw us when we were walking through town yesterday."

"Not likely at all," Bob observed. "We're too far off the beaten path. Could he have found out from your roommate?"

You could call and ask her.

"It would depend on how chatty Yuko was feeling. Jeff can be quite the talker when he wants something, and he may have wormed the information out of her without her even realizing it. She might not have seen anything wrong with it because I never told her about what he did."

"You mean kicking the dog?"

"No. I mean beating me up . . ."

Why not leave him? Or break his jaw?

". . . and I just wanted to forget it ever happened, so I quit talking about it to anyone." Marmalade was crawling up into Glaze's lap, and she reached out to help the furry purr-box over her knees. "The only reason he could get away with it was that I had pretty rotten self-esteem. That's what depression does sometimes. Usually. Now, I can't imagine letting anyone treat me that way. But back then . . ." Her eyes looked out of focus, and I knew she was seeing the old Glaze, the one who had tried suicide three times. "Back then, I kept dating him even after he'd given me two black eyes."

'That's just what we need in our don't-lock-your-doors town,' I thought. Marmalade, who I'd assumed was going to sleep in Glaze's lap, surprised me by hopping down and walking over to where the phone cord was dangling over the edge of the counter. She batted at it idly. Leave it to a cat to want to play all the time.

Glaze tilted her head to one side. "Good idea, Marmalade. Maybe I should call Yuko to find out if he's been around there."

Glad you got the message.

Even as she spoke, she was standing up and heading for the phone. Within moments she had reached her roommate, asked the questions, and received an answer she didn't like. "Well, that's it, then. He called her up last Wednesday evening and she guesses she might have mentioned where I was."

"All she'd have to do was say the name of the town. He could look it up easily. We may be small, but we're on most of the maps."

"Yes. Once he got here," Bob added, "he just *might* have seen the two of you on your walk. It sounds more believeable that way. But why would he want to find you anyway?"

"That's his style," Glaze grumped into her mug. "He's done it every six months or so for the past five years. Calls and leaves suggestive messages. Runs into me on my way home in the evening. I put him off for a week or two, and then he'll be gone for another six months. About two months ago he started getting a lot more obnoxious. Not enough to file a complaint about. He'd just pop up anywhere, anytime, as if he'd been following me all day." She ran her left hand through her hair, this time leaving it rumpled.

Bob stood up. "I'm going over to the station to run a check on this guy. Do you know an address or phone number or anything?"

"No. He moves around a lot." She thought a moment. "He used to live in some suburb north of Philly, on Parkinson Street. I remember that because he used to joke about the name. He'd start shaking his hands and his head and saying he lived on a street named for a disease. He thought he was being funny. I thought he was being heartless."

"I'll start there. I'm going to take the drawing off the mailbox. Maybe we can get some fingerprints," Bob said, as he walked out of the kitchen. He came back almost immediately with the cordless phone from the living room. "Keep this right next to you," he said, plunking it down on the table between us. "I've got my pager. I'll lock the door after myself. Keep it locked," he added unnecessarily, since we had no intentions of unlocking anything.

Marmalade, who had stopped playing with the phone cord as soon as Glaze called her roommate, jumped up onto the bay windowsill, meowing loudly. I glanced out, and saw a flock of sparrows chipping away at the seeds in the feeders. "You keep an eye on them, Marmalade." At least something was normal around here.

You are blind! He is leaving, and I have a human who is blind!

We just sat there for a very long time, looking at the watercolor, looking at our teacups, flexing our fingers or rubbing our chins. Finally, Glaze asked, in a strained voice, "Do you hate me for getting you into this?"

"Of course not, and you haven't gotten us into anything. So what about the mailbox? It's been painted dozens of times, and always survived."

"You know what I mean, Biscuit. This is something more than decorating a mailbox. The fact that he followed me here feels somehow threatening, but I don't know what to do about it. Jeff doesn't give up easily . . ." She broke off in a strangled groan as our phone began to ring. I smiled a little too brightly, and picked up the handset in a firm grip.

The voice was almost an anti-climax. It didn't sound sinister. Along with the raspy quality of a long-time heavy smoker, it sounded rather as if he hadn't talked much for a long time. "I'm looking for Glaze McKee."

Why on earth hadn't I let the machine answer? Why hadn't I taken a moment to figure out what I'd say if he called? Why should I have expected him to call? "Who did you want?" I asked, to gain some time.

"The lady visiting you," Jeff said, and gave a little chuckle. "The one wearing the orange shirt. Hand her the phone please."

That 'please' didn't sound very polite to me, but I found myself handing over the phone without arguing. "It's Jeff, and he wants to talk to you." Glaze looked at me as if I were sending her into a lion's den. I covered the mouthpiece with my hand and whispered, "He knows you're here. He said to give the phone to the one wearing the orange shirt. He must have seen us out by the mailbox."

Glaze's face turned a shade paler as she glanced down at her orange pullover. I had a feeling she'd give it to Goodwill the next time there was a clothing drive. Good idea, since it's not her shade anyway. And I'll donate this gray one, too. No sense in wearing something that doesn't feel wonderful. She took the phone, though, with a surprisingly steady hand, and said, "Hello, Jeff." After a short pause, she said, "Of course I wasn't expecting to hear from you. . . . Yes, I saw your little present, as you call it." Glaze took a deep breath. "Jeff, I want you to hear this and believe it. Go away. Don't call me any more. Don't try to see me. Stay away from me." Her voice was getting louder with each clearly enunciated sentence. "There is no hope. I'll never change my mind. Do you understand that?" She listened for another few seconds, then pushed the 'off' button.

Her eyes strayed up to the sulphur mine on the wall, and in an almost normal tone of voice, she said, "The thing I hate about cordless phones is that there's no way to slam them down when you want to hang up."

I took the now quiet handset from her and placed it in front of me, with its antenna pointed skyward. "Did you ever hear Grandma talk about how growing up without telephones had been so restful?"

"No. I never heard anything about that."

"She said that there was never the sense of being at the mercy of a ringing box. But, I think Grandma was wrong. There have been many times when I've chosen not to answer a phone – if I'm up to my elbows kneading bread, if I'm playing dominos with little Verity, if I'm reading a really good biography."

"I know. I do the same thing."

"But if someone comes to visit, it's hard not to answer the knock on the door. If Jeff had come to the door . . ." I met Glaze's eyes, knowing that we were thinking the same thing. If Jeff had come to the door, we might not have been able to keep him out.

Marmalade chose that moment to jump up into my lap and start kneading doughballs on my tummy.

I could have jumped at his eyes and ripped them out of his head. I could have clawed his ears off. I could have bitten his nose. I could have shredded his legs. I could have done to him what I did to Whitewhiskers. I could have made him leave you alone.

What a comfort she is. What a dear sweet, gentle comfort. She's so good-natured. It's a joy to have a friendly cat. Her purr is so loud sometimes she almost sounds like a lion.

She didn't want to stay in my lap, though. After a few moments, she hopped down and headed for the door. I wanted to put in a kitty door as soon as I moved in, but it would have to wait until we actually owned the house. I stepped over to the back door, took a quick look through the peephole onto the porch, unlocked the door and opened it. "Don't stay out too long, Marmalade."

I do not know why not. I do not think you will be going anywhere soon, and I have some tracking to do.

"You know what we need?" I asked Glaze as I turned back into the kitchen. "We need to get busy on those curtains. That was, after all, one of the reasons you came a week early. Let me punch down the bread dough and get it ready for the second rising, and then we'll head upstairs."

I felt like the engine to her caboose as we trooped up to the sewing area. While Glaze made sure there was thread and a fresh bobbin in the machine, I rummaged through the shelves of fabric for the big pieces of chintz that I bought last month when I first moved in. "Guess which ones we're going to make this afternoon?"

Glaze looked at the yards of yellow-flowered chintz. "The café curtains to match the kitchen chairs?"

"You got it, sweet pea, except they're going to be full-length. I bought LOTS of material, and I'm feeling the need to block prying eyes." Glaze frowned at this reminder, and her eyes strayed over to the window that overlooked the front yard and the mailbox. "I've got the window measurements all sketched out right here. We'll just need to lengthen the curtains some. I never felt all that much need for curtains before. I'd been thinking they'd just be for show, but now I want a way to close up the view, especially at night."

"This is all my fault."

"Baloney-feathers! We were going to make the curtains anyway." I did some quick calculations. "We have the blinds on the front windows, so we'll start with the three back windows, especially the bay. It'll cut out some of the light, but we'll feel a lot safer. There will finally be something to match the seat covers. I made those the second week after I moved in – once the compost bin was finished."

There's something about women sewing together that heals hurts. Throughout history, women have gathered in circles to sew, to quilt, to mend, to spin, to weave, to knit. In extended families, years ago, women used to progress from learning the basics of carding wool when we were little girls, to spinning and weaving it as we grew older. In old age, surrounded by daughters and nieces, daughters-in-law and granddaughters, to whom we had taught the skills of sewing, we might have turned again with wrinkled hands to the simple activity of carding the wool – combing it to align the strands and remove debris caught in the fibers. We felt stronger when we were connected.

Men respond to threats with the fight or flight syndrome. Women gather and nurture, befriend and tend. Even now, with a Singer instead of a spinning wheel, and with just the two of us rather than a whole clan of women, Glaze and I turned to sewing to ease our minds.

We pulled out the folded-up hobby table, spread out the fabric, and set to work with the measuring tape and scissors and pins. We decided that the fancy valances to cover the curtain rods could wait. It was fairly mindless work, which kept us from getting frazzled; but it took some concentration, which moved our thoughts away from what we were curtaining out. The old Singer hummed and buzzed, the scissors snipped and clacked, and we gradually shed the immediacy of fear and anger as we worked on the castle defenses.

"Biscuit?"

"Hmmm?" I said as I took the straight pins out of my mouth. I know you're not supposed to hold pins between your lips, but I don't know one single woman who doesn't do it. I should make myself one of those cute little stuffed pin holder jobs with elastic to fit on my wrist. I'll need to build in some sort of sturdy base so I don't stab myself.

"Tell me something else you like about living here away from the city."

I thought a moment, and said, "Chickens."

"Chickens?"

"Yes. How much do you remember Grandma Martelson?"

"Not a lot. I know she dragged you to a funeral home when I was pretty little, and I know she was a farm wife from way back. I think Mom was afraid of her, but I don't know why."

Glaze looked at me over the pile of fabric she was feeding into the hungry mouth of the sewing machine. "What does Grandma have to do with living in Martinsville?"

"Well, Grandma raised chickens that used to scare the pee-turkey right out of me when I was little. They were in that chicken coop that smelled to high heaven – surely you remember *that?* Grandma expected me to go in there and reach underneath the laying hens to pull out their eggs. The trouble was, the nests were up on risers, which meant the hens could look down on me. I just figured that put my eyes right in pecking range."

I had to shake my head to rid myself of the image of those angry hens who were out to get me. Take a deep breath, Biscuit McKee. "Nowadays I sometimes think I'd love to have a couple of chickens, but it's simpler just to have neighbors who have chickens. I think I like the *idea* of raising chickens better than I'd like the reality of it. Maggie Pontiac, up the street beyond Mr. Olsen, has chickens. Didn't you hear the rooster this morning? Our eggs are always fresh, and I don't have to get my eyes pecked out! If I lived in a city, I couldn't have neighbors with chickens. If I lived on a farm, I'd probably have to raise them myself."

The stories flowed as we gradually pieced together what we remembered about our childhood. Her memories were so different from mine, we might have been raised in two separate families. Within a couple of hours we had the fabric pieces hemmed all around, gathered into pleats at the top, and strung on the rods. After I took a break to deal with the bread-baking, Glaze and I made tie-backs for the curtains.

"The curtains are going to be closed all the time, so why are we making tie-backs?" Glaze had objected.

"Because I want them, we're not going to have to keep the curtains closed forever, we have the time to do it, and it'll keep us busy. Is that enough reasons? Here's some yellow rattail for the piping. I bought it when I chose the chintz. By the way . . ." I handed her the roll of rattail, the heavy string that would pad the long bias strips of fabric before we sewed them into the seams along the edges of the tie-backs, " . . . it's a little late to ask, but are you comfortable sewing with your finger in a cast?"

"Sure. I'm left-handed, remember?"

"Yes, and do *you* remember those awful green plaid pillows with the orange piping? You made them in seventh-grade home ec class."

"Oh my gosh, they were horrible," Glaze groaned as she began spreading the chintz and marking it to cut bias strips. "I can't believe you're reminding me of them."

"Only because it proves you know how to do piping, and that you owe me one, bigtime! I actually put that ugly pillow on my bed!"

Like a lot of laughter between good friends, what we were saying wasn't that funny, but the guffawing was a good release of tension. Glaze chuckled, too, as she turned back to the Singer. Even if we weren't planning on leaving the curtains open for now, I had to believe that Bob would catch the elusive Jeff. We would be safe, soon. We would. And we'd tie our curtains back to catch the morning sun.

Every time I think of the morning sun, I remember growing up in Braetonburg. We had a living room with a big window that faced due east. Across the room from that window was a long wall. My dad, who would have been perfectly at home living at Stonehenge, one year started marking the position of the sun by drawing a vertical line before breakfast every Sunday to show where the northern edge of the window cast a shadow on the far wall. The first line he drew was on my fourth birthday.

We had dozens and dozens of lines, all labeled with dates. That's how I learned about the gradual shifting of the Earth's alignment with the sun. Back and forth, back and forth. The farthest south the shadow ever went was around December 21st, when the sun began rising a bit farther to the south each day, which sent the shadow lines scurrying back northwards until around the third Sunday in June, when the sun would head toward the north, making the shadow line veer southwards again.

> From the Statement of Martha "Maggie" Pontiac
> to the Georgia Bureau of Investigation
> Wednesday, May 3, 1995
>
> Yes, this house is just one block up Beechnut from
> Matthew and Buddy, but you already know that. I
> don't know why I'm rattling on like this. . . . Oh, I
> knew Harlan really well. He spent one whole Sat-
> urday morning taking pictures of my chickens.

Those four over there in the white frames are my prize hens. The picture in the middle, in the brown frame, that's Doodle-Doo, my rooster. I'm going to miss that boy. He really had class, if you know what I mean. . . . He was smart with his hands. He had a good heart, even if he didn't have a fancy job. . . . Well now, I usually wear an eight. Why are you asking that? . . . Library? No, I don't know why he was in the library.

Thursday, February 9, 1995
Garner Creek

The pictures were more than Sid had expected. He was right. Something was definitely going on, but it was the man's face that surprised him. It was the guy in the gray suit from the bank. There were a few photos in a little restaurant. Then there were two pictures of her getting into a car. Only one of these showed the man's face clearly. He'd toss the other one. Finally, there was one picture of them going into a motel room and one of them coming out of that room. That was enough. He'd make photocopies of the pictures so he could show them to Mr. Bigshot and see just how much it was worth to keep quiet. He wouldn't hand over the negatives, though. Not right away. No need to tell Sarah about this. He'd just make sure the meetings stopped.

In the meantime, these needed to be in a safe place. Wouldn't it be funny to put them in the safety deposit box in his own bank? Right under his nose, and he wouldn't be able to get at them. That's called ironic, Sid thought. That's what that is. He wouldn't say a word until the negatives were safe. This was going to be a very good year.

Sunday, April 21, 1996
Martinsville

By the time Bob came over on Sunday evening, it was after dark. Marmalade had scratched at the door to come back in shortly after she went out, so I fed her the rest of the salmon that Tom had donated. Bob had called three or four times, just to make sure we were okay, and to reassure us that he had his pager and was close by in case we needed him. He told me he was planning on staying the night, just in case. "I'll sleep on the couch, and Glaze will be a good-enough chaperone that nobody will be scandalized." I appreciated his attempt at lightening the situation. When he walked into the kitchen, we were munching slices of fresh bread, slathered with butter. I could make a whole meal out of bread and butter. Comfort food.

I stood up for a kiss, while Glaze tactfully pretended that the butter dish needed a close inspection.

"I like the yellow curtains, Bisque. You two did a great job."

"Well, we had planned to sew them starting tomorrow. We just moved the schedule up a day. Now we're that much readier for the weekend. They do make the kitchen look cozier." What they really did was make the kitchen look closed in, but I wasn't about to voice that opinion. "This way we won't see the reflections of the kitchen lights on the glass at night." This way we won't see the stars, or the raccoons who raid the seed that falls off the bird feeder.

This way you will not see who is sneaking around in the back yard. I will have to wiggle behind the curtains to watch.

This way we won't see anyone who's sneaking around our back yard. Yikes! This way of thinking is an instant formula for paranoia. I drummed my fingers on the table, took a deep breath, and asked, "Did you find out anything of value?"

No. He drove off in a blue pickup truck before I caught up with him.

"No, I just started a lot of balls rolling. I eased the drawing off the mailbox, which was easy, since I could just peel off about five layers of paint along with it. That side of the mailbox is orange and green and lavender now, until I can paint it over."

"Why don't we paint the whole thing lavender? I'm tired of black mailboxes – they're boring. Lavender brings back some good memories."

I stood up to get the tea and to slice some more bread. When I was thirteen years old, my mom said I could paint my room any color I chose as a "coming of age" present. I chose lavender. I had always liked my room. The light blue I'd had in there as a younger child was restful, and it was easy to decorate, since blue seemed to blend with anything I chose to put in my room. But the lavender for my teen years made it truly mine, and it seemed to be a particularly daring choice, since my mother was all oranges and yellows and browns, colors that made her golden complexion come alive. We even had a brown couch. Ugh. She had probably hated painting my room blue when I requested it as a three-year-old. Ten years later I still preferred colors that would have drained my mom, but mom didn't have to live in that room, and I did.

I saved pretty purple wrapping paper to line the drawers in my dresser. I lavished all the care I knew how to give on my bedroom, making it truly a place of comfort and peace. When I broke up with George in eleventh grade, and when Peter didn't ask me to the prom until I already had another date - each time, I threw myself on my purple and blue quilted bedspread, sobbing until the peacefulness of that room soaked into my pores and told me everything would be alright.

When Glaze made those horrible pillows and gave me one for my birthday, I martyred myself by putting it on my bed, where it clashed for seven whole months until I took it to college with me and gave it to the gold-brown-green-orange girl whose room was just down the hall from the one I shared with Karla.

"Earth to Biscuit McKee."

Startled out of my reverie, I looked up at Glaze, wondering how much I'd just missed. I've always had this ability to sort of drift away from other people in my mind, and I've gotten used to coming back into a conversation that's already looped around three more subjects, without my knowing what they were. When I was a kid, the word "huh?" was a frequent part of my vocabulary.

I can't remember when I wasn't fascinated by words, and – other than "huh?" – I seldom used a word that I didn't understand completely. I thoroughly enjoyed looking up words in the dictionary, and I could spend long stretches of a Saturday afternoon, leafing through Merriam Webster, the way my high school friends leafed through Seventeen Magazine. In fact, when I was in seventh grade, Miss Johnson, my English teacher, told me that the first time she'd met me, she'd thought that I was fairly persnickety. I had no idea what that meant, so I went home and looked it up, only to find that the correct word was *pernickety*, without an S in it. Of course, when I told Miss Johnson the next day what I had found out, she burst out laughing. It wasn't until years later that I realized I had simply confirmed her opinion of me.

"Earth to Biscuit McKee. Again."

"Sorry. I was off on one of my English-major jaunts through the woods of language. Did I miss some earth-shaking revelations?"

"No, your fiancé and I have just been sitting here marveling at how you do it. Of course, I was able to confirm that you came by it through genetics, since Dad always did the same thing."

"He did?"

"Biscuit McKee, do you mean to tell me you're almost fifty years old and you never even noticed that our dad was in a fog half the time, dreaming of conducting the symphony?"

I felt sheepish at having to admit that she was right. Probably because I was dreaming at the same rate he was, during the same conversations.

"Bob, get me out of this pickle. What did you find out, and what do we do next?"

"I wish I had a plan of action. Basically we just sit and wait for some of the balls I sent out today to bounce back. Hopefully by tomorrow there'll be some up-to-date information we can use. In the meantime . . ."

Keep the doors locked!

"We know," we both chimed in as Marmy meowed loudly. "We keep the doors locked!"

The three of us managed to turn the rest of the evening into a semblance of normalcy. We studiously ignored the threat of the dark night, stayed inside our sunny chintz-lined nest, played our own brand of Charades. Around 11:00 most of the "sounds like" clues began to look like "Yawn" – lawn? fawn? prawn? dawn?

"Speaking of which," Bob interrupted the silliness, "it's going to come a lot sooner than we think – dawn, that is. I'm camping out on the couch."

We didn't try very hard to talk him out of his suggestion, because both of us wanted to retreat upstairs to a more secluded room. Bob had brought over some of his stuff, his toothbrush, some pj's, his favorite pillow. As he started lifting his things out of his small zippered bag, he shooed us up the stairs. "You two be sure to sleep, now. Don't stay up half the night talking."

"Don't worry about that, honey. We're too tired to talk any more." Great words, but they weren't true. As soon as our heads landed on the pillows, we were wide awake. Glaze turned her head, looked at me, and burst into a giggle fit. "Shhh! You'll wake up Bob, and he'll think we're dying up here. Don't you know you're in grave danger?" I mouthed as I waved my hands, monster-like in the air. "Don't you know that any moment, the boogieman could come stomping up those stairs searching for both of us?"

I have two humans who have gone berserk. I wonder if I should call on Softfoot for help.

Marmalade was crouched between us, looking from my sister to me, probably wondering if we'd lost our minds.

"Did you see what I saw?" Glaze asked between giggles. "Bob had a gun hidden in his towel. He was trying so hard to be nonchalant about it, but the handle was sticking out from under his rolled-up pajamas."

I hadn't seen it, but I couldn't join in her laughter. I guess I'd lived in a small town long enough not to take guns for granted. Bob never kept his gun at home. He must have brought it back from the station when he came here this evening. If that was the case, he was a lot more worried that he pretended to be.

I slid my arm over Marmalade to wrap it around my sister, and I told her how much I loved her and how glad I was that she wasn't facing this alone. We went to sleep like that, with the purring cat between us, holding each other for comfort, for safety, for kinship, for love.

Snuggling between Widelap and Smellsweet is very comfortable, since they do not wiggle much, but something tells me I ought to be downstairs with Softfoot. There is something in the air that I do not like, a tremor passing through these three people I love. They smell like mice do when they know they are being watched. Even their laughing has an edge to it, like that human kitten I found once under a desk. I could smell her fear before I saw her, and knew that she had frightened herself with her hiding game.

Ah. Now they both are asleep. I ease off the foot of the bed, and walk quietly downstairs, expecting to find Softfoot asleep, too, but he is sitting up, rubbing his hands over his eyes. He must have just set aside the book he was writing in. I can smell the pen-smell on his fingers. I hop up on his lap, nuzzle my head against his arm, and give him what comfort I can. I reassure him that we are all in this together.

"You must have read my mind, little one. You knew I was lonely, didn't you?"

Yes.

"I've been sitting here thinking about your mom."

Widelap. You think about her often.

"Did you know that the first time I ever met her, I talked about urine? I was positively tongue-tied. I could tell from the moment I saw her that she was exactly what I wanted in a wife, and I was afraid of scaring her away. I can't believe I talked about pee."

That is okay, Softfoot. She thought it was an interesting conversation. And you sure got her attention.

He talks a while longer, quietly telling me things I do not think he would tell Widelap or Fishgiver.

"Thanks, Marmalade. Talking to you makes me feel better, even if you don't understand a word."

Mouse droppings! Of course I understand.

"What a sound! Are you singing?"

Finally he stretches out to sleep, and I watch and listen through the night, but all is well.

Tuesday, February 14, 1995
Garner Creek

"I may be up here in Garner Creek tomorrow at lunchtime. How about I drop by the dress shop and we'll get some lunch?"

"Sid, that's a wonderful idea! Is this my Valentine's present?"

"What? Oh, yeah, it is."

"I can't leave the shop before one-thirty. Would that be okay with you?"

"Yeah." Sid looked at Sarah closely, not sure whether there was any disappointment on her face. 'She won't be able to see Mr. Bigshot Loverboy tomorrow, and I'll be talking to him on Friday,' he thought. 'One look at those pictures, and he'll stay away from my wife.'

Chapter 11

Monday, April 22, 1996
Martinsville

Marmalade woke me up early by burrowing under the covers and kneading my tummy. Glaze couldn't sleep through that amount of activity, so we took turns patting the cat and using the bathroom. I'd forgotten to write my gratitude list last night, so I picked up the little white fabric-covered journal with the big orange sunflower design on the front, and wrote:

> Sunday gratitude list (written early Monday morning)
> 1. Fresh bread
> 2. Bob's presence
> 3. Glaze
> 4. Baby birds that flew the nest
> 5. Marmy

That was my five, but I decided that today we could use some extra thankfulness, so I added:

> 6. Rain
> 7. Doughnuts
> 8. Safety
> 9. Soup

> *good eyesight*
> *good hearing*
> *good sense of smell*
> *whiskers*
> *claws*
> *I will add:*
> *leftover salmon*

It had rained off and on all night, but wasn't raining now. Some light thunder was still rumbling in the distance. A good day to stay indoors, which is what I wanted to do anyway. A good day to sew more of the curtains. Maybe we could even tackle making a couple of valances today. Some people like those elaborate ones that look like an interior decorator came in to top the curtains with waves of cloth, usually surmounted by at least three enormous fabric rosettes. I go for the simpler stuff. It wouldn't take us long to make some quiet little drapings to hide the curtain rods.

Glaze was beginning to come to life slowly, brushing her hair and watching me rummage through the closet. I chose a pair of soft cotton slacks, a white teeshirt that says *Relax and Breathe* over the pocket. On the back, in bigger letters it says *for the REST of your life*. Then I pulled a soft lightweight pink cardigan out of the third dresser drawer. As I opened the top drawer to pull out undies and socks, Glaze brightened visibly and hopped off the bed where she had been snuggling in the flannel sheet. I like flannel, even in summer.

"We're going to look like a mirror today," she chuckled as she did her own rummaging. "Where on earth did I put my . . . Phooey! She sure did move things around."

"She? Who's *She*?" I asked.

"Oh, the nurse who re-packed this for me. The cop who came to the scene brought my suitcase to the clinic. Nice of him to do that. It had popped open during the wreck, and he must have crammed everything back in." As she was talking, she pulled out a pair of gray cotton pants, a plain pink crew-necked top, and her own cardigan that could have been a twin of mine except that it was white. It was the one she'd worn to CT's on Saturday. "See?" she chirped. "Pink-white, white-pink."

Just then Marmalade hopped up onto the windowsill by the bed and started doing her own chirping, a sort of sing-song whine. I stepped around to the dormer window, looked down at the birdfeeder, and saw two male cardinals disputing the back-yard territory. Marmalade put her paws on my arm and looked up at me expectantly. "Do you want to go outside, sweetie?" I asked her.

Yes. Now!

"It looks pretty damp out there, but I'll let you out for a while when we go downstairs."

We would have made a grand entrance, except that Glaze tripped somehow as she turned on the landing to head down the second flight. I tried to catch her, but she bounced smartly down the eight steps and landed in a heap at the bottom. Of course, Bob and I both rushed to her, and we managed to bump heads as we leaned over her. Glaze laughed at us, claimed she was okay, tried to stand up, and grimaced as she put weight on her left leg.

"I think I twisted my ankle as well as my dignity," she said. "This'll be great for the wedding. A Maid of Honor in an ace bandage."

"Take a big breath," I told her, "and stop worrying."

"Don't worry about the wedding," Bob agreed, now that we were sure she wasn't too badly damaged. "You can be my best man, and Tom can be the maid of honor for Bisque. That way you won't have to walk down the aisle."

We looked at him in astonishment. Actually it wasn't a bad idea. We might as well give the town something to talk about for the next ten years or so. He and I maneuvered Glaze into the kitchen, propped her foot up on one of the yellow chairs, smoothed on some arnica cream, gave her a few drops of Bach's Rescue Remedy® and applied an ice pack. Bach's is one of the best herbal remedies I've ever found. I always keep it handy.

Then I took a good look at Bob. He hadn't shaved yet, and he looked a bit the worse for wear. "You didn't pull out the bed, Bob? Don't tell me you slept cramped up on that couch." I felt a pang of remorse that I hadn't even thought to help him make up a bed last night. In fact, I'd been too anxious even to give it a thought.

"I was fine. Marmalade makes a pretty soft pillow, and the rain played me a lullaby."

"Do I detect a smidgen of sarcasm, dear sir?"

"Not even a whiff of it. Actually I slept pretty well. I had planned on sitting up to watch, but Marmalade talked me out of it. That purr of hers is hypnotic. Once I shave I'll feel 100% better. By the way, I squeezed some orange juice for all of us while you two were being lazy."

"Bless you, oh loved one," I said, and started over toward the coffee pot, but he reached out and pulled me to him in a long, slow hug that was sheer comfort. Then he went to do his whisker thing.

I would like to go out now.

Glaze pointed over at the back door, where Marmalade had curled up in her meatloaf position, looking for all the world like the pillow Bob had said she was. A pillow with ears. And whiskers. Meowing loudly.

I walked over and looked out the peephole again. No sense in being casual about somebody who'd beaten up my sister, although I didn't want to think about that this morning. Marmalade scooted out the door, which I then locked behind her. "I'll get the pancake ingredients together."

"Can you bring in the paper first?"

"What do you mean, bring in the paper? Here, if you want the paper, you walk a couple of blocks to the grocery store. What do you think this is, a suburb? We *do* have fresh orange juice, though, since Bob is spoiling us. I was going to get you to squeeze it, but now you can just relax and . . . " I paused, looking down at the front pocket of my shirt. ". . . just relax and breathe!"

Wednesday, May 3, 1995
Garner Creek

It was a Wednesday. They never had lunch together anymore. It all had ended that day they went to the Hideaway. But today, Sarah decided to go back to the little diner across from his bank. She felt summer-time free, even though it was only early May.

When Sarah went in, the yellow-haired waiter brought her decaf. It was good to be remembered after three whole months, but her usual table was occupied, so she sat near the front door. This time she could take a whole hour almost and eat at a leisurely pace. She leaned back in her chair and looked around. She smiled at Pamela, Marcia, and Helen. Marcia, she noticed, was wearing her new silk scarf, tied in a simple square knot. Sarah felt good about that, and she'd gotten new business for Mabel's, too.

Glancing farther to her right, she noticed that, even in the warm spring weather, the older man with the crooked nose wore a sweater with leather patches at the elbow. The sweater looked new somehow. She was glad he was doing well.

Sitting at the table to her left was the same man in the same black teeshirt, looking rushed as usual. From where Sarah sat it was hard to see the whole room. She turned a little in her seat. Yes, there was the student with her tote bag, still wearing a denim dress, although this one had short sleeves, which was more appropriate for summertime.

She'd heard that the young man with the long face had been murdered last week. That was so sad. She still thought of him as one of the regulars here at the diner. Although, now that she thought about it, she'd seen him only a couple of times. And then, of course, she'd seen him last Friday at Cherokee Motors. On her anniversary. Ha! What a laugh. Some anniversary. She'd gone home after dinner and straight to bed. She hadn't even heard Sid when he came in. He said he had tiptoed in about 9:15, not wanting to wake her. That *was* nice of him. Maybe there was hope after all. She stirred more cream into her decaf and ordered a turkey sandwich on rye.

Monday, April 22, 1996

Thank goodness there is a gap in the fence. I do not mind hopping over it, but I got a foot caught in the wire once, and that was no fun whatsoever. The gap is much easier. He was hiding in the trees out back. That is how he could see Widelap and Smellsweet in the kitchen yesterday. They should have noticed him sneaking along the fence line behind those tall trees that smell so good.

I told them he was here yesterday. Why did they not listen to me? Too bad I lost him when he got into his big truck. I will keep hunting him, though. Maybe today . . .

This is where he jumped over yesterday, and he came this way again this morning. There is a big dent in the grass where he landed.

He stepped on one of her baby bushes. That will hurt Widelap. Her face will crinkle, and her eyes will bunch in from the sides, and her nose will go a little flatter. Widelap spends a lot of time on her knees talking to all these plants, and patting them and fussing with them, but she does not always seem to hear what they are telling her. This one that he stepped on needs more light. He did not kill it, but it is going to grow up lopsided, leaning out to try to catch the sun.

This is so easy it is absurd. Up the hill, along the sidewalk, across the street. Uh-oh, I had better run – there is Looselaces in her yellow car. Now across this street and into the place where they plant the bodies in boxes.

Well, well, well. There he is sitting on the back flap of his blue truck, stinking up the world with his smoke. I think a little leg-shredding is called for. I will move a bit closer first . . .

I'll teach you a thing or two, you lousy dog-kicker. How dare you sneak around and scare my people?

&$^$@(%#&^^" " (^%^*&()%^" ^&%&

Ouch!

From the Statement of Esther Anderson (Mrs. Leon Anderson)
to the Georgia Bureau of Investigation
Wednesday, May 3, 1995

No, I hardly knew him. He never came here to the library. . . . Yes, I volunteer here with Sadie Masters and Rebecca Jo Sheffield. . . . Yes, I think a lot of the new librarian. . . . My shoes? Size seven or seven and a half. It depends on the style . . . . No, I don't know how he got into the library, unless it was through the back door. Biscuit, the new librarian, that's what we call her, always locks up the front door real tight. . . . Everybody in town knows about that door. I don't think it's ever had a lock on it. . . . No, I don't know why he was here.

Monday, April 22, 1996
Martinsville

By the time Bob emerged, clean-shaven and smelling like Old Spice, the coffee was dripping and we had already started on the orange juice. It had taken me a while to explain to Glaze that I followed the food-combining principles that say that fruit of any sort needs to be eaten (or drunk) half an hour before any carbohydrates or proteins are put in the stomach. Helps the digestive processes immensely.

When I told Bob about it almost a year ago, he agreed to give it a try. Luckily, he liked the results, which, since they had to do with the end results of digestion, were better left undiscussed during breakfast. Heaven keep me from the belief that the activities of my bowels are of vital interest to every person I meet. Years ago, thinking of my great-grandfather on my dad's side, I told Sandra and Sally both that if I ever start a conversation with, 'So, have you had a bowel movement yet today?' they are to COMMIT ME instantly. Either that or take me out into the hills in the middle of winter and leave me for the bears. No, they would be hibernating, so it would have to be wolves. I hope they eat me fast, so it doesn't hurt too much.

So we drank our juice and sat talking of simple non-digestive things until it was time to start the pancakes.

After breakfast, Bob left for work, reminding us again to keep the doors locked. Although I thought Glaze should stay in the living room rather than tackle the stairs again, she insisted on hobbling back up. "I left my toothbrush up there, for one thing, and I've brought some things for you that I keep forgetting to get out of my suitcase. Not wedding presents, just some fun stuff."

I held her left arm and she leaned on the bannister with her right arm as we inched up the stairs.

Chapter 12

Monday, April 22, 1996

Sadie Masters, determinedly steering her old yellow Chevy up Juniper, noticed an orange and white cat trundling across the street. It paused in the middle of the road, looked her way, and then ran across to the other side. "Why look," she told herself. "It's Jelly, that sweet little library cat." That didn't sound quite right to Sadie, who had never been one for remembering details of any sort, except epitaphs and funeral attendees. "It's around all day, underfoot most of the time. Why can't I ever remember its name? Honey, or Maple Syrup, or something like that."

Sadie carefully braked as she approached Third Street, looked both ways, and saw that the cat, off to her left now, was doing the same thing. Pausing with her foot on the brake, Sadie continued to comb through her memory. It was some kind of jam or jelly. Raspberry? Loganberry? Kudzu? She laughed to herself, easing her foot off the brake and applying just a little gas. Sharon Armitage had actually carried fancy little jars of so-called Kudzu Jelly in her gift shop last year. Any fool could tell it was only mint jelly just by looking at the color, although they might have thrown a kudzu flower in the batch just to be truthful on their hand-written labels, she supposed.

By the time she maneuvered her car around the left turn, the library cat was just slipping through the open gate to the cemetery.

"Now who would have left that gate ajar?" Sadie questioned out loud to no one in particular. "Oh dear, I'm talking to myself again. That gate is always left closed. Not to keep anyone out. No, no. There's no lock on that gate. This is such a friendly town, where nothing bad ever happens . . ." Sadie had again eased her foot onto the brake, stopping in the middle of Third Street as she looked over toward the cemetery.

Mrs. Martha Pontiac – everybody called her Maggie – who was cutting through the Town Park on her way home, paused in the shade of the big Tulip Poplar that grew near Third Street and Juniper. There was Sadie, she noticed, stopped again in the middle of the road. How that woman ever avoided being run down, she'd never know. If she wasn't stopped, she was weaving. When she wasn't weaving, she was usually in the wrong lane. Not that it mattered much around here, but down on First Street along the river, that woman was a holy terror. It was bad enough that there was getting to be so much traffic in town, without Sadie Masters causing calamity everywhere she went. 'Of course, to be entirely fair,' Maggie thought, 'I have to admit that I've never heard of Sadie actually having an accident.' Shaking her head, she crossed Juniper, heading away from Sadie. 'I don't think she's ever really caused an accident either, and if that's not proof that angels exist, I don't know what is.'

Sadie corrected herself. "Nothing bad happens here except that terrible murder last year." What was his name? Harry something or other? He was such a nice young man. He'd helped her carry her groceries into her house once when he and that Olsen boy were walking up the street. Harmon! That was his name! Who'd name anybody Harmon? Sounds like a church organ. Sadie, momentarily distracted from the open gate, nudged her car forward slowly as her mind continued to mull over the crime. 'We never, ever had anything bad happen around here until then, and now somebody goes and leaves the cemetery gate open.'

Happy that she had found her train of thought, Sadie passed across Dogwood. As she approached the dangerous turn onto Magnolia Way, she marveled again that someone would build a street at such a funny angle. The exigencies of slopes and rock outcroppings and such made no difference to Sadie. It seemed for her inconvenience alone that Magnolia Way ran up the hill from northeast to southwest, unlike Juniper that climbed straight east to west up from the river on a gentler slope than the part of the hill that Magnolia surmounted. Sadie came to a full stop in front of CT's, that wonderful restaurant where she'd been to dinner once or twice, but the menu was confusing, to say the least, all those foreign words.

Turning left, she suddenly began to chuckle. "Maybe the cemetery gate," she reasoned, "was always closed to keep people IN, not OUT! Ha-ha! That was a good one. I made a joke!" She shivered deliciously as she thought of the appreciative oohs and ahh's from the other girls next week at the Reading Circle. She passed perilously close to a car parked outside that sweet young doctor's clinic – she was just going to have to get him to meet her niece from Memphis. They'd make such a nice couple. Then she paused a moment to imagine describing her vision of ghostly spirits being stopped by that simple iron grating. 'Whatever am I thinking?' Sadie reined in her imagination. That gate wouldn't stop anybody. The cat could have just ducked under it, if it had been closed the way it was supposed to be. Maybe she should drive back and shut it out of respect for the dead.

Her younger brother Eustace was buried there, next to their parents. And, of course, little Samuel was there, too. Sadie always kept the plots tidy looking, with fresh yellow flowers from her yard each time she visited, which hadn't been very often recently. How had she gotten off her twice-a-week schedule? "I know!" she remembered. "It was when I started working at the library on Wednesdays and Fridays. Wednesday always used to be cemetery day. That and Sundays after services. So poor Eustace has suffered a bit for the past year." Well, she supposed it wouldn't hurt him to miss his flowers once a week. He had a whole eternity ahead of him. She did idly wonder if her good friend Esther Anderson might think a wee bit less of her for neglecting the grave.

Maybe she'd just turn left and head back that way. She could take a few moments to tidy up Eustace a bit and then be sure the gate was closed on her way out. "Esther probably pities me having to walk all the way to the top end of the graveyard to tend my family. But I like the way Mama and Daddy and Eustace and, of course, little Samuel are sort of tucked into the corner with the dogwood branches hanging out over them. It gives such lovely shade on hot summer afternoons. Not that I ever try to walk up there at that time of day. No, early morning is the best time to visit poor Eustace and the rest of them."

By this time Sadie was back on Juniper where she had started. Martha Pontiac was happily out of view, so no one noticed that Sadie appeared to be going in circles again. Sadie pulled up onto the curb just past the church and stepped carefully from her car. She smoothed out the front of her yellow housedress. She always wore her seatbelt, but it did cause wrinkles. Sadie closed her car door carefully, so she wouldn't disturb the stillness of the morning.

As she was stepping gingerly up onto the curb, a blue truck gunned its motor off to her right, startling Sadie to a standstill. The truck raced around the corner and almost rammed Sadie's Chevy. She caught a quick glance of an angry-looking dark-haired young man behind the wheel. "Oh land sakes alive, was he making a rude gesture at me?" Sadie gasped, and then felt another delicious shiver go up her spine as she thought of the sympathetic murmurs of support she'd get when she told the girls about her close call. 'Some people though,' thought Sadie a bit uncharitably, 'shouldn't be allowed to drive.'

After stepping through the little gate, Sadie closed it after her, then continued her slow walk up the narrow winding pathway. She paused respectfully for a few moments at the Martin Memorial, almost in the center of the graveyard. "Poor young men," she mumbled, as she sat down on the wide stone wall that surrounded the grave plot. She took a few minutes to re-tie her shoelaces. "And their poor mother and grandmother. Nobody should have to lose a child. Nobody else. Ever." Getting to Eustace took her a bit longer than usual, as she felt compelled to say a few words of greeting to so many of her old friends as she passed. "Hello, Mrs. Perkins. You were the first dead body I ever saw. I was only four when my Mama made me kiss your hand when you were laid out in your front parlor. My how times have changed," she muttered to herself. "Now there's that fancy funeral home, and we can't prepare people properly – wash their bodies and dress them in their finest clothes and sit by them through the night. Now we leave all that to strangers."

'Well,' she thought, 'not that Marvin Axelrod is a stranger. I've known him ever since he was knee-high to a grasshopper. But now we have to wait for viewing hours. Bunch of nonsense!' By this time she had reached her family's grave, and there was no one else around – 'at least nobody who's standing up!' Sadie laughed to herself. Another joke. She was sure funny today, if she did say so herself.

As she turned to look back across the little hillside cemetery, she noticed a movement off to her left. It was that library cat, who seemed to be acting very strangely. As Sadie watched, the cat was trying to stand up. It lurched a bit, and then sat down suddenly in the middle of the old Axelrod plot. Sadie hoped it wasn't going to do its business there. But no, the cat stood up slowly, looked around at Sadie, turned back toward the church, and carefully picked its way between the head stones. Sadie could have sworn the cat was limping. Was it hurt? Was it sick? She called out, wondering if she could do something, but the cat ignored her and kept up its painful trek down the hillside.

There is Looselaces again . . . here to give more dead flowers to the . . . bones in the ground. She cannot help me though. I need to get back to Widelap. One step . . . at a time. I can do it . . .I can do it . . .

The mid-morning sun glinted for a moment off the cat's tawny fur. "Now I remember," exclaimed Sadie. "It's Peach Preserves! Strange name for a cat."

From the Statement of Sadie Marie Masters
to the Georgia Bureau of Investigation
Wednesday, May 3, 1995

Has the date for the funeral been set yet? . . . Well, of course I need to know. I want to be there to tell his mother what a sweet young man he was. . . . My shoe size? What does that have to do with anything? Five. Well, sometimes a six. . . . Never! I don't believe in tottering around on those pointy things. It's not safe. Give me my tennis shoes any day. . . . Yes, I knew him. He helped me carry my groceries into the house once, and he spent one whole Sunday evening taking pictures of my yellow dahlias. . . . I'm really sorry she gave him such an unfortunate name. . . . His mother. . . . My goodness, you do change the subject a lot. Yes, this is Peaches, the cat that found the body. . . . No, he was never here in the library before. I would have noticed him. . . . I'm very observant.
You did not ask me.

Monday, April 22, 1996

"I stuffed a couple of good books in the zippered side pocket just in case I couldn't find a library."

"Very funny."

Glaze was talking as she squeezed out some toothpaste. "I brought you a new biography and a great Elizabeth Peters book. I hope you haven't read it yet. Why don't you get them out so I don't forget and take them back home with me?"

I opened three zippers before I found the right one. There was the biography - some poet I'd never heard of. Then the Peters book, which I'd already read. I noticed that there was something else underneath them, so I tugged on it. It was a small paperback cookbook. "Do you read cookbooks for fun?" I asked.

She poked her head through the bathroom door and mumbled through her toothbrush, "No, why?"

"Because you have a cookbook in your suitcase."

"No I don't."

"Yes, you do," I said, holding it up for inspection. "Chicken recipes."

"Let me see that," Glaze said after rinsing and spitting." She hobbled over to where I was perched on the side of the bed. "Oh my gosh, it's Sarah's book. You know, the woman in the blue car that ran into me? I remember picking this up off her night table to look at, but I don't think I ever read any of it. I must have just fallen asleep. How the heck did it get in my suitcase?"

"You said the nurse packed up your stuff for you since you had your finger in a cast. Maybe she stuck it in by mistake." I looked through the first few pages. There were some interesting recipes in there. "Maybe I could copy some of these before you return it."

"I don't know how to reach her."

"Sure you do. Look here. Her name and number are on the inside cover. Sarah Borden. The number's in our area code."

"Yeah, she said she lived nearby in Garner Creek. She was on her way home for lunch when she hit me."

"Why don't we call her and see if she can drive down here? You're in no shape to drive twenty miles with your ankle the way it is. You sit here, and I'll hang the rest of these clothes up so they don't get wrinkly. I should have done that for you two days ago." I picked up a lime green short-sleeved pullover. How can she possibly look good in that color? I tried wearing a lime green dress once, and my kids actually laughed at me. Pathetic.

"Why would she drive all this way for a cookbook?"

As we chatted, Glaze had been idly turning more pages of the cookbook. There was some sort of heavy bookmark, something wrapped in a piece of plain white paper. It slid out of the book and landed on the braided rug.

"What's that?" Glaze asked as I bent to retrieve it for her.

"I don't know, should I open it up?"

"No, you shouldn't. It's private property. Give it to me and I'll open it up."

It was a small square of white paper, folded around a single key. "Now we really have to call Sarah," I said, heading for the phone. "It looks like it might be her safety deposit box key. She'll want it back right away. Poor thing. She must be worried sick."

"Imagine using it as a bookmark. Isn't that pretty careless?"

"Only if you run a red light and end up in the hospital next to somebody who steals books," I teased as I handed her the phone. "Here, prop your foot up and get this ice bag on it before you call."

A few moments later, Glaze was talking to an answering machine. "This message is for Sarah. This is Glaze McKee. I was in the hospital with you last week, and I ended up with your cookbook in my luggage by mistake. Your safety deposit box key was in it. I would offer to drive it up to you, but I've sprained my ankle. I'm going to be here another couple of days visiting my sister in Martinsville. Could you drive down tomorrow or Wednesday? We'll even serve you lunch or dinner! It's just the two of us, and we don't have any other plans since I can't move very fast." She chuckled as she admitted, "We're using a couple of the recipes, I hope you don't mind. I promise to leave the book and your key right on the kitchen counter so they don't find their way back into my suitcase again by mistake. Give us a call anytime today or tomorrow." She gave the address and phone number, then said a cheery goodbye.

"I love machines with long message tapes," she remarked as she gave me the handset. "I hate it when it goes beep and I have to call back again. Now we just wait to hear from her. How about a rousing game of Scrabble before we start on the office curtains?"

The Scrabble game was a success. Glaze and I sat side by side on the little loveseat in what I'm calling the sitting room. Eventually, once we own the house, Bob and I are going to take out the wall and merge this room with the bedroom to make a huge master suite. For now, this is just a pleasant room to sit in for reading or garden planning. Or Scrabble.

Glaze and I have never followed the rules. We didn't play together much when we were kids, but when we did, we never counted up scores. Sometimes we helped each other out if one of us had a strange combination of letters. Now that she had her ankle to contend with, she left it propped up on the ottoman, sticking out to the left of the coffee table, and I placed all the words. She handed me an O and told me to put it in front of the "micro" I had just formed.

"That's not a word!"

"It will be when you put this N at the end of it."

I looked at the resulting word. Omicron. Greek letter. "Smartiebritches," I said over my shoulder.

We never bother much about what words to accept. French, Spanish, Latin, Greek, contractions, abbreviations, whatever. If we can look it up in a book, we let it count. I think that's a much more civilized way of playing the game. I do the same thing when I play that trivia game with all the little pie pieces. Yes, I play it by myself. I always substitute a science question if I land on a sports square. To give myself a chance, though, I read the sports question first, just in case. As if I care who won the open in 1956. And I could use help on the entertainment questions. That's about the only disadvantage I can think of for not having a TV set. That, and not being able to watch operations on that surgery channel I've heard about. Wouldn't you love to see an appendectomy?

"How about taking a break for some tea and cookies?" Glaze interrupted me just as I was contemplating the best angle of incision for that appendix.

"Sure." I put the scalpel down on the sterile cloth. "You sit here, or better yet, stand up and do some stretches. I'll be back in a jiffy."

Monday, April 22, 1996
Dr. Nathan Young's Office, Martinsville

"Come right back this way, sir. I need to check your weight. Step up here carefully. . . . 194. . . . Now if you'll come in here and sit up on the table. . . . Thank you. I'll put this around your arm.

Don't worry about the blood. We'll clean it up later. That's a nasty gash. It's amazing you were able to drive here with your leg in that shape. . . . Now, quiet for just a moment . . . hmm . . . 157 over 95. . . . I hope you have another pair of pants in your car, because we'll probably have to cut this pant leg off."

"Yeah, I have a pair of shorts I can use."

"Are you allergic to anything Mr. Winslow? . . . good. . . . Any medicines you can't take? . . . Okay. . . . You just wait here a moment and the doctor will be right with you."

Jeff couldn't believe this. 'I've probably got rabies,' he thought. 'I hope I ruptured something big when I threw that . . .' His thoughts wallowed in obscenities until a young, brisk-looking man wearing a white labcoat walked in. Jeff could tell right away he was a friggin pansy. 'Great,' he thought. 'Now I'll have AIDS *and* rabies.'

Dr. Nathan Young looked at this new, walk-in patient, and recognized the mixture of pain, fear, and disdain in his eyes. He sighed, and breathed a quick prayer of gratitude that he was being given yet another chance to help the healing along. 'This guy looks like he could use a lot of healing.' That thought was there before Nathan could censor it – a postscript to his prayer.

"So, you said you were attacked by a wildcat?"

"Yeah. Are you going to put gloves on before you touch me?"

'God give me patience . . .' "Yes, Mr. Winslow. Do you have any idea what your usual blood pressure is?" he asked as he glanced over Polly's concise notes.

"No, why should I?"

"It would just help me to know whether this high pressure reading was caused by your injury or whether it's in your normal range."

Jeff's thought was clearly visible on his face. 'It's probably up a lot since I'm gonna have a queer touching me.'

Dr. Young turned abruptly, opened the door, and called out, "Nurse Lattimore, could you please come in to assist me? Bring a large pair of scissors." Ordinarily, he would have taken a pair of scissors from the second drawer and cut off the pant leg himself. But he wanted a witness around.

'Nurse Lattimore?' she thought. 'He's calling me Nurse Lattimore? Whatever happened to *hey, Polly, can you help me out here?*' Sighing, she realized he probably just wanted some moral support – and maybe a witness. Anybody with a ghastly tattoo like this man had, needed watching. She laughed to herself, picked up the desk scissors, and went to Nathan's aid.

As she entered the pleasant little examining room with its watercolors of daisies and lilies on the light blue walls she heard Dr. Nathan – whoops! she'd better remember to call him Dr. Young – explaining, "Don't worry, Mr. Winslow. There hasn't been a case of rabies in this county in decades. Thank you, Nurse Lattimore." He reached out a gloved hand to take the scissors, barely suppressing a wink as he did so. "Would you please help me get this pant leg cut away?"

The man had obviously been attacked by something that didn't like him very much. There were some deep-looking puncture wounds that were already beginning to bruise around the edges. Too bad he hadn't been wearing heavy jeans. These lightweight chinos weren't a match for teeth and claws.

The claw marks were long, but fairly closely spaced. 'Cancel wildcat and substitute housecat,' Nathan thought. Out loud he said, "So where were you when this wildcat attacked you?" He and Polly, also gloved, continued to clean and examine the multiple wounds as the patient complained.

"I was just sitting on my tailgate, minding my own business up . . ." He was about to say 'up behind the cemetery' but checked himself. He'd had to drive over a couple of flower beds to get his truck in there out of sight of the streets. ". . . a couple of streets over. I saw your sign when I drove into town, so I knew right away where to come to get patched up."

"Where are you staying?" Polly couldn't help but ask.

"In a motel about twenty miles up the road."

'Good,' she thought. 'He won't be hanging around here then.'

"This may hurt a bit, Mr. Winslow, but it's important that we clean this up thoroughly. Nurse Lattimore will give you an injection once I get this bandaged. You'll need to see your own doctor if you notice any signs of infection. Please examine your leg thoroughly twice a day. If you see any red streaks, or if any more swelling occurs, get to your doctor immediately."

Once all the bandaging was in place, Nathan wrote a prescription and some instructions in a surprisingly legible script, while Polly gave the injection of antibiotics.

Nathan handed over the two sheets of paper, with near certainty that they would not be followed. He paused at the door, turned around, and said, "Thank you for coming in, Mr. Winslow. I hope your leg heals quickly."

"Yeah, right." He followed the nurse down the short hallway, gave her a credit card, signed the receipt, and stuffed his copy in his wallet. He limped through the waiting room, past three small giggling children, a woman in an armchair, and an old lady who was reading what looked like a library book. Nothing interesting there.

At the curb, he leaned into his truck, extracted a wrinkled pair of khaki shorts, stomped back into the little house with as much dignity as he could muster wearing three-fourths of a pair of slacks, with the left leg cut off at mid-thigh and fat bandages winding down his leg. When he told the nurse he needed to change, she led him back to the same little examining room.

While he was changing, he glanced around and took a moment to open drawers and cabinets. Nothing interesting, except that he saw a pair of scissors in the second drawer. Stupid pansy doctor didn't even know he had a pair of scissors right under his nose. So Jeff took the scissors, figuring they wouldn't be missed. They'd make a nice souvenir. He slipped them into the front pocket of his shorts and left his mutilated pants on the floor.

Once again he passed through the waiting room. The old lady was gone, but the woman with the kids was still there. As he walked by her, he muttered, "I hope you like queers, lady." The woman was so startled, she looked up at Polly, who simply shrugged and said, "Goodbye Mr. Winslow."

"Yeah, right."

Just as he was getting set to slide into the driver's seat, he remembered the scissors, and removed them from his pocket in time to avoid another nasty puncture wound.

Chapter 13

Monday, April 22, 1996

Glaze and I managed to get some simple café curtains made for the office, but our hearts weren't in the sewing, and we gave up after that. Her ankle had swollen quite a bit, and I finally talked her into letting me drive her over to Nathan's office. I stuffed two of the loaves of bread into bags, one for Nathan and one for Polly, then got Glaze into the car. Before I pulled away from the curb, though, I saw Marmy dragging herself across the street toward me. I don't think I've ever jumped out of a car faster than I did then. Thank goodness Sadie was nowhere around. By the time I reached Marmalade, she had collapsed in the middle of Beechnut Lane.

I was afraid to scoop her up, afraid even to touch her. "Poor sweetie! What happened to you?" Had she been in a fight?

Yes.

I bent down next to her and ran my hands gently over her, careful not to push too hard. She was breathing, but it seemed labored. Her ears were hot. That could be the weather. It could be that her blood pressure was up. Her whiskers looked wilty. I sure will be glad when Holly gets her degree and starts her clinic here.

There didn't seem to be any fur missing, so it probably wasn't a cat fight. No blood, thank goodness. Her right rear leg was definitely hurting, though. When I touched it, her ears twitched and she shifted as if to move away from me. "Don't worry, little one. I'll be gentle." I lifted her carefully. "Why can't you tell me what went wrong, sweetheart?"

Try this: a big man with an ugly tatoo on his arm grabbed my leg and yanked really hard. I bit him first and shredded his leg some, so we are even. He will think twice about coming here again.

Her purr was weak, but she settled into my arms nestling her head into the crook of my elbow. I carried her to the car and placed her gently on Glaze's lap.

By the time I drove the three and a half blocks to Doc's office, Glaze had drops of sweat beading her forehead, and Marmalade looked awfully limp. I had to run inside and get Polly to come out and help me get the two of them up the walkway and straight into an examining room.

Nathan strode almost immediately into the attractive little room, and went straight to Marmy. I had laid her as gently as I could on the paper-lined examining table. "I know you're not a vet," I started to say, but Nathan hushed me with a wave of his hand.

He used a disposable dropper to place a few drops of a clear liquid into Marmy's mouth. I recognized the brown bottle, but held my tongue as he put his stethoscope under Marmalade's chest and listened carefully. "When I was in med school, I volunteered at the local animal shelter," he said as he gently felt Marmalade's back, neck, ears, legs, tail. "And I've been a fan of Marty Goldstein's holistic approach to treating animals ever since I heard him speak at a conference last year."

Glaze looked a little confused, so as Nathan continued with his exam, I told her that if she ever adopted a cat or dog, she had to get *The Nature of Animal Healing.*

Nathan straightened up and asked me to tell him what I knew of the injury. Which was precisely nothing, other than that I'd found her struggling to get across Beechnut. He asked me if I thought Marmalade would lie still for an X-ray.

Yes.

"Yes, I'm sure she will." Polly helped Nathan transfer Marmalade onto a rolling cart that they had cleared of its usual load of bandages and bottles and swabs. They had covered it with a big soft white towel. Then Glaze and I had to just sit and wait. I scooted out to the car to retrieve the two loaves of bread, and returned just as Nathan reappeared with a very quiet Marmalade in his arms.

"I took two X-rays, and don't see anything broken, but her right hip was dislocated badly. This is one brave, smart cat. I explained to her what I needed to do, and told her it would hurt, and I think she actually understood me . . ."

Well, of course I did.

". . . because she stayed perfectly still while I eased her hip back into position."

Thank you. You have gentle strong good hands.

"There's going to be some swelling and discomfort for a few days. If she didn't have all this heavy fur, we'd probably be seeing a lot of bruising. The good news is there's no external bleeding. I need to warn you, though; there may be some internal injuries that don't show up on the X-ray. My best guess is that she was hit by a car."

Bad guess.

"What else should I do for her?"

"Just try to keep her as quiet as possible. Put an icepack on her bed and let her lie against it."

"Will she do that?"

Yes.

"I think she will. It'll probably feel good to her. Cats are smart about tending their wounds. She'll let you know when she's ready to start moving around. Until then, just spoil her rotten."

Good idea. How about some chicken?

As I stood there holding Marmy and stroking her gently, Nathan turned to Glaze. "I wanted to meet this sister from Philadelphia, but I didn't expect it to be under these circumstances." He took her hand in a gentle handshake, raising his eyebrows at the bandaging.

"Car accident last week," she said. "Someone ran a light and plowed into me. But that's doing fine. It's my ankle that brought me here today. I fell down the stairs this morning. Ice took care of it for a few hours, but now it's swelling and hurting a lot more."

"I put some arnica on it, too."

"Did you give her some of the Bach?"

"Of course. I keep that stuff handy all the time."

"What does music have to do with all this?" Glaze asked through gritted teeth.

"Not Bach the composer. Bach the herbalist. Edward Bach was an English physician in the early part of this century, who discovered remedies made from flower essences. He invented a formula that can be used to lessen the effects of shock on the body.

"Dr. Bach," he said as he made a few notes on a chart, "wrote that the main reason for the failure of modern medicine is that it deals with results and not with causes. That was 1931, but it's still true today. That reminds me," he said as he glanced up at me. "Keep treating Marmalade with the Bach remedy for a couple of days. I already put a few drops under her tongue to ease the shock."

"Should I put some in her water, too?"

"If she'll drink it. Try a little and see how she likes it."

I like it. It feels right.

Nathan kept up a gentle banter as he removed my sister's shoe and examined her foot and ankle. "This has been a busy day. You're the second new out-of-town walk-in patient today. That's something of a record around here."

I was curious as to who the first one was . . .

It was Tattooman. I can smell his stink in here even now.

. . . but didn't ask because Nathan never talks about his patients, just one of the many things I admire about him. "It looks like you're going to be fine, but I think you've been overdoing it. I'm not trained in acupuncture yet, so we'll have to rely on bandaging to give you a little more support. The icepack seems to have helped, and I'd like you to keep it iced as much as possible for the next twenty-four hours. Hopefully it'll be good as new by the wedding."

"I was a little worried about having to limp up the aisle."

"I'm not saying you won't be limping a bit," Nathan said. "This is a usual medical disclaimer, you know." He smiled. "But you should at least be able to walk."

Once her ankle was securely bandaged, she *could* walk a bit more comfortably. We thanked Nathan for working us in, paid the bill, nodded at Polly's reminder to keep a cold pack on both patients as much as possible, and left in considerably higher spirits. "What a pleasant man," Glaze said. "I compliment you on your choice of doctors."

Yes. So do I. Goodhands is his name.

"He may be the only doctor in town, but I'm convinced he's one of the best anywhere." I paused a moment, debating whether or not to tell the juicy tale. Oh, what the heck. "Do you remember Sadie Masters?"

"How could I forget? She's the yellow Petunia who can't drive straight."

"That's the one. She's been trying for three years to fix our doctor up with her niece who lives in Memphis."

"You've got to be kidding! Doesn't she realize . . . ?"

"Obviously not."

When we reached home, I looked around before I opened the passenger door. The only thing moving was – of course – Sadie's yellow Chevy. She waved airily as she passed us, meandered more or less up the center of Beechnut Lane, turned right onto Third Street, running a back tire over the curb, and disappeared from view. I picked up Marmalade and held her as I helped Glaze up the walk. As we passed the mailbox, I noticed that it was completely lavender. When had Bob found the time to paint it? I love that guy! When we walked into the vestibule, I locked the door behind us.

Oh, I forgot to tell you – you need to move the little plant with the white bell flowers. It needs more light, especially since Tattooman stepped on it.

Wednesday, April 17, 1996
Garner Creek

Ben took a deep breath as he walked back through the First Community Bank lobby toward his office. 1996 was going to be a good year after all. Sarah had been so willing to help him when he'd called her last week. Having to do that had been infuriating. It was bad enough having Sid walk into his office on the first Friday of every month, close the door, and hold out his hand for the envelope of cash. He'd had to pay it. He couldn't risk his wife thinking that he had cheated on her. It had been dumb to go to that motel, but he'd thought he was attracted to Sarah, and he'd been surprised when all he'd wanted to do was talk. Amazing. He'd even cried. Thank goodness they hadn't been in the diner when that happened.

He had never admitted to Sarah that her husband was blackmailing him. It didn't seem the right thing to do, to worry her about something like that. Anyway, it was embarrassing.

But Sid had told him two weeks ago, that first Friday in April, that the negatives were 'right under your nose, Mr. Bigshot, and whaddya think about *that*?' He had asked for more money, too. Well, that was just too much. That was why Ben had called Sarah at work the next Monday and asked for her help.

He hadn't talked with her in such a long time, so he'd wondered if she'd be willing to help him. After all, she'd been the one to stop their weekly meetings. He smiled as he remembered how solemn she had been. How fortunate he was that they had remained friends. She always said hello when she came in to cash a check, but they hadn't talked in over a year. Until he asked her to get the key. She'd been furious to hear about the blackmail. Somehow she thought that she was responsible for getting him into all this, and she'd apologized again and again. It wasn't her fault, but why on earth had a nice person like Sarah married a creep like Sid anyway?

It had taken her eight days to find where Sid had hidden the key, but she'd called Ben this morning and made an appointment with him at 1:45 to get into her safety deposit box.

He was so glad Sarah had found the spare key somehow. Just now, during her lunch hour, he had escorted her back to the vault, where she had opened her deposit box. That was legal. She was, after all, one of the signatories. Now he had the negatives, which had been in a plain envelope marked with his initials. It had been tucked underneath a roll of film.

"Film?" Sarah had said when she noticed it. "That's funny. This key was hidden in Sid's big toolbox underneath a camera. I wonder if the two are connected?"

While they had the box open, after she'd given Ben the negatives, Sarah had slipped a ring out of one of the envelopes. "Now," she said, "all I have to do is get the key back into the tool box, before Sid gets home from work."

Yes, this was going to be a better year from here on. Ben and his wife were getting along well now, and their first baby was due in a few weeks, so he was relieved to have the negatives. He felt very grateful for the sweet friendship of such an understanding woman as Sarah, who had helped him see how he could save his marriage.

Ben smiled, remembering how Sarah had whispered to him a few minutes ago, as they were closing the box in the vault, that she'd arranged to go visit her aunt in North Carolina for a couple of weeks. She was thinking that she just wouldn't come back after that. "I can't live with a sleazy blackmailer," she said. They had shaken hands before she left the bank. She had to hurry to get the key home and get back to work before two-thirty.

'Sarah may be little,' Ben thought, 'but she has guts.'

Monday, April 22, 1996
Martinsville

About six o'clock, Glaze sat in the kitchen with the icepack on her ankle, while I put together a simple meal. "Soup?" she asked.

"My own chicken noodle soup, of course," I replied as I walked over to the cushion where Marmalade was lying up against an ice pack, and handed her a bit of the chicken. "It's good for healing."

Thank you.

"Is that why you're giving some to the cat?"

"Well, it can't hurt, and it might help. I'm adding some leeks and a few mushrooms to the soup for us people. I hope you like it. And we'll have a side salad with the radish sprouts on it."

Even though Glaze said, "That should wake me up," by the end of the meal we headed upstairs, and when Bob arrived about 8:30 to stay for the night, we were ready for bed. This time, though, I helped him make out the sofa bed, kissed him a fond good-night, and carried Marmalade upstairs while he headed into the kitchen to make himself a snack. I warned him about the fridge light being out. "I flat forgot about getting a replacement bulb, " I said. "What with Glaze's ankle and Marmalade's hurt leg, I just never thought about it."

"Don't worry about it," he volunteered. "I'll pick one up tomorrow."

I love that guy. Maybe just one more quick kiss . . .

He's nice to take such good care of you.

Later, as Glaze and I settled in for the night, she turned to me and said, "You had your soup today. I wish I'd had a milkshake!"

"Go to sleep, silly. I'll get you a milkshake tomorrow."

Gratitude List – Monday
   1. Bob, for painting my mailbox lavender
   2. Soup and salad and sprouts
   3. Dr. Nathan

4. Polly

5. Radiant good health for all of us, including Marmalade

a successful attack
tombstones to hide behind
Widelap and Goodhands
not having to catch my own food
chicken

Marmalade woke me twice during the early part of the night. She seemed restless, and I hoped her leg wasn't hurting her too much. "Poor honey," I murmured to her, as I looked at the clock. Eleven-thirty-six. "Go back to sleep." I heard a car headed up the street. Maybe that was what had woken her.

At one-fifteen, she woke me up again, stepping on my neck and tickling my face with her whiskers. Not content with waking just one person, she proceeded to walk across Glaze's face, too.

"Are you awake, Biscuit?"

"Yes. Marmalade took care of that. She must be feeling better."

No, I'm not, but you need to go downstairs.

"As long as we're awake, could we make some hot chocolate?"

"You can't walk!" I was trying to keep my voice at a whisper.

"Yes I can," she whispered back at me. "My ankle feels a lot better with this bandage on it."

Well, a cup of cocoa did sound like a good idea. I supposed we could sneak down quietly without waking up Bob. "It's a deal, but only if your ankle feels all right when you try to stand on it." The night air was chilly coming in through the open window, so I pulled the two bathrobes out of the closet and held one of them for her to put on. She managed a pretty fair imitation of a normal walk, so I picked up Marmalade. I figured I might as well give her a little more chicken. We crept quietly from the bedroom and tiptoed down the stairs. I couldn't believe that we hadn't woken Bob. Maybe he was just pretending to stay asleep so he wouldn't interrupt our she-nanigans.

There was enough moonlight outside that, even with the chintz on the windows, we could see vague outlines of everything in the kitchen. I put Marmy down in her basket by the side counter, settled Glaze into a chair by the bay window nook, and crept around getting together the saucepan, cocoa, cinnamon and some extra sugar. Might as well live it up. The dark refrigerator gave up the carton of goat's-milk. Luckily I remembered right where it was in the door. I started the milk heating on the stove, and went to sit down next to Glaze for a minute.

"How's your ankle holding out?" I whispered.

"It's doing fine," she whispered back. "I'll be good as gold by tomorrow. Well, maybe by Wednesday. In the meantime, I'm hungry. How about a sandwich?"

"At this hour of the night?"

"Yes. If I'm hungry, I'm hungry. It doesn't depend that much on the clock. Anyway, I was hurting too much to eat a full dinner."

"Okay. What do you want? I'll get it out."

Still whispering, she decided on a sandwich of peanut butter, ketchup, mayo, and radish sprouts on pumpernickel. "You have to be kidding," I gasped in a strangled whisper. "That sounds awful!"

It sure does.

"No, it's really good. You bring me the stuff and I'll make the sandwiches, a big one for me and a little one for you."

"Maybe I can just try a tiny bite of yours."

I would rather have chicken.

"Fraidy cat," she whispered at my back as I rose to rummage through the darkened fridge to find the ketchup. While I was at it, I pulled out a little bite of leftover chicken for Marmalade.

Thank you.

I couldn't find the mayo. How on earth was Bob sleeping through all this? We were being quiet, but surely he must have heard us by now. I put a plate, a knife and the heavy glass ketchup bottle in front of Glaze and turned to find the bread and peanut butter, but before I had reached the cabinet, I heard Glaze's quiet "Shhh!" It didn't sound like a joke. I froze in place and turned my head just enough so I could see Glaze outlined vaguely against the light yellow chintz on the bay window and could tell from the angle of her head that she had heard something on the verandah outside the other window.

She sat there, not moving. There were quiet footsteps creaking across the verandah. Those boards had been squeaky ever since I'd moved in – and probably for years before that. Now someone was inching his way across the porch, toward the long yellow-curtained window that was directly behind Glaze. I could see her lift a hand to her lips. She stood up slowly, swaying a bit as she tried not to place her weight on the damaged ankle. I barely heard her as she whispered, "It must be Jeff!"

As we watched in horrified fascination, there was a sharp cracking of glass, and the curtains billowed out as someone stepped over
the low sill of the tall window. I could see where his head was pushing against the fabric, obviously looking for a way around or through
it. I suppose I should have screamed or something, but the whole
night went into slow motion. I saw Glaze reach behind her, pick up
the ketchup, and smash it onto the bulge in the chintz where Jeff's
head was. As he crashed to the floor, his body tangled in the curtain,
I stepped across the kitchen and flipped up the light switch, calling
Bob's name as I did so.

I paused a moment, waiting for Bob, but he didn't appear. Jeff
was starting to thrash around. "Help me with this," Glaze called,
and I quickly realized that she was trying to roll him up in the curtain like a paper towel tube. Fine with me. Marmalade was trying to
help by balancing on top of the heaving pile of fabric and angry
man. I grabbed his legs, not an easy task since he was kicking like
crazy. Together we rolled him two full turns. Luckily his arms were
trapped. Otherwise we might not have succeeded. Once he was thoroughly trussed up, Glaze sat down on him with a resounding thump.
"Serves him right," she crowed.

This was when I noticed a note propped up in the middle of the
big table. I unfolded the single sheet of paper and read, "Biscuit, I
got a page at 11:24. Melissa reported a prowler over at Doc's. I'm
headed there now. I have my pager on me – silent operation. Buzz
me when you get this note if I'm not back already. Keep the doors
locked!"

Great. So much for police protection. I read the note to Glaze,
who was still sitting on Jeff. By this time he had started to holler. I
could tell Glaze was considering hitting him again, but I warned her
that killing him after he was already trapped in the curtain might be
frowned on by the authorities. Instead, she leaned closer to the head-
end of the bundle, and said, slowly and loudly, "I've got a gun, and
I'll use it if you don't shut up right now!"

Silence. Good. "Now, what do we do with him?"

"I don't mind sitting here until Bob comes."

"Since we worked so hard to make the tie-backs, we might as
well use them," I said, pulling several of them from their hooks on
the window molding. One around his ankles, two looped together to
reach around his midsection. We had to push him around a bit to
accomplish that, and the shouting was muffled but thoroughly

indignant and mostly profane. Then, there didn't seem to be anything left to do. I congratulated Glaze on not having broken the jar.
"I didn't know those bottles were so sturdy. We should write the
company with a testimonial." Ketchup would have ruined the curtains. As it was, we'd probably have to press them before Saturday,
but that would be a breeze.

"Aren't these bottles usually plastic?" Glaze asked me as she sat
back down again, rubbing her ankle. It must have started hurting
again. If Nathan thought she'd been overdoing it before, he should
have seen her rolling Jeff up in the chintz.

"Tom gave me this one from the restaurant."

I moved over to the phone and paged Bob, leaving a message
that said, "Glaze and I are up. Give us a call." By now it was after
2:00. I poured two mugs of cocoa, and handed one to my still sitting
sister. The phone rang almost immediately. "What are you two doing up?" he asked without preamble.

"We're drinking hot chocolate."

"Well, save me some. I'm on my way. I have some good news for
you and your sister."

A few more threats from Glaze kept Jeff quiet as we waited for
Bob to arrive. When he walked into the kitchen, I lunged into his
arms. He seemed surprised, but cooperated efficiently. Obviously he
didn't see Glaze right away, since she and Jeff were tucked in the
little alcove behind the counter where the sink is. And since his face
was buried in my hair. "I have some great news for you," he said, as
I finally let go. "Melissa saw a prowler at the clinic, and I got there
in time to catch him red-handed. On my way there I called out Tom
to be my unofficial deputy sheriff, since he was close at hand, and
we nailed the guy for burglary." He moved over to sit down at the
big table, pulling my chair out for me first. "Before we got there he
had pretty much ruined a couple of doc's cabinets, but we've got
enough fingerprint material to put him away for quite a while, especially since his pockets were stuffed with stolen narcotics."

"Who was it?" I asked.

Bob seemed to notice for the first time that Glaze wasn't right
there with me. "Your sister will be delighted. It was Jeff Winslow.
It'll be a long time before he bothers her again."

Glaze's stunned voice issued from behind Bob, causing him to
turn around suddenly, looking for her. "If you've got Jeff Winslow
locked up, then who am I sitting on?"

It took a fair amount of explaining about the cocoa and the fridge light and the whispering and the footsteps and the shattered window and the ketchup bottle, but between the two of us we managed a relatively coherent story. Meanwhile there was some man rolled up in the chintz curtains, tied up with matching, piped tie-backs.

Bob helped us untie and unroll the man, who sputtered up into the light to look straight into Bob's gun barrel. I hadn't realized he still had his gun with him, but I was glad when I saw how quiet it made the man. Being tied up in a curtain must be a difficult experience. He was looking pretty sickly, whoever he was.

"Sid Borden?" exclaimed Glaze as his head came into full view. "What on earth are you doing here?"

"You know this guy?" Bob asked.

"Of course. I bought my green Honda from him. He sells cars over in Hastings. He's Sarah's husband."

Tuesday, April 23, 1996

Word travels fast. Melissa Tarkington showed up about 8:30 on Tuesday, bringing breakfast with her. She'd heard about the break-in from Hubbard Martin's wife, who had apparently called everybody in town. Since I hadn't had a chance to take Glaze over to the bed and breakfast yet – things had just been too busy – we sat and chatted for an hour or so, reliving the excitement of the night before, and giving two of my favorite women a chance to get to know each other a little better. Glaze is the sister I was raised with. Melissa is the sister I chose.

An hour later, Melissa was walking out the front door as the phone rang. It was Sarah Borden. She had driven home from her aunt's that morning, planning to move some of her things out of the house while Sid was at work. She heard the message on the answering machine, erased it, and called us to find out what was going on.

When Glaze told her on the phone that Sid had been arrested for breaking and entering, but that we were all okay, she asked if she could drive down and explain what had been happening on her end. Of course, we took her up on the offer. Anyway, I figured Bob would want to hear her side of the story.

I invited her to come for lunch, cold cucumber soup and a big salad from the garden, then called Bob at the station and told him what was going on. "Let me know when she gets there, and I'll stop by. We found some physical evidence that's very interesting."

"What is it?"

"Can't say, but you'll find out eventually."

Friday, April 28, 1995
Garner Creek

"Can I buy you lunch? I've got another job for you." Sid had walked up beside Harlan as he waited at the corner for cars to pass.

"Sorry. Can't do it," Harlan said, looking from side to side, waiting for a break in the unusually busy traffic. "I just got a call from Buddy, my friend in Martinsville. His dad's out of town, and he's been called out on the road, so they need somebody to feed the parakeet. I'll be gone a day or two, and then I may take a few extra days off to go camping. Business has been slow here."

"That's for sure. Well, we'll take a rain check on lunch. Maybe when you get back from your camp-out."

"Yeah, maybe." The traffic flow opened up, and Sid turned away as Harlan crossed the street. No sense in wasting lunchtime if he couldn't get any work out of the guy. This particular job could wait. It was just a minor case, but it might pan out. You never knew with this kind of work.

At 5:15 Harlan was putting away his tools, when Tony stopped him. "Would you tell your mom that me and Arlene can't make it to dinner tomorrow?" Arlene had been Tony's girlfriend for fifteen years. She'd been introducing him as 'my fiancé' for the past eleven years. Neither one of them seemed inclined to change the status quo, though. She kept wearing the ring, and seemed happy enough with the situation. Tony must have been getting what he wanted out of it. That seemed kind of sad to Harlan. As much as he wanted to date Miranda, she was still just too young. Of course, she'd be out of high school in a couple of months. Time enough.

"Can't do it, Tony. I'm on my way out of town right now. Heading over to Buddy's to house-sit for a couple of days while he's out of town."

"I thought he lived with his dad," Tony said as they began walking out to the parking lot.

"He does, but his dad's in Ohio, and won't be back for a couple of days. Then, if it's okay with you, I thought I'd head up into the woods for four or five days. We're pretty well caught up in back, and business has been slow."

"Yeah. Maybe I should run the ad before the 11:00 news, too; I need to drum up some more business. Yeah, good idea, maybe I should re-do the ad. Use a drum instead of a hatchet."

"Whatever you think, Tony. You're the boss." Harlan noticed an auburn-haired woman getting out of her car in front of the dealership. He recognized the way her hair waved across her forehead.

"Go ahead and take off," Tony said. "I'll call your mother myself."

"Tony, do you know who that woman is?" he asked, gesturing to her as she walked across toward the door, just as Sid Borden came through it from inside the showroom.

Tony glanced up, nodded, and said, "Sure, that's Sid's wife. Don't see her around here very often. I wonder what's up?" He raised his voice and called, "Howdy, Sarah! How's it going?"

Sarah turned, smiled briefly in Tony's direction, then paused as she recognized the young man with the aristocratic nose. She'd seen him in the diner a couple of times. She waved, but Sid suddenly stepped forward and took her arm, pulling her into the showroom.

"I wonder what that was about?" Tony mused.

"Beats me," said Harlan, turning to walk away.

At his apartment, he quickly packed a small backpack, then cleaned up and changed out of his Cherokee Motors overalls, making sure that his medicine pouch was tucked in his shirt. His camping gear always stayed stowed in his car, so he was ready for a trip at any moment. He wouldn't have time to eat at the deli. It would be closed by the time he got there, but he could call Miranda at work. She always left late. Maybe they could meet later this evening for a cup of coffee or something. It would be nice to see her. He opened the top drawer of the little table where the phone sat and lifted out a napkin that had the deli's phone number on it. The last time he'd been there, a couple of weeks ago, Miranda had given him the number in case he was in town and needed to order a sandwich.

The phone rang four times before she picked it up. She sounded out of breath, as if she'd been lifting the heavy trays out of the commercial dishwasher.

"DeliSchuss, Miranda speaking."

"Hey, Miranda. It's Harlan." He hated it when people said 'it's me' on the phone, as if they expected you to know their voice. Several times he'd talked to people thinking they were someone else. He always identified himself. Seemed like good manners. Maybe he was old-fashioned that way. "I'm headed out to house-sit for Buddy and his dad. I thought maybe we could get together for some coffee. Will you still be at the deli for a while?"

"I can't do it, Harlan. I'm running so late today." He thought he heard real regret in her voice, but maybe he was only imagining it. "We had a bunch of last-minute delivery orders come in, and I'm trying to get them packed and clean up this place so I can deliver before I go home."

"Can't you get Cory to do the deliveries?"

"No. He's not here, and Mama is expecting me to cook dinner with her tonight, too. Her brother's in town, and we're having a family get-together."

Harlan took a deep breath. Was she putting him off for a reason? He'd never know if he didn't try. "I'd really like to see you. Could we meet somewhere after you have your dinner? Maybe I could pick you up and we could come back to Mr. Olsen's."

"Are you kidding? Mama would kill me if she found out. You know how proper she is." There was a long pause. Harlan wasn't sure how to proceed. He didn't want to push her, but he didn't want to give up either. "Maybe," she said at last, "I could sort of leave the house late and we could meet somewhere. I'd have to sneak out. How about 11:30 or so? Is that too late?"

There was another long pause. Harlan's head told him yes, it was too late. But everything else told him that he was tired of waiting. "No. That's not too late. Where do you want to meet?"

Miranda picked up a towel and began to polish the already gleaming surface of the coffee maker. "How about the library?" she asked.

"Won't it be closed?"

"Yes, but there's a back door that doesn't have a lock. Everybody in town knows about it, but nobody ever uses it. It's behind a great big bush. You just walk around the left side of the building and duck behind the bush and feel for the doorknob."

"I'll be there early, and I'll wait for you."

Harlan turned away from the phone and pulled his deerskin vest from the closet. 'I might as well wear this for good luck,' he said to

FRAN STEWART   - 186 -

himself. Then he lifted the medicine pouch out into view. It went
well with the vest, and he thought Miranda would like seeing it.

From the Statement of Miranda Schuss
to the Georgia Bureau of Investigation
Friday, May 5, 1995

Yes, sir. I was home all evening. My uncle was here
visiting, and I helped cook a big dinner. . . . The
last time I saw him? It was on a . . . Saturday two or
three weeks ago. He and Buddy stopped in . . . at
the deli. . . . Yes, sir. They . . . they came in a lot. .
. . Sandwiches and coffee, usually . . . . Yes, thank
you. I *do* need a tissue. . . . Well, I remember it
because . . . because Harlan said he had gotten some
. . . some really great pictures that morning out in
the hills west of town. He told me he thought I'd
. . . he thought I'd like one of them. It was of a
couple of fawns. . . . No sir, that's not unusual. He's
given pictures to lots of people in town. . . . No, sir.
I never saw the picture of the fawns. . . . What? . . .
Five or six. It depends on the style. . . . Yes, sir. I
considered him . . . a very . . . good friend . . . . The
library? No, I don't know . . . why he was in the
library.

Chapter 14

Friday, April 28, 1995

"I told you never to come here," Sid hissed at Sarah as he gripped her arm and led her away from the showroom doorway.

"Ow, you're hurting me."

"Why did you come here?"

"It's our anniversary, Sid. I thought I'd surprise you. Maybe we could go out to dinner."

"You surprised me all right. I don't like mixing family and business. As long as you're here, we'll go grab a quick bite somewhere, but I don't want to see you here ever again."

Sid slid a few papers off his desk and put them in the top drawer. Then he grabbed his suit jacket and steered Sarah out the side door. They agreed on a restaurant, and went in their separate cars.

Dinner was a bleak affair, particularly after Sarah asked, "Who was that young man standing next to Tony in the parking lot?"

"Harlan Schneider?" Sid shifted to his salesman's voice. "Now, why would you want to know that?"

"Oh, no particular reason. I just thought I'd seen him . . ." She was about to say in the Creek Diner, but thought better of it. ". . . somewhere around Garner Creek. He works at Cherokee?"

"Yeah. Now order so we can eat and get out of here."

'Our anniversary,' Sarah thought.

As Harlan drove the few short miles to Martinsville, he began to think about the strange behavior of Sid at the dealership. Sid had told him that the woman was suspected of selling some sort of secret information, but Tony had said she was Sid's wife. What on earth was going on? He didn't mind not being told everything about a case, but he didn't like being lied to. That crud Sid told him was obviously false. Why would he want pictures of his own wife? Of course, she'd gone to that Hideaway, so maybe she was . . . As Harlan worked it out, he became more and more angry. Sid wasn't a private investigator at all. He was a lousy snoop. No wonder his wife was cheating on him.

Harlan pulled up in front of the Olsen house. The door was never locked, so he walked around to the back porch and let himself in. He first said hello to Mr. Fogarty, as he reached into the cage to scratch under the little bird's chin. 'I really like this silly bird,' Harlan thought. Mr. Fogarty cocked his head from side to side, guiding Harlan's finger to just the right spots. Harlan laughed and said, "You know, Mr. Fogarty, tomorrow morning, when the first light comes through that big old window over there, I'm going to take your picture. You'll be immortal in the Parakeet Hall of Fame." Mr. Fogarty bounced his head up and down, muttering his agreement, or so it sounded to Harlan. Before he refilled Mr. Fogarty's seed and water, Harlan took a few moments to park his backpack in the guest room, where he always slept. It was so good to feel a part of a family like this. 'Someday soon, I'm going to have a house of my own,' he thought later as he scrounged in the fridge and made himself a meatloaf sandwich. He'd been looking at a couple of places over in Garner Creek. Maybe he'd get a dog for company when he had a back yard.

His thoughts returned to Sid, and he crossed to the kitchen phone and dialed the number for Cherokee Motors. There was no answer, so he picked up the sandwich and walked out onto the porch, where he waved to Mrs. Hoskins next door. She waved back, pointed at her bright orange mailbox, and gave an elaborate shrug. Harlan laughed and nodded. He noticed there was still enough light for some good black and white shots, one of the few good things about Daylight Savings. He had plenty of time till he had to go to the library. So Harlan ducked back inside for his F-1 and headed up Beechnut Lane to where it lost its pavement and merged gently into a path that led through the woods surrounding the little town. Maybe he'd try that copse of river birches where he'd seen the deer a couple of weeks ago. He could get some good texture shots. He'd have it out with Sid when he got back to Garner Creek next week.

From the Statement of Elizabeth Hoskins (Mrs. Perry Hoskins)
to the Georgia Bureau of Investigation
Saturday, April 29, 1995

Of course I recognize that knife. Where did you find it? . . . It was my late husband's hunting knife. See the monogram on the handle? . . . Oh, for years and years. He received it as a birthday gift from his Uncle George when he was nineteen years old. . . . Oh, everybody in town knew about it. Perry was always showing it off. . . . The last time I remember seeing it? A couple of days ago, I guess. Yes, it was Thursday evening, because I was separating my daylilies out by the mailbox, and I went running in to answer the phone. It was my sister from Topeka, calling to sing me Happy Birthday, even though she can't carry a tune in a bucket with a lid on it . . . . I must have left it there and forgot about it because it got dark while I was still talking to her. . . . I remembered it this morning and went out to get it, but it wasn't there. . . . I wear a size eight usually. It depends on the style. . . . Yes, of course I knew him. He was such a friend of Buddy's, the boy next door. He was so gentle and patient. He spent a whole afternoon once taking pictures of Barley. . . . My dog. I've got the nicest picture framed on my bedside table upstairs. . . . Yes, I did see him yesterday evening. It was when he left Buddy's house about seven or seven-thirty. I was out at my mailbox. Somebody spray-painted it orange. Harlan waved at me and I waved back. . . . Uphill toward the woods. . . . Yes, as a matter of fact I do remember. He was carrying his camera. . . . Library? No, I don't know why he was in the library.

Friday, April 28, 1995

"You go on home and I'll be there later. I forgot something at work, a contract I have to write out. I may be late, so don't wait up." Sid watched her drive off, then headed back to the dealership, where he picked up a rental car and drove toward Martinsville. He couldn't risk letting Harlan do too much thinking. He hoped the kid hadn't already called somebody about this, but he'd just have to take his chances. He was pretty sure that Harlan was the kind of guy who'd have to think about a deal for a while before he made his mind up. Tomorrow might be too late, though, so he'd have to stop him tonight. 'There's no way I'm going to jail for blackmail,' Sid insisted to himself.

He had brought along the gun he kept hidden under his spare tire. It wasn't registered, but he didn't have a silencer, so he'd be running a risk to use it. Luckily Martinsville was a podunk little town, and he knew Harlan's car by sight. "Hope it's not in a goddam garage,' he thought. But Sid was lucky that night. He spotted the car in front of a corner house after driving up only two or three streets. He parked the rental car down a block or so, then walked up toward the house. Just as he was passing a virulent-looking orange mailbox, another car pulled into the curb ahead of him. Sid bent down as if he were tying his shoelace, while a tired-looking guy carrying a suitcase and a big heavy book limped up the walk and let himself in the front door.

Off to his side a bit, Sid noticed the late evening sun glinting off something under a messy-looking bunch of flowers. Without even pausing to think, he reached out and lifted a heavy hunting knife from among the green leaves. "Well, well, well, what have we here?" he muttered to himself. "This looks like the answer to a man's prayer." Slipping the knife under his dark jacket, he crossed to the other side of Beechnut and ducked behind some dense shrubs that formed a loose hedge in front of a darkened house. 'Hope nobody comes home while I'm here,' he thought.

Sid was somewhat at a loss. Blackmail he could handle, but he'd never killed anybody before. Of course, he knew how to do it, especially now that he had the knife. He'd read about it in those magazines he'd bought in the city last year. Could you believe it? They actually printed directions on the best angle to use to get under the

ribs and into the heart. He'd read those very, very carefully because
they seemed really interesting at the time.

He'd have to wait till it got darker, then sneak over and find out
which room Harlan was in. It couldn't be that hard to break in a
window. Sid's mind was wandering a bit when he looked up and saw
Harlan walking into the house across the street. Damn! Where had
he been? Well, at least now he knew for sure where the kid was. In
the meantime, he'd head back to his car, drive it around so nobody
would get suspicious about a parked car. He knew what these gos-
sipy little towns were like.

When he headed up Beechnut Lane, he found that the road just
dwindled down to nothing but a crooked path, so he pulled off into a
little space between some darkening trees, turned off the engine,
and waited. He even snoozed a bit. 'Might as well be rested when I
go to do this,' he thought.

A little before eleven Sid came to with a start. About time to
reconnoiter. Leaving his car in the woods so he wouldn't make any
noise, he walked the few blocks back to the little house on the corner, keeping to the opposite side of the street. Just as he was getting
ready to cross the street, he saw the door open. Harlan walked out
onto the front porch, looked around briefly, then headed to his left,
down toward the river. He never looked around, never even suspected
he was being followed. Sid had never been quieter. Thank goodness
he had these soft-soled shoes on.

At the corner Harlan turned to his right, crossed the street, and
continued walking for two blocks. Sid stayed on the upper side of
the street, keeping an eye out for stones or pine cones on the path
that might go crunch and give him away. There was just enough
light from the moon for him to see that Harlan had his camera bag
hanging across his right shoulder.

In the middle of the next block Harlan suddenly turned off the
sidewalk and headed off to the side of a big old house. There was
some sort of sign out front, behind a picket fence, but Sid couldn't
see what it said. He could follow the light-colored shirt that Harlan
was wearing, and it disappeared around the back corner of the house.
Sid was so afraid of losing him that he hurried across the street and
loped up the lawn beside the house. As he eased himself around the
corner, he heard a door open and close. The lights were all off in the
house. 'What's this guy up to?' Sid wondered. Well, he certainly
couldn't wait to find out.

There wasn't a back door. Sid had expected some sort of side-walk leading up to a porch, or a door with little bushes on each side of it to hide the foundation. There was nothing like that. Only a wide expanse of wall with a few windows down at the other end of the house. There was a great big bush bunched up against the middle of the blank wall. But Sid had heard a door close *nearby*, so there had to be a door in this section of the wall. He just had to find it. Going back to the corner of the building, he felt his way along in the deep shadows. The moon was too high and too far over that way to lend any light back here.

His hand brushed a frame of some sort, and only a moment or two passed before Sid was quietly opening the hidden door. He passed into a room that had windows high on the wall all the way around, making it fairly easy to see that he was in a living room of some sort. Lots of benches and low tables and easy chairs. Slowly he drew the knife from under his jacket, then steered his way between the chairs toward the doorway he could see in the opposite wall.

Ahead of him he heard Harlan moving around. Barely breath-ing, Sid followed the sound. As he rounded a corner he could hear Harlan's footsteps on the wooden floor. He'd have to be very careful. He hoped the floor didn't creak. The footsteps changed. Harlan was climbing stairs. No telling where he was headed. Once again Sid didn't want to lose him, so he hurried to see just where the stairs were. He could see Harlan turn, up above him, almost at the top of the stairs. "Miranda?" The quiet voice floated down to where Sid, moving through the shadows, had scuffed his foot against a table leg.

Harlan started quickly back down the stairs. Sid could see him smiling. Sid wondered who this Miranda was. 'Even pretty boy here is getting some tail,' he thought as he flew at the stairway, meeting Harlan just below the landing. Sid's outstretched arm, holding the heavy hunting knife, hit Harlan below the rib cage. At that angle, it was just like the magazine said it would be.

He hated to leave the knife, but what was he going to do with it? So he wiped the handle clean. The kid's camera had fallen off to the side of the stairs. No telling what was in it. Sid picked it up, walked out the way he had come in, found his way back to his car. Before he got in, he threw up at the base of one of the big pine trees.

Saturday, April 29, 1995

Saturday morning, Sarah woke up early. Sid was snoring, so she eased out of bed. She was in the kitchen, wrapped in her orange terry cloth robe, when Sid stumbled in about eight o'clock. "You must have been on tiptoes when you came in last night. I never heard you."

"What time did you go to bed?"

"I was out like a light by 9:00."

"Did you sleep well?"

"Sid, you haven't asked me that in three or four years! Yes, I slept sound all night long."

"That's good. That's good. I got in around 9:15."

"Did you finish the contract?"

"The what? Oh, yeah. Yeah, I did, and it went fast because I was home by quarter past nine and in bed by nine-thirty. Too bad you were already asleep."

Sarah made his breakfast, wondering if things were getting better between them. He was acting so sweet and concerned about her.

Tuesday April 23, 1996
Martinsville

Sarah told us at lunchtime all about the safety box key and how her husband had blackmailed Ben Alexander, the banker. I asked her if she thought Ben would be willing to testify against him. Sarah wasn't sure. She thought Ben would probably just want to keep the whole thing quiet, now that he was back with his wife, and they were expecting a baby. "I hope that won't make it too difficult for you. I'd be willing to testify, but I guess I can't since I'm still his wife until I can get a divorce. I don't want to be married to a crook."

Bob leaned back in the kitchen chair and cleared his throat. "Actually, you could testify if you wanted to," he said to Sarah, "but that'll be up to you. In the meantime, don't worry, because we have some physical evidence that should keep Sid locked up for a very long while."

I'd been wondering about Bob's earlier comment, and all of a sudden the pieces clicked together. "I know what it is! His finger-

prints match the partial, right?" Bob actually scowled at me. I guess
I should have kept my supposition to myself. But from the look on
his face, I knew I was right. So I turned to Sarah and explained,
"Bob just found out that Sid killed a young man in the library a year
ago. He left his fingerprint on the blade of the knife."

"Biscuit, I didn't say that."

"You didn't have to. What other reason would you have to lock
him up for a long time? It has to be a murder, and what other murder
could he have committed that you'd know about except for Harlan
Schneider?"

"Harlan?" Sarah's voice went up at least an octave. "He killed
Harlan? He *killed* Harlan?"

"Did you know him?" Glaze asked her.

"He worked at the car lot where Sid worked. I heard he'd been
killed. I never met him, but I saw him around town a few times."

I saw him once for a whole night.

The rest of lunch was extremely subdued, with Bob sending dis-
approving looks my way. I hoped I hadn't compromised the investigation. I was glad Marmalade was sitting on my feet. It was somehow comforting.

You are welcome.

Bob took down Sarah's name, address, and phone numbers to
pass on to the GBI. Right after lunch, he said his goodbyes to the
group, and I followed him out onto the verandah. "I'm sorry, love. I
shouldn't have blurted all that out about the murder. Did I really
mess things up?"

"Yes, but I think I can find it in my heart to forgive you."

And then I found out, not for the first time, that Bob's arms
around me are just as comforting as Marmalade on my feet, if not
more so.

They are?

When I joined Sarah and Glaze, we just sat there in awkward
silence for a short while. What do you say to a woman who's just
found out her husband is a murderer? There was an inane etiquette
book all the girls in my sixth grade class were given in 1958. It told
us such vitally important tidbits as how to freshen up a hat veil using a light bulb. Just what we needed to know. Along with it was a
booklet called *Growing Up and Liking It*. Sandwiched in between

rather clinical sketches of ovaries and Fallopian tubes, were veiled hints about what it meant to be a woman.

Neither the etiquette book nor the other had shed any light on how women support each other through murder trials or planned divorces. Ah well, we just serve tea and listen, I suppose. I liked Sarah well enough, but could tell that she and Glaze had a potential for a long-term friendship.

"What are you going to do now?" Glaze asked Sarah.

She took a deep breath and let it out slowly . . .

Good. She is breathing.

'. . . At least she's breathing,' I thought.

"I'm feeling a little numb right now, but I do know I'm calling my lawyer today to speed up the divorce process. I've said all along I wouldn't be married to a black-mailer, but I *certainly* won't stay married to a murderer!" Sarah had tears in her eyes, but she had determination in her voice as she continued. "I suppose that after I get the divorce, I'll figure out a way to go back to school." She paused to gather her thoughts, while Glaze and I just sat quietly, nodding our heads in support. "I think," she said slowly, "I'd like to be a counselor."

"What a wonderful idea, Sarah." Glaze leaned forward and placed her hand on Sarah's arm. "You'll make a very good counselor."

Eventually Sarah gave all her address info to Glaze. We remembered at the last moment to return her cookbook and the key Sid had been trying to retrieve, and then waved to her as she drove down Beechnut Lane.

Gratitude List – Tuesday
1. Integrity
2. Logic
3. My new lightbulb in the fridge
4. A wonderful guy who knows how to replace a broken window
5. Ketchup bottles

people who get up when I tell them to
those yellow curtains
feet under tables
breathing
my window sills

Wednesday, April 24, 1996

In a small town like Martinsville, it's practically impossible to keep such juicy details quiet, so by Wednesday, the word was out. Mostly the story was told the right way, but a few fantastic details did slip in here and there. Glaze and I, it seemed, had rounded up an intruder and kept him cowering in a corner as we pointed a shotgun at him. I thought that "armed with a ketchup bottle" was much more interesting, but not everyone had the imagination to see the lyricism in that version of the tale.

We learned later from Bob that Wednesday afternoon, Miranda Schuss from the deli had shown up at the police station with her mother in tow. "I told her to be quiet about this," Margot Schuss complained. "She never had to say a word, and everything would have been all right."

Miranda was ready, finally, to face the consequences. She told Bob her story in a steady voice, explaining her early fascination with the soft-voiced, gentle young man, telling how she had gotten to know him and like him a lot. He used to come to town to spend time with Buddy Olsen, and she'd met him at the movies one Friday night more than four years ago. They'd come to like each other, but there was so much difference in their ages. Last year, when she was just about to graduate, when he'd been here to fill in for Buddy as a house-sitter for a few days, he'd called and asked her out.

Miranda told Bob, "I couldn't meet him earlier, so I snuck out of the house. I'd already told him about the back door to the library. We were planning to meet there at 11:30, because Mama would never have wanted me to go to Buddy's house, but I didn't get there until way after midnight because my folks were talking to my uncle, who was visiting. When I got to the library," she added in an almost imperceptible whisper, "he was dead. If I . . ."

"Yes?"

". . . if I hadn't agreed to see him, he'd be alive."

Miranda stopped her monologue, wiped her eyes with her hand, and looked up to meet Bob's eyes. "You can arrest me now, Mr. Sheffield. I'm ready." He opened the bottom drawer of his desk and handed her a box of tissues. He's kept them stashed there ever since last pollen season when I told him between sneezes that it was frustrating to need a tissue and not be able to find one. "Nobody's going to arrest you, Miranda, but I'd like to know why you didn't tell us all this last year?"

"When you and those detectives came to the deli and asked us about him, I was really scared, but Mama did most of the talking, so I just answered a few questions and then stayed out of the way. I was crying a lot, but most of the other kids in town were, too. Everybody liked Harlan. Later, I told Mama, and she said that we might as well leave it all alone, since I didn't know anything about who might have killed him."

"Did you take anything from the body?"

"No!" Miranda was horrified even at the thought.

"What did you do with the shoes you were wearing?"

"I saw that I'd stepped in . . . stepped in his . . . in his blood. So I went home and washed off the shoes and hid them in my closet. Then, about a week later, I told my mother. She helped me get rid of them. We drove down to Athens and threw them in a dumpster."

"Well, there aren't going to be any consequences, other than the work of your own conscience. It's not a crime to sneak out of your parents' house at night; it's not illegal to find a body. But you did withhold material evidence that might have simplified the investigation, and you'll have to testify when this comes to trial. You can expect a very stern lecture from the judge."

"Yes, sir. I'm really sorry."

Bob had her sign a statement, then he wished her well and sent her on her way.

Meanwhile Glaze had been sitting on a lawn chair in the shade – thank goodness we weren't into the scorching summer heat yet, and there was a lovely breeze blowing up from the river. She held Marmalade in her lap and kept her leg propped up while I puttered in the yard. The little *Pieris floribunda* I'd planted just a month ago under the big maple on the west side of the house near the fence, had a broken stem. Poor little thing. I felt like crying. I'd looked such a long time for it. It's hard to find, even though it's a variety of *Pieris* that's native to the southeast, and it's much better suited to the Georgia climate than the Japanese shrubs. In some places it's called a Fetterbush. I wonder why? Even as little as it was, there were a few small bell-shaped white flowers clustered on the one stem that wasn't broken. As I was wondering what to do, Marmalade hopped very carefully off Glaze's lap and headed straight to me. She oozed her back along my knee, where I knelt beside the tiny bush.

It needs more light. I already told you that.

It occurred to me that, although native pieris are shade-loving plants, this one might need a bit more light. I dug it up while I was thinking about it, and took it to the edge of the woodsy area in the back yard, where it would catch the morning sun. I decided to plant it on Barley's grave – he was such a nice old dog. Marmalade walked along behind me, limping only a little bit, and tried to help me dig the hole. I'm so glad she's beginning to feel better.

It is about time! Whitebell will be fine now.

Gratitude List – Wednesday

1. My yard
2. Springtime
3. Marmy
4. Healing
5. Planting

people who listen to me
digging
helping Widelap
getting my ears scratched
cool breezes

Chapter 15

Thursday, April 25, 1996

Thursday afternoon at 2:15, Mom and Dad drove up Beech-nut Lane and parked behind my Buick. I hadn't seen them for several months, since they'd been driving around the Maritime Peninsula, falling in love with Halifax, reading "Evangeline" to each other in the evenings, strolling on the lovely sand beaches of Cape Breton Island. Despite the thousands of miles of driving, they looked rested and, at seventy-four and seventy-six years of age, still in their prime.

After we chatted for a while, and told them all about the excitement of the past few days, Mom and Glaze and I took a good look at the curtains that I had folded up on Tuesday morning and set aside. They were embedded with slivers of broken glass, so we decided to ditch the whole thing and leave the window uncovered. The Lady Banks Rose was all the curtain that window needed anyway.

Bob's mother came over for dinner. We had arranged for Mom and Dad to stay with her through the weekend. Introducing them almost didn't need to happen, since they all felt an instant connection that lit up their faces and brought a warm glow to the whole gathering. We tried to get Mom and Dad to tell us all about their trip, but aside from mentioning a few high points and a couple of funny stories, they begged off, saying that they'd tell us all about it later. "It's a whole story by itself," Mom said, as Dad nodded in agreement.

Gratitude List – Thursday

1. Mom
2. Dad
3. Curtains/no curtains
4. Flexibility
5. Roses

seeing Sunsetlady and Dreammaker again
fresh water to drink
birds to watch
listening to happy people
open windows

Friday, April 26, 1996

Bob and Tom took Dad fishing early on Friday morning. Guy stuff. They think it's fun to get up before dawn and go shiver on the bank of some pond tucked up in the hills. Glaze and I slept uninterrupted and woke up at a reasonable hour. Mom was, we assumed, having breakfast with Mrs. Sheffield – I wonder if I should start calling her *Mother Sheffield?* No, sounds too much like a nun. After a breakfast of yummy homemade toasted bread dripping with fresh unsalted butter, I gave in to chores and scurried a bit doing last-minute fix-up projects around the house, getting it ready for the influx of family on Saturday. Marmalade was sociable for awhile and then she disappeared upstairs. I found her sprawled out contentedly in the middle of the bed when I went up there to iron Glaze's dress. Glaze's ankle was still too sore for much walking, so once all my chores were done, I drove Glaze and Mom the two and a half blocks down to Sharon's for hair-washing and such. Marmy didn't even say goodby . . .

That's because I was much too comfortable.

. . . and by 5:00 we were all cleaned up and ready for the wedding rehearsal.

We rehearsed it the way we'd decided on Monday. Glaze stood with Bob at the front of the church, while Tom walked down the aisle, preceding Dad and me. We had a lot of laughs over it, imagining what the town's reaction would be. Reverend Pursey, used to more conventional parishioners, couldn't think of a valid reason why not, so he went along with us. We hadn't been able, amidst a riotous amount of laughter, to decide whether Tom should carry the ring and Glaze the bridesmaid's bouquet, or whether she should hold the ring and he the flowers. We tried it both ways, leaving our options open until the last minute.

We had no idea how many people would show up at the wedding. It was pretty much understood that we were inviting the whole town and everybody we'd ever known. Invitations had been phone calls and "spread-the-word" tactics. Perhaps it was a bit tacky. Okay, I admit it – it was *very* tacky, but we decided that this way we wouldn't offend anyone by forgetting to address an envelope. We put an open invitation in the church bulletin, and one over at the Catholic Church as well. The head table at the reception would be just family – we made that clear right from the start. Then we had to realize that 'family' by this time meant Tom, too, especially since he was my bridesmaid!

At the rehearsal dinner afterwards – at CT's of course – it was just Mom and Dad, Bob and me, Glaze and Tom. Tom was ready to carry Bob's 'best man' from the car, but he restrained himself admirably, and simply offered his arm for her to lean on. During dinner, he had arranged to have Billy Smith bring Glaze a vanilla milkshake. I looked at Bob with my now-do-you-see-what's-happening look, and he pointedly gazed back at me over his glasses with his now-don't-jump-to-conclusions look. But I was right.

Gratitude List – Friday

1. Laughter
2. All my dear family
3. Having beautiful hair
4. A clean house
5. A long warm shower

laughter
all my dear people
food from Fishgiver
this soft bed
long naps

Saturday, April 27, 1996

Early the next morning, my daughters and their families descended en masse. Even Scott, my son, made it in from Alaska. A wonderful surprise. Brighton Montgomery had driven to the airport in Atlanta on Friday evening to pick him up. Blessings on good neighbors. Scott called me from Brighton's house to say he'd see me at the church, since all the menfolk were gathering for an early Saturday breakfast at Tom's. I was sure that Bob would tell my son all about the time he and Tom went cave exploring on the other side of the Metoochie when they were twelve and got stuck in a small dark cavern. Finally they dug their way out and came home covered with bat poop.

Then, maybe, Tom would tell Scott never to play cards with Bob because he cheats. Of course, Bob will swear that he never cheats, but will modestly admit that he just remembers every card that's ever been played. No telling what Scott will think of my groom and my 'bridesmaid' by the end of the breakfast.

Tom had asked me if, as my bridesmaid, he was required to help me dress on Saturday morning. I sweetly declined the offer, for which he pretended to be deeply disappointed. Now, how much help does a forty-nine year old woman need in getting dressed, even from a female bridesmaid,when all she has to deal with is a simple off-white long frock, with hand-made lace at the neck and the hem?

You look beautiful.

Marmalade even joined in the festivities, playing quietly with the long pieces of ribbon we cut for her from the large roll we had used to trim my bouquet. Melissa Tarkington had come over at dawn to help Glaze and me. We gathered dew-covered flowers from my own yard. We made almost a ritual of it, and each of them tucked a tiny daisy in my hair and wished me all happiness. My sister, and my sister-by-choice.

The bouquet turned out beautifully, and each of my girls brought some flowers from their own yards to add to the display. So we spent most of the time snacking and laughing, remembering the old family stories about weddings, like when Auntie Blue married Uncle Mark in 1942 during a huge thunderstorm, and the lightning hit the church in Braetonburg. The volunteer fire brigade, many of whom were guests at the wedding, put out the very small fire that resulted, while everybody huddled under umbrellas outside. Then, after a quick consultation, they all trooped, dripping, back inside and continued the rites. Mom and Dad were courting at the time, and they thought the huddle under the umbrella was the best part of the afternoon.

The next year, when Mom and Dad got hitched, they couldn't get wedding rings because of war shortages, so they borrowed Blue and Mark's rings for the three days until Dad was shipped off to basic training and on to the South Pacific. "I didn't get pregnant during those three days," Mom said, heaving a sigh and running her hand along Marmalade's back. Pause of five seconds. "But it wasn't for want of trying!" Her belly laugh held all the joy of a woman who was wise about her world, who loved her husband, who appreciated her womanhood. How could I have been so fortunate to have been birthed by this woman?

Sunsetlady is what I call her, and you are fortunate.

I looked over at Glaze and realized that she, too, was recognizing her incredible fortune in having such a mom. I'm putting both of them on my gratitude list tonight. If I remember to write it...

As Mom was finishing that particular tale, amid hoots of laughter, we heard loud voices downstairs hollering, "Where's that bride-to-be?" I recognized my friend Glenda Harvey's voice, of course, but what surprised me was Karla Michaels. I'd grown up with her, but I hadn't seen her in the twelve years since she left Braetonburg after her divorce. We'd written and called each other, of course, but just never found time to drive or fly between Arizona and Georgia. So, the number of "family" members at the reception increased by two. She and Glenda had cooked up this surprise visit as their wedding gift to me. Good fortune again.

About ten o'clock, most everybody trooped up to the church. Glaze and Mom and I followed half an hour later, when Dad came to pick us up in the sturdy old Lincoln that had ferried them to Nova Scotia and back down the east coast without a bit of trouble.

At eleven o'clock on a sunny Saturday in late April, almost one year to the day after Bob and I met in the library over the body Marmalade discovered, I stepped into the aisle of the Martinsville Community Church with my dad. We paused at the door, looking at the congregation; most everyone in town had come to see the librarian and the town cop get hitched. As Tom started down the aisle, surrounded by shocked expressions and some laughter, I looked beyond him to see Bob standing there in his dark gray suit beside Glaze, smiling expectantly. I turned to my dad, remembering his question twenty-five years ago, about my feelings for Sol. The question was still a good one. "Guess what, Dad? Bob makes my heart sing."

The End
Not quite.

Topics for Your Book Club's Discussion of
Orange as Marmalade

If you've never belonged to a book discussion group, now may be the time to join one. If you can't find one, why not get a few friends together and start one? A search of the Internet for *Book Discussion Clubs* will give you a good starting point.

There are, of course, many topics for discussion in any good book. The following list is intended to be used as a springboard for conversation about *Orange as Marmalade*. Please feel free to bring up your own questions. It helps if everyone in the club has read the book to be discussed, and many people like to make notes in the book margins as they read, to make it easier to find specific passages that relate to the topic under discussion.

Sisters
• Do you have sisters by birth, sisters by choice, or both?
• Would you trust your sister if she had failed you somehow in the past?
• Has the age difference between you and your sister affected your relationship? If so, how?
• Are you closer to your sister now than when you were growing up? Why or why not?

Parents
• If you have children of your own, did having them change your opinion of your own parents?
• Describe your parents in terms of what lessons they've taught you.
• When you were young, which set of parents in your neighborhood would you like to have had?
• What did you learn from those people?

Cats / Pets
• Did you have a favorite pet as a child?
    I hope so.
• Do you have an animal that brings richness to your life? In what ways?
    I have some special humans in my life.

• What is the most important lesson you've learned from an animal?
Think carefully about this one.
• How do you balance meeting the needs of your pet with meeting the needs of your family? Has this been easy or are there challenges?
Does your animal have a Goodhands to help?
• What has been your experience with receiving messages from your special animal friend(s)?
It is much easier if you relax your heart and LISTEN.
• Throughout *Orange as Marmalade*, Biscuit McKee writes a gratitude list at the end of each day.
So do I.
What has been your experience with gratitude lists? Are there other ways in which you can increase your awareness of the positive elements of your life?
Those are good questions.

Neighborhoods/Towns
• In what ways are you supported by the people in your neighborhood? How would you rate your neighborhood on a scale of 1 to 10? In what ways do you contribute to a sense of connection with your neighbors?
• If you have lived in both cities and towns, how would you compare these experiences?
• Is there one thing you could do to increase the "neighborliness" of the area in which you live?
• Is your neighborhood ethnically diverse? Are there many different religions represented? How would you rate the "tolerance level" of your community? How could that level be improved? What one thing could you do this week to make a difference?

Jobs
• What was your very best after-school job?
• What have been the best lessons you've learned from working?
• What advice would you give a new parent about how to instill a work ethic without overdoing it?
• What are five ways you can increase the amount of joy you have in your current job?

Hobbies
- What is your experience with photography? gardening? cooking? decorating? birding?
- If you could spend time increasing your skills in one area, what would you choose to do?
- Did you grow up in a family where hobbies were encouraged? In what way?
- Have you ever considered writing a book that relates to a hobby of yours?

Motherhood / Career
- What was your own mother's way of handling motherhood and career?
- Did you or would you choose to do it differently? Why or why not?
- If you have a daughter or a favorite niece, what can you do to help her prepare for the time when impending motherhood might conflict with her chosen work?

Bipolar Disorders
- Has anyone close to you ever been diagnosed with bipolar disorder? If so, how would you characterize the impact that person had on you or your family?
- Are you familiar with the signs and symptoms of depression? A confidential screening for bipolar disorder is available from the Depression and Bipolar Support Alliance at www.dbsalliance.org or toll-free 1-800-826-3632. Lists of symptoms of depression and bipolar disorder are available from the National Institutes of Mental Health at www.nimh.nih.gov or toll-free 1-866-615-6464.
- There are many illnesses, disorders, or dis-eases that affect family members. Have you ever had to deal with a family member who had a long-term physical, mental, or emotional challenge? If so, what were the specific challenges, and how did your family cope with them?

Zany Family Members
- Who's the zaniest relative you have? Is it yourself?
- What have you learned from that person's life experiences?
- Do you have any relatives you don't claim in public...or at all?
- What have you learned from them?

Wedding Memories

• What's your favorite family wedding story?
• If you are married, is there one thing you wish you could have changed about your wedding?
• Describe your idea of the ideal wedding.
• Do you know anything about the weddings of your grand-parents? If it's not too late, can you find out the details from them or from someone who knew them? Why would this be an important project?

The End
For now.

About the Author (By the Author)

So, who am I, anyway?

In this country, we usually answer that question by saying what we *do*, which is not the same as *who we are*. Hopefully, though, who we are and what we do are connected in some way. So, besides being a writer, I am a breath coach and a nationally certified neuromuscular massage therapist. My practice is limited to women only. I'm a Reiki Master (in case you're wondering, reiki is pronounced "ray-key" with the accent on the first syllable), and I was ordained several years ago as an interfaith minister through the Universal Brotherhood Movement.

I live with nine cats (all of whom are indoor critters now) who showed up in my life at just the right times. They've taught me a lot about the important things in life—self-esteem, boundary-setting (when to hiss and when to walk away), and naps (on something soft in the summer shade or the winter sun).

I am a member of the Georgia Writers Association and the Atlanta Writers Club. I sing alto. I laugh a lot, and I write for the sheer joy of it. When I was in seventh grade at East Junior High School in Colorado Springs, I had a wonderful English teacher named Miss Helen Johnson. She taught me to love Shakespeare, to write from my soul center, to appreciate classical music, and not to make excuses for myself when I blew that test (for which I had not studied). She listened with an understanding heart. I kept in touch with her by snail-mail for the rest of her life, and always knew that she was one of those amazing women who paved the way for me.

Since I was an Air Force brat (a term proudly used by service kids - not the pejorative townies think it is), I don't have a home town, unlike Biscuit McKee. I attended four different schools 9th to 12th grades. Went to Illinois Wesleyan University for two years (and consider it my true alma mater, even though I didn't graduate from there). Took a very long sabbatical. Got married. Seven years later, had a couple of kids. Then I went back to school part-time for seven years, and graduated from Trinity College in Burlington, Vermont. Trinity, by the way, closed its doors several years ago. I now have a Masters degree and a Doctor of Divinity degree from Universal Brotherhood University.

I've had people ask me if my D. Div. is just a piece of paper. No. In order to earn my degree I had to create something that would make a positive difference in the lives of the people who read my dissertation. The doctoral process for UBU requires that one document a product or project that goes out into the world and helps people who may not even have heard about the Universal Brotherhood Movement.

My resumé is a catalog of small jobs, since I chose for a long time to be a stay-at-home mom. I sold various stuff (and will never again try anything multi-level as long as I live, so don't even ask), worked in a women's shelter, edited a couple of newsletters, taught color analysis, was a substitute teacher in Vermont. Finally, after 25 years of marriage, I realized that I wasn't very good at being a wife. I wrote a series of songs that I now call *Happily Single: a Sing-Along for Women Who Are Divorced*. At the time I simply called them my sanity songs. I ended up using them as the basis for my Masters Thesis. Someday I may even record them or find someone to record them for me.

Since 1993, I've lived in Georgia, northeast of Atlanta, where my house is surrounded by a bird and butterfly sanctuary that I created from essentially bare ground (three tall pines and a sick azalea), in large part because I read **King Solomon's Ring** by Conrad Lorenz when I was a young girl. I was fascinated by the idea of working *with* nature instead of against it. Since then another book that has become a beacon for me is **Noah's Garden by Sara Stein**. I use no pesticides in my yard and no fertilizers other than compost. Yes, like Biscuit McKee, I built my own three-bin compost pile. My favorite magazine is **Mother Earth News**.

My idea of redecorating is to get another bookshelf (one the cats can sit on top of).

Why is this such a long *About the Author* blurb? I always want to know more about my favorite authors than those little bitty descriptions, and I figured you might want that, too.

Orange as Marmalade is the first in the Biscuit McKee Mystery series. Look for *Yellow as Legal Pads*, scheduled for release in the last half of 2004.

Follow Biscuit and Bob on their journey to a small hotel north of Savannah, Georgia, where they find another body and once again try to figure out *whodunit* and why and how.

Marmalade, of course, will be offering her comments throughout this honeymoon escapade.

Visit our website often for the latest update on the availability of **Yellow as Legal Pads** and other upcoming adventures of Biscuit and Marmalade. Each book in the Biscuit McKee Mystery series will add clues to the mystery surrounding the 1745 founding of the town of Martinsville, Georgia. The 200-year-old puzzle will finally be solved in **White as Ice**, the eighth book of the series.

http://www.doggieinthewindow.biz

You may learn more about Fran Stewart through her website at:

http://www.franstewart.com